VICIOUSLY YOURS

FAE KINGS OF EDEN
BOOK ONE

JAMIE APPLEGATE HUNTER

Viciously Yours

Fae Kings of Eden Book One

CONTENTS

DEDICATION

For everyone who hates the word cock—

I have devastating news.

WORLD GUIDE

HUMANS

- No magic
- Not immortal
- Do not have fated mates

NON-ROYAL FAE

- Stronger and faster than humans
- They can glamour small areas around themselves.
- Their glamour works on humans and animals.
- It takes their magic thirteen years to fully manifest.
- They do not have fated mates unless mated to a royal fae.
- Not immortal

ROYAL FAE

- Stronger and faster than non-royal fae
- Their glamour works on every living creature, including non-royal fae.
- Their glamour is stronger than non-royal fae (they can glamour entire kingdoms at one time).
- They have fated mates.
- Royals traditionally only have one child.
- It takes twenty-five years for their magic to fully manifest.
- They cannot leave their kingdoms until their magic fully manifests at twenty-five years of age.
- Royal fae heirs take over the throne at twenty-five years of age.
- They receive a *familiar* and *familiar* mark on their fifteenth birthday
- Not immortal

MATES

- Only royal fae have fated mates (their mate can be a non-royal fae).
- On a royal fae's thirteenth birthday, the name of their fated mate is whispered into their minds by the gods.
- Fated mates can feel each other's stronger emotions.
- A mate bond can be broken if one of the mates marries another person before the two fated mates marry.
- A mate bond does not make them love each other.
- Mate bonds are the strongest form of pure magic from the gods and were created to ensure the strongest royal fae heirs.

FAMILIARS

- An animal bonded to a royal fae on their fifteenth birthday.
- The "bonded" (royal fae) can see and hear through their *familiar*.
- The bonded receives a tattoo of their *familiar* on their upper left chest at midnight on their fifteenth birthday, and their *familiar* finds them within a few days.
- *Familiars* and their bonded can communicate telepathically.
- *Familiars* live to be as long as their bonded.

KINGDOMS

- Mountain Kingdom (fae—cold, snowy, mountainous)
- Desert Kingdom (fae—desert land with mountains and plateaus, hot days with cold nights)
- Tropical Kingdom (fae—thick canopy of tropical trees, humid, mild temperatures, borders the ocean)
- Garden Kingdom (fae—lush flowery greenery with comfortably mild temperatures all year)
- Human Kingdom (human—surrounded by the four fae kingdoms. Made up of all four habitats, depending on which fae kingdom the human regions border).

Note: Fae kingdoms possess magic that the Human Kingdom does not. Their vegetation, animals, bodies of water, etc. are different and can be dangerous to humans.

THE BARRIER

- A magical wall that protects the humans from the dangerous fae lands
- Fae can pass through the barrier freely, but humans require a fae escort in order for the magic to allow them through.
- The five kingdoms agreed to erect a wall along the barrier with only one gate to each fae kingdom.
- Any fae or human who passes through the barrier must have a legal permit to do so.

KEY

BORDER

BARRIER

N
W E
S

HUMAN
KINGDOM

GARDEN
KINGDOM

NOTE

Content warnings can be found on the last page.

IF YOU ARE LOOKING FOR A LITERARY MASTERPIECE, THIS MIGHT NOT BE FOR YOU.

This is not your typical fantasy romance novel in the way that there is minimal world building, no overarching background plot, and no big villain.

The plot focuses solely on the romance between the two main characters because it is a **romance** book. If you're thinking, *"There's no way someone could write a fantasy romance book without a fantasy plot,"* you're wrong.
I can, and I did.

The main characters make a few morally black choices in the name of protecting their relationship (never toward each other), and at some point you might think,
"That might be too far."

Do not take this book too seriously, as it was written to be a fun, quick read with a bit of *"that's fucked up"* thrown into the mix.

There is a 50/50 chance you'll have a good time reading it.

Good luck.

PART ONE
THE LETTERS

1

THIRTEEN YEARS OLD

Rennick didn't know which frightened him more; the voices in his head no one else could hear, or the name those voices whispered and what it meant.

"Amelia," he murmured to himself, running a hand through his dark brown hair.

It was the prettiest name he'd ever heard.

As a royal fae, Rennick didn't have a choice in who he would marry, and he'd been preparing for this day since he was old enough to understand what a mate was.

At midnight on a royal fae's thirteenth birthday, the gods whispered the name of the royal heir's fated mate for only them to hear, creating a bond between the two before they ever met.

Amelia.

Royals possessed stronger magic than other fae, in addition to superior physical strength and speed. His father said the gods ensured the royal bloodlines stayed strong and left nothing to chance. That's why royals had fated mates. There was no stronger magic than that of a royal's mate bond, thus making the strongest offspring possible.

The thing about mates that Rennick didn't understand was

that the bond didn't make them love each other. *Wouldn't that be easier?* he thought begrudgingly.

The gods decreed that royals *had* to marry their fated mates, no matter what. It didn't seem fair. Regardless, his father said he had a duty to his mate and his kingdom, and Rennick would do his best to make him proud.

Rennick's father, Callum, chuckled, pulling him from his thoughts. "I know that look." Callum gazed lovingly at his wife. "I remember hearing your mother's name for the first time." He winked at her. "*Helena.*"

Helena smiled and rolled her eyes before turning to Rennick. "Who is she, sweetie?"

Rennick's wonder gave way to anxiety. What if he didn't like Amelia when they met? Doubt threatened to overpower him, and he drew in an unsteady breath. "Amelia. I've never heard of her."

He knew most people his age in Vale, the capital of the Mountain Kingdom, and since mates were born on the same day, he'd taken note of girls who shared his birthday.

"That's normal," his father assured him. "It's not likely you'd meet them naturally."

Rennick's face paled. They might not meet?

Would that really be so bad?

"Callum." Helena leaned across the small dining table in Rennick's rooms to pat his hand. "What your father meant is there are many people throughout the four fae kingdoms, and it's not unusual for your mate to be someone you don't know; there are too many people in this world to encounter them all." She squeezed his hand reassuringly. "You will find her. The gods ensure it."

Meeting Amelia for the first time would be uncomfortable at best. All the heirs from other kingdoms were boys, meaning she was a normal fae and wouldn't know he was her mate. She would feel his stronger emotions, but the gods only spoke to royals. She probably wouldn't understand what the extra emotions meant.

What would he say? *Hi, we're going to get married. By the way, my name is Rennick?*

What if she wasn't from the Mountain Kingdom? His mother grew up in the Garden Kingdom, and she didn't mind the cold, but if Amelia lived in the Tropical or Desert Kingdoms, she would freeze to death.

He would have extra coats and blankets stashed around the palace, just in case.

"I know you don't understand now," his mother said gently, "but one day she will be the most important person in your life. It will be your job to protect her if she cannot protect herself."

He puffed out his chest and sat taller. "I will do my duty and protect her."

Even if we never fall in love.

ONE WEEK LATER

Rennick and his best friend, Finn, stood in the middle of the training arena, panting after their last round of sparring. Rennick began warrior training when he was old enough to hold a sword, and Finn's father, one of the Mountain Kingdom's best warriors, brought his son to train alongside the other trainees. They'd been best friends ever since.

The impossibly tall stone walls of the arena formed an oval structure far outside the palace. The open space could fit an entire legion of warriors, as well as trainees. Rennick and Finn spent every bit of free time they had either training with the other trainees or watching the warriors train.

The large colorful trees filled with rainbow leaves and capped in snow provided shade on cloudless days, but even they weren't enough to filter out the blistering sun today. Sweat coated Rennick's lightly tanned skin, and he swiped at his damp forehead, but the leather of his sleeve stuck to his skin, making it worse. Finn's warm umber skin glistened as well, and Rennick knew it was time to go inside before one of them died of a heat stroke.

The Mountain Kingdom was cold and covered in snow, but its location high in the mountains placed them closer to the sun. On a clear day, it felt like the seven rings of hell, especially when weighed down by armor. It didn't help that Rennick's father had increased the training schedule for the trainees and newer warriors.

New rebel factions had popped up throughout the four fae kingdoms. They attacked at random and grew bolder by the year. In history classes, they learned that with each generation came new waves of unrest, but no matter the era, the rebels' goals remained the same: to extinguish the royal bloodlines.

Rennick once asked his father why the rebels hated the royals so much, and his father said, *"You will always be someone else's villain, whether you deserve the title or not. Your duty is to ensure their hate is unjustified."*

They could thank the stupid rebels for their mandatory extra training.

As Rennick and Finn left the training arena with dirt coating their sticky skin, all Rennick could think about was soaking in a snow bath.

Finn jogged alongside him to keep up with his long strides. At thirteen, Rennick already stood six feet tall, with broad shoulders that rivaled those of fully grown men.

"When does your father leave?" Finn asked between pants.

Rennick continued his hurried pace in silence.

Finn punched Rennick's arm. "Answer me."

Rennick punched him back, dodging when Finn swung again. "Tomorrow morning."

Rennick's parents had spent the last few days checking the Mountain Kingdom's birth registry for anyone named Amelia with the same birthday as Rennick, but they'd found nothing. Tomorrow, his father would leave for the other kingdoms to check their registries as well.

Once a royal fae heard the name of their mate, they needed to find them as soon as possible and move them to their kingdom's capital for their own safety. The quickest way to end the royal lines was by killing a royal's mate or a young royal heir.

"Your Majesty," Rand, Finn's father and one of the king's most trusted generals, called out to Rennick. The look on his face had both boys pulling up short. Something was wrong. "A group of rebels breeched the palace walls. I need you two to come with me."

"How?" Finn asked as they followed Rand back toward the palace.

"They managed to slip into the garden," Rand replied, his eyes distant.

The garden. On sunny days, his mother spent hours in the gardens. Rennick sprinted toward the palace walls as the other two ran after him, yelling his name.

His chest tightened as he closed in on the palace gates. *Please be okay*, he chanted silently as his feet pounded against the ground. A guard moved into his path with his hand out, and something within Rennick went wild. They'd not keep him from his mother. An explosion of anger had him slamming the guard against the stone wall.

"Unlock the gate," he commanded in a voice he didn't recognize, scaring himself.

"Yes, Your Majesty." The guard waved his hand to another. "Let him in."

If the rebels had hurt his mother, she'd be in the infirmary. He took off in a sprint, praying she wasn't there. Guards jumped out of his way, and when he rounded the corner of the service wing, he saw the familiar silhouette of his father entering the infirmary. A flash of red hair dangled from his arms.

Rennick's blood ran cold, and he skidded to a halt outside of the infirmary door. "What happened?" A guard stepped in front of him and braced his hand on Rennick's chest. Through the gaps between the guard's body and the door, Rennick watched his father lay his unconscious mother on a bed. Time stopped.

"*Mom!*" He should have been embarrassed by the desperation tainting his voice, but the vision of his mother's lifeless body killed whatever pride he had.

The guard spoke in a deceptively soft voice. "The best thing you can do for the queen is let the healer and his staff do their jobs uninterrupted."

Rennick tore his gaze away from his mother. "What if she dies?"

The guard pinched his lips together and glanced over his shoulder into the room for a long moment. With a sad sigh, he turned and motioned for Rennick to follow him inside.

Callum turned on them with such fury and pain in his eyes that Rennick almost stepped back. He took tentative steps to his father's side and stared at his mother with abject horror.

The healer and nurses switched out blood-soaked towels at an alarming rate in an attempt to staunch the bleeding. Fae were stronger and faster than humans, royals even more so, but they weren't immortal, nor did they heal rapidly, like the human fairytales claimed. The healer hung his head and stepped away.

Rennick moved to the other side of the bed and tenderly took his mother's hand in his.

"I love you, Mom," he choked out while tears streamed down his dirty face.

Rennick's father leaned forward and kissed her forehead, murmuring, "Goodbye, love," and when her chest rose for the last time, a sob ripped from his chest.

Rennick's ears rang, and his legs gave out, sending him to his knees.

He didn't know when Finn arrived, but his friend grabbed him by the arms and hauled him to his feet. Rennick's father remained hunched over his wife, his body shaking with anguished sobs.

Rennick allowed Finn to lead him toward the hall in a daze, but he paused at the door and took one last look at her rapidly paling face. Grief filled his veins, pumping through him at a rapid pace. *Thirteen years' worth of memories,* he thought bitterly. That's all he had left of his mother. Their future memories bled dry at the hands of the rebels. Hatred joined the grief within him, and he reached for it, latching onto the dark emotion with everything he had.

Finn guided him down the halls toward the royal wing, but Rennick barely registered his surroundings. He thought back to the last conversation he'd had with his mother. That morning, at breakfast, she'd chattered excitedly about Amelia and how she'd always wanted a daughter. She wondered which kingdom she came from and what things she liked to do.

Pain lanced through him.

She wouldn't be there to weep at his wedding like he knew she would have, and his mate would never know the joy of having his mother as her own.

2

SIX MONTHS LATER

"Can't you send one of the guards?" Finn asked, looking more annoyed with each passing second.

Rennick shook his head. "I don't trust anyone but you, and Dad said we can't tell anyone about her."

Amelia.

It took months, but his father found Amelia living in an orphanage in the Human Kingdom after receiving a tip from an unexpected source. He petitioned Charlotte, the human queen, to bring Amelia to the Mountain Kingdom palace immediately since she had no family to speak of. The queen refused to let his mate cross the barrier until Rennick took the throne.

When she explained why, his father agreed, but upon finding out the news, Rennick destroyed his father's study in a fit of uncontrollable rage. He understood she was safest hidden amongst the humans, but he had a duty to her, and he couldn't protect her from a kingdom away.

Royal fae needed to be at their full power to protect their kingdoms once they took over, and because of this, the gods bound them to their own kingdoms until they took the throne at twenty-five. Fae pulled magic from their lands, and leaving fae lands before they were fully grown would weaken their magic. For normal fae, they came to full power at thirteen, and even if they left before then, it didn't mean much. For royal fae, the stakes were higher, and because they were stronger, it took longer for their power to fully manifest.

Rennick placed his hand on Finn's shoulder. "Something happened yesterday. I felt it." He tapped his chest where Amelia's agony had knocked the air out of him the day before. Her strong emotions resonated in him like his own. He didn't like it.

He'd been trying to convince Finn to take Amelia a letter for the last hour. Only he, outside of a select few of his father's inner circle, knew Amelia's true identity. If anyone caught wind of who she was to him and he wasn't there to protect her, she would be killed, and he wouldn't allow that to happen.

His mother's death hung over their heads like a guillotine. It did not matter that Amelia was only a thirteen-year-old girl, killing her would weaken, if not exterminate, the Mountain Kingdom's royal bloodline.

"How am I supposed to sneak into an all-girl's orphanage?" Finn demanded. "I'll be arrested."

"You know how to pick locks," Rennick reminded him, "and you can glamour yourself to be invisible." All fae possessed the ability to use glamour, a magic allowing them to make any non-fae person or animal see what they wanted them to.

"And if she shows someone your letter or someone snoops around her room and finds it?" Finn looked pointedly at the black envelope in Rennick's hand. "They'll think she's lying, or worse, that she's telling the truth."

Rennick *knew* she wouldn't tell. He couldn't explain how, but he had never been more sure of anything in his life. "I won't tell her who I really am or what kingdom I'm from," he said, slightly offended his friend thought him that dense. "I won't even tell her what I look like. And when she finishes reading the letter, use glamour to take it back."

Finn ran a hand over his short, dark, curly hair with a groan. "Fine, but you owe me big."

Rennick's relieved smile faltered. "I need to send her a gift."

Finn looked ready to strangle him. "Why?"

He motioned for Finn to follow him back toward the palace. "I missed her birthday."

Amelia trudged home from the library through the slushy snow, wishing the walk wasn't so far. In this region of the Human Kingdom, it was cold year-round, and during the snowy season, it became downright miserable.

The coat she currently owned was too snug and thin, doing nothing to block the chilly wind. The orphanage she lived at didn't have the luxury of buying everyone new clothes and relied on donations. One of the house mothers taught the girls to sew the hems of their dresses shorter to keep them from dragging through the snow because there was nothing worse than a wet dress sticking to your legs.

She could have gone home right after school today when the sun was still high and streaming through the tall evergreens, but she'd read her entire stack of books from the library and needed new ones. Without her books, she'd be bored to tears.

It was her own fault she had no friends. Instead of joining her classmates outside during breaks, she chose to read at her desk, preferring fictional worlds to the real one. It wasn't that she didn't want friends. She did more than anything, but their school wasn't very big, which limited her options. Then the only two girls her age at the orphanage, Ana and Farrah, were awful.

She was well-liked, and she liked most of her classmates, but she had nothing in common with the other girls, and the boys made her nervous. Amelia needed to learn to face her fears if she wanted to live like the characters in her books.

Lately, she'd been reading adventure books with epic romances, and while she'd always wanted to live in the fictional worlds she read about, she longed for a love like in her stories more than anything.

Thirteen was too young to worry about marriage and a family of her own, but Amelia could think of nothing else. She wanted to love someone who loved her back and often wondered what it would be like, since she hadn't the slightest clue what any type of love felt like.

Almost thirteen years ago, someone left her on the front stoop of the orphanage with nothing but a blanket and a copy of her birth record with no parents listed. While the house mothers she had over the years treated the girls well, stepping into the matronly role they all needed, no one stayed forever.

She sighed and climbed the porch steps, ready to dive into another book.

A dream hovered just out of Amelia's reach as she teetered on the edge of consciousness. A whisper that she couldn't make out in her hazy dream state until it fizzled away all together, replaced by the sun's bright rays assaulting her senses.

She and the other girls were fortunate to have their own rooms, but the spaces were small, leaving her no choice but to position the bed directly across from the window with no spare blankets to hang over the glass.

Rolling over, she grabbed her pillow and smashed it over her head to ward off the morning, but the crinkle of paper against her cheek made her jerk back.

She swiped her long blonde hair out of her face and, after

rubbing her eyes to ensure she wasn't seeing things, stared at the crisp black envelope.

Where had it come from? Had it been there last night, she would have noticed when she fluffed her pillow.

Someone came in my room while I slept.

Tentatively, she reached for the envelope, inspected the fancy-looking paper, and pried it open without grace. A single piece of paper waited inside. With shaky hands, she unfolded it, furrowing her brow at the messy penmanship filling the page.

Hello, ~~Human Mate~~

Have you ever had to tell someone something, but you didn't know where to start? That's how I feel right now. I figured meeting you in person for the first time would be awkward, but I think writing this letter is way worse. (words are hard)

I'm messing this up. You don't know me, but what I'm going to say will change your life. (I'm fae, by the way)

You're my fated mate, and that means a lot to fae.

It means you are mine, and I am yours (whether we like it or not) and as mates, we can sometimes feel each other's emotions. Since you don't have magic, I don't know if you can feel mine, but I can feel yours.

A few days ago, I almost cried in front of my friends. I'm assuming that was because of you. It was embarrassing.

Either way, I hope you are okay now.

Happy (late) thirteenth birthday. I hope you like the gift.

~~Your Fae Mate~~

Nick

P.S. This might sound stupid, but when I'm upset, I sit outside and talk to my mother. My father says she can hear us in the heavens. You should try it. She'd probably like to hear from you, too.

. . .

Amelia read the letter again. And again. And again.

After her tenth read through, she deduced that Nick, whoever he was, had the wrong person. Why would a fae think *she* was their mate? It wasn't even addressed to her.

She'd read about soulmates in a few romance books, but she hadn't thought they were real. *Assuming that's what he meant.* Human schools didn't teach much about the fae. Other than folklore, not much was known about the mysterious people with pointed ears because they rarely crossed the barrier.

A wall reinforced the magical barrier separating the Human Kingdom from the four fae kingdoms. Fae could pass through the barrier by themselves, but humans couldn't get through the magic without a fae escort, but magic or not, everyone was required to have an official permit to pass through the gates. Amelia didn't know what happened if they caught someone without a permit.

Jacob, a boy at school, claimed humans were never seen again if caught crossing illegally, but that couldn't be true. There were no *real* horror stories about the fae; they stayed on their side of the wall, and humans stayed on theirs.

Glancing toward the window, she noticed a white box with a red bow balancing precariously on the sill. She set the letter aside and crossed the room to inspect the mysterious package.

A heavy object shifted inside as she shook the box. Curious, she untied the bow and wiggled the top free. A scream escaped her upon seeing the horror inside, and she threw the box on reflex.

Her heart raced as she stared at the floor, knowing, without a doubt, that someone had played a cruel joke on her. She'd been stupid to think a fae would... what? Claim her? Pre-love her? The letter hadn't explained much.

Slowly, she toed the box out of the way and bent over the

creepy doll on the ground. It had white porcelain skin with red dots on its cheeks, unmoving blue eyes, and long, dark hair.

She'd never liked dolls and never understood how they didn't scare other children. Even at thirteen, she wanted nothing more than to set it on fire. Huffing, she stomped to her bed to grab the letter... but it was gone.

Spinning around, she scanned every surface in her room. *Where did it go? Letters don't magically disappear.*

Unease slipped down her spine, and her eyes slid back to the doll. Perhaps she'd been half asleep and imagined the letter.

"Were you really sad a few days ago?"

She had been. Earlier that week, while walking home from school, Amelia found a poor rabbit half dead in the snow. Unable to leave it, she'd carried it all the way across Friya, the small village she lived in, to the livestock healer.

He'd taken one look at the helpless creature and said it was cruel to let it live. Its injury was too severe, and it would suffer a slow death.

Amelia cried when the healer carried it away. She'd never liked seeing animals hurt, and while she knew hunting was crucial to survival, when hunters carted their kills through the village, she had to look away.

It was possible Ana or Farrah saw her crying and wrote the letter, but not even their evil could make letters disappear. More proof she'd imagined it. Looking at the doll again, she gritted her teeth because, letter or not, someone snuck into her room.

But if the letter *had* been from a fae, he might have enchanted it. Taking no chances, she walked to her tiny desk and pulled out a piece of paper, an inkwell, and a quill.

Dear Nick,
Screw you.
Not Sincerely,
Amelia
P.S. I'm sorry about your mom.

She folded it neatly and set it on her windowsill. If "Nick" came back, she wanted her message received loud and clear.

The first light of dawn filtered through the rainbow leaves, creating a kaleidoscope of colors above Rennick's head on his morning run. On an average day, he waited until the sun rose completely before running through the dense forest, but he'd been out there most of the night.

Sleeping or sitting still proved to be impossible, and he thought training would help tire him out.

He'd thought wrong.

Another several hours of running, climbing, and any other training he could do alone to help pass the time, droned by slowly. Finn should have returned from the Human Kingdom, and Rennick's patience wore thin.

They'd decided Finn would leave early enough the night before to arrive at the orphanage by dinner time, then he'd glamour himself to slip in unnoticed and figure out which girl was Amelia because they had no idea what she looked like or which room was hers.

Once Finn gathered the information, he was to stay the night at a local inn and return to the orphanage before dawn to deliver the letter. He'd have to wait for her to wake up and read it before stealing the letter back and heading home, and Rennick hadn't considered that Amelia may be a late sleeper.

"He's almost home," a warm voice said.

Rennick spun around to face his father. "Who?" He couldn't mean Finn. No one knew of their plan.

His father laughed, the sound deep and comforting. At six foot four with a wide frame, his father looked like a larger, older version of Rennick. His dark hair had hardly any grey, but his eyes showed evidence of his humorous nature.

Those eyes crinkled now, and Rennick knew he'd been caught.

"Did you think my warriors would allow a thirteen-year-old boy across into the Human Kingdom with a permit signed by you and not tell me?"

He should have forged his father's signature.

"Forging my signature wouldn't have worked," his father said knowingly. "A child crossing alone would have raised flags, regardless."

"Something happened. It hurt," Rennick said softly, placing his palm against his chest. "Not physically, but she was upset, Dad. I had to do something."

"I think writing her letters is a good idea." His father's words surprised him. "The humans don't teach much about fae, and it's a good idea to tell her as much about us as you can."

"She can't know who I am." Rennick raked a hand through his sweaty hair. "If someone found out, she might get hurt." *Like Mom.*

The unspoken words hung between them, and his father's face softened.

"I know, son, and that's why she cannot write you back. If another fae, even a palace maid, were to see a letter from her in your room, where she calls you her mate, or intercept it somehow, it would put her in danger."

"I'm not going to write to her again," Rennick told him. "I can send her a history book on fae."

His father studied him for a moment. "I think the letters will help keep you two connected. You don't want to be detached and forget the importance of your bond."

Rennick pulled himself up to his full height. "I would never forget. I know my duty."

"And her?" his father asked. "If she never hears from you again, there is nothing stopping her from falling in love with another and marrying them before you can retrieve her."

He'd not thought of that. What would he do if that happened?

"The royal bloodline would weaken," his father went on. "We cannot allow that to happen, and I don't want you to miss out on the joys of marrying your fated mate."

"Just because she's my mate doesn't mean I'll love her." Rennick set his jaw stubbornly. "That's not how the bond works."

"Even if you do not love her romantically, you will love her deeply. Your souls are one and the same."

"I can't stop her from marrying someone else if I'm not there." Rennick silently implored his father to refute his claim.

He did no such thing. "You're right. You've been dealt a bad hand, son, but that doesn't mean you roll over. The least you can do is try." His father's eyes glazed over briefly before clearing. "We need to head back. Finn and Reyna just arrived."

"Reyna?" Rennick echoed.

Reyna was his father's *familiar*. The snow leopard's head came to Rennick's chest, and her teeth looked like rows of triangular ivory razor blades. Her eyes were pitch black against her solid white fur, and had Rennick not grown up with her, he'd be terrified.

"I glamoured her," his father assured him.

Royals could glamour entire kingdoms if they needed to, and with Amelia's village being only an hour away from the barrier on horseback, glamouring Reyna that far away was nothing for the king. Only one thing gave Rennick pause.

"You can glamour past the barrier?"

His father looked amused. "The barrier does not affect fae, son."

Rennick knew that, but it still surprised him. He hadn't really thought about it.

His father's eyes glazed over momentarily. "Finn is almost to your rooms."

Rennick nodded and followed his father home with a new fear. What if his mate fell in love with someone else? What if *he* did?

SIX MONTHS LATER

Amelia sat on a worn settee in the common room of the orphanage with a new book. The dark wooden walls and mismatched furniture felt cozier than her small room, and the fire roaring in the stone fireplace gave off a warm glow alongside the lanterns adorning the side tables. But the best part was that she wasn't alone. Clover, a girl her age who'd joined the orphanage a few months ago, often read quietly in the large room, too.

Amelia and Clover sat together many nights, sharing a lantern to read by without saying a word. Did that make them friends? Amelia wasn't sure, but the prospect of finally finding someone who enjoyed the same things she did, mainly reading and talking about books, was exciting.

Clover stayed in the classroom during lunch too, opting to read or draw rather than join the other students outside for fresh air. Amelia didn't know if she was painfully shy, preferred the quiet like Amelia did, or just hated people in general.

Amelia's heart sank each time she tried to start a conversation, but curiosity replaced her disappointment when she realized

Clover always found her way to Amelia, no matter the circumstance.

They didn't look alike, but they did have a few of the same attributes, namely long blonde hair and tall statures, but that's where their similarities ended. Clover's skin was a shade darker than Amelia's own light beige and their bone structures were completely different. Where Amelia had soft features and a round face, Clover had high cheekbones and a defined jawline.

They ate, read, and walked to school together, all while Amelia talked and Clover listened, occasionally commenting here and there. They'd go to the library together, and if Amelia wanted to stop somewhere on the way to or from school, Clover followed without complaint.

Clover looked up from her book and caught Amelia staring at her. Embarrassed, Amelia turned back to her own book.

"Hey," Clover called in her whisper-quiet voice. She hopped up from where she sat and held out her open book to Amelia, tapping on a paragraph. "This is my favorite part. I think you'll like it."

Amelia leaned forward to read the passage and realized she'd read the book several times before, and to her surprise, it was one of her favorite parts, too. The scene always made her laugh, and the fact that Clover thought she would like it and chose to share it made her laugh harder than usual. She beamed at the mysterious girl, who returned her smile and retreated to her spot.

Amelia had all the confirmation she needed that she'd officially made her first real friend.

❄

FOURTEENTH BIRTHDAY

Letter #4

Happy Birthday, ~~Darling,~~

I'm sorry I haven't written much. I don't know what to talk to you about because you can't reply, and I feel stupid telling you about myself when you didn't ask, but for the sake of the bond, I will.

I do normal things like hang out with my friends or go hunting with my best friend, Finn, and our other friend, Ora. She's a terrible shot, but we're teaching her to track so she doesn't accidentally put an arrow through one of our necks. I'm not hopeful.

Finn and I have to train a lot, but Ora says it's too hard to fight in a dress. She could wear pants like the female warriors, but when Finn told her that, she cried. ~~Girls can be weird.~~

I swear I do more than two things. I just can't think of any others right now.

Some of my hobbies might not match up with yours, or maybe they will. I guess we'll see one day. If not, we can find other things to do together that we both like. I'll ask Ora to help me think of things.

I have to study, or my father will tan my hide, but I'll try to write more.

~~Your Mate,~~

Nick

P.S. I felt you laughing yesterday. I wish I could have heard you too.

4

ONE YEAR LATER

Rennick inspected the bow and quiver full of arrows appreciatively. "And you're sure she'll like it?" he asked Ora.

Ora's father, Tully, had been the king's advisor for years, and since she and Rennick were the same age—the *exact* same age—her father brought her to the palace almost every day. They'd known each other for almost seven years, and wherever Finn and Rennick went, Ora followed.

Finn crossed his arms, looking skeptical. "I told you to do something else. You don't know if she likes to hunt."

Ora mirrored his stance and threw her long, dark hair over her shoulder. "And I said it's exactly something she'd want. What do you know about girls?"

Finn stared her down in a battle of wills. "My sister hates it."

"Not all girls are the same, *Finnigan*," she sneered.

Rennick ignored them both. They were always at each other's throats for one reason or another.

Two weeks prior, Ora had confronted him because she'd overheard her parents discussing Rennick finding his mate. As the king's advisor, Tully knew Rennick's mate lived in another kingdom and wouldn't move to the Mountain Kingdom until he took the throne, but that was it.

Thankfully, Tully didn't know Amelia's real name or which kingdom she lived in. Rennick's father told most of his advisors Amelia's name was Orissa, and that her family insisted on staying in their fae kingdom until Rennick took the throne.

Had it been up to Rennick, they wouldn't know anything, but his father explained that he had to tell them something. It was unusual for an heir's mate to not be found within the first few months of their thirteenth birthday, and the council had had questions.

The knowledge that information about his mate, even false knowledge, had been easily overheard stoked a familiar rage within him. His father spoke with Tully on the matter, but if it happened again, Rennick would handle it himself.

When Ora asked him about "Orissa", he'd sworn her to secrecy and threatened to cut out her tongue if she dared utter a word. He'd never so much as raised his voice to her, nor had he ever been a violent person, but something in him had changed following the death of his mother.

Ora had agreed to his terms, and when he told her the fabricated story of finding his mate, Ora's eyes flashed with something he couldn't name.

"Orissa is close to Ora," she'd said lightly. "Are you sure you heard correctly? It can't be a coincidence that our birthdays are on the same day."

He'd furrowed his brow, confused at her statement. "I'd never mistake the name of my mate, and there are several girls in the kingdom who share our birthday."

She never mentioned it again. Instead, she smiled brightly and said she knew just the thing a fifteen-year-old girl would love. Which led them to this moment, inspecting the new hunting gear commissioned specifically for Amelia.

"Stop fighting," he told his two friends. "I need to find a way to wrap this."

Ora looked pleased with herself and gave Finn a smug smile. "She's going to love it."

"I'll tell my mother they're for Ora's birthday and have her wrap them," Finn offered reluctantly.

Rennick smiled. "I don't know what I'd do without you two."

Reminiscent of the night of his thirteenth birthday, Rennick watched the seconds tick away on the clock. Only one minute left until he turned fifteen and received his mark.

When royal fae turned fifteen, they bonded to an animal companion for life—their *familiar*. Magic marked them with a tattoo of their *familiar's* species. A short time later, usually a few days, their *familiar* arrived and the bond completed. Along with enhanced magic and mate bonds, familiars were exclusive to royal fae.

Individuals with a *familiar* bond had the ability to see and hear through them and mentally communicate with them. The *familiars* couldn't say anything back, but their bonded could sense their thoughts. *Familiars* also assisted in battles should the need arise, and Rennick wanted something fierce, like his father's snow leopard.

Rennick hissed as his skin burned from the left side of his chest all the way up the side of his neck. It took his breath away.

"The pain will be over soon." His father's voice was calm, but it didn't make his chest hurt any less. "Breathe through it, son."

Rennick closed his eyes and grabbed the arms of his chair, refusing to double over from the pain. It felt like someone held a hot iron to his chest. As the pain subsided, his breathing slowed, and he opened his eyes.

Unable to contain himself, he jumped up and ran to his dressing room with his father close behind. He stood in front of the mirror and stared at the large tattoo adorning his chest in utter disbelief.

Etched in his skin was the side profile of an owl in flight. Its large wings stretched over Rennick's collarbone and up the side of his neck, and its rounded head with large eyes covered the front of his shoulder. The rest of the owl's body covered the entirety of his left pectoral.

He turned back to his father, his fury building. Everything the gods blessed him with came with a bitter twist. First his mate, and now this. That familiar darkness crept into his soul, and he itched to carve the image out of skin. "A fucking owl?"

He'd wanted something that could instill fear in his enemies or protect his mate when he wasn't around. A wulfer or even a serpent, would have been better than a bird the size of a breadbox.

His father chuckled. "Do not be disappointed with what the gods have blessed you with. They know exactly what you need."

Rennick scoffed. "Do they think I need a bag of birdseed? Because that's about the only thing I'll gain from this." He motioned to the marking on his chest. "What is an owl going to do? Peck someone to death?"

His father took measured steps toward him. "Serpents," his father replied. "Rats. Other birds. Fish."

Rennick furrowed his brow and turned back to the mirror to examine his mark again. "What are you talking about?"

"You said bird seed." His father stopped behind him. "But owls eat other animals. They are fierce predators." Their gazes collided in the mirror. "They swallow their food whole, and when someone threatens what is theirs, they attack without question." His father smirked. "Seems perfect to me."

FIFTEENTH BIRTHDAY

Letter #16

Happy Birthday, ~~Kitten~~
I commissioned you a special bow and a quiver full of
arrows this year. I didn't really know if you liked hunting or
not, but Ora said all girls do (even though my mother didn't)
and I chose not to argue.
When we're together, we can go hunting as much as
you'd like.
I got a big ~~mark~~ tattoo today. It's an owl covering the
left side of my chest. Between you and me, I wish I'd gotten
something else, like a panther or ~~wulfer~~ wolf, but I'm stuck
with this big-headed bird. I hope you don't hate it.
Eat some cake for me today.
~~Your Friend,~~
Nick
P.S. I think about you a lot. I wonder what you look like
or sound like or if you snore. And I wonder if you think
about me too.

5

EIGHT MONTHS LATER

For the past couple of months, Rennick woke every morning before dawn and spent bonding time with his *familiar*, Greta, a large, snowy white owl. He'd lay in his room with his eyes closed and tap into their bond.

Greta's thoughts felt similar to Amelia's emotions traveling down the mating bond, but clearer. With emotions, it could be hard to decipher exactly what the emotion was and what caused it, but with *familiars*, their thoughts and feelings came through like a sixth sense.

That morning, he'd let Greta lead them wherever she wanted, and when she flew through the barrier into the Human Kingdom, he'd expected their connection to sever. But it didn't. She admitted she was curious if it would hold since he was only fifteen.

You could have told me that's what you were doing, he'd grumped down their bond.

Greta ignored his attitude. *I didn't want to get your hopes up.*

Rennick made a mental note to ask his father more about the limits of their *familiar* bond.

After his connection to Greta survived the crossing of the

barrier, it'd taken him a moment to realize the implications—the possibilities—but once he had, he knew exactly where he wanted to go. He and Greta agreed to get a *quick* glimpse of Amelia and leave.

Over the years, Rennick had asked Finn what his mate looked like, and Finn, being Finn, said she was tall, blonde, and pretty. That was it.

That morning, he'd watched the girls from the orphanage walk to school and, just his luck, there were two equally tall, blonde girls who looked his age. They walked together, separated from the others, and a tiny, big-eared fox trotted beside them. Rennick had no way of knowing which girl was his mate.

But the more he watched them, the less he cared who was who because he couldn't take his eyes off the one whose face lit up as she talked, moving her hands more the more excited she became.

She was the most beautiful person he'd ever seen. Looking away felt impossible, and when a classmate called her name outside of the school building, confirming she was Amelia, everything faded to the background until only she remained.

Once Amelia went inside, Greta perched on a branch outside of Amelia's school. That was hours ago. Yet Rennick still stared through the owl's eyes, completely mystified.

Tall windows lined both sides of the school building, giving him a perfect view of his mate. He greedily soaked up everything he could in the short amount of time he had.

When the class broke for lunch, most students left, but Amelia and her friend from that morning stayed at their desks. His mate reached into an old lunch pail, pulled out a book, sandwich, and apple, and set them neatly on her desk. Her hair swung with the movement, and Rennick longed to run his fingers through it. She wore a simple blue dress that strained against her soft chest and hovered well above her ankles.

Everything she did mesmerized him, even the way she ate her small sandwich.

Is that all she brought to eat? he wondered with a frown.

Greta bristled, no happier with Amelia's meager lunch than he was. *Feed your mate.*

I will, he promised the owl, who was poised to attack if anyone tried to take Amelia's apple.

Seeing Amelia for the first time was unlike anything he'd ever experienced, and he knew, without a doubt, that he would love her more than anyone had ever loved another.

Letter #24

> *Hello, Love,*
> *My imagination did not do you justice. You are beautiful.*
> *Yours,*
> *Nick*
> *P.S. Are the other girls at the orphanage taking your food? I've included a basket of things for you to keep in your room, just in case.*

Amelia stared from the letter in her hand to the giant basket of food sitting on her desk, unsure which oddity in his letter to address first.

He said he'd seen her, but how? She always assumed he used magic to deliver the letters, but maybe he slipped in and out of her room without her knowing? No, that couldn't be it because he claimed to not have seen her before now. Nothing about Nick and his letters made sense.

She glanced down at her body. Why did he think she was

starving? Once again, she had the uneasy feeling that the letters weren't meant for her. After two years, he still hadn't used her name.

The only thing giving her hope was that he always wished her a happy birthday. She didn't know when the other girls' birthdays were—birthdays weren't celebrated at the orphanage since some of the girls didn't know theirs—and she didn't want to ask, afraid of the answer.

She stared at his signature. *Nick.* "Who are you?"

The paper crinkled slightly in her hand when she pressed the letter to her chest, hating that she couldn't keep it.

Nick wrote to her every month, and a few months ago, she'd held onto one of the letters and tried to copy down what it said, but it'd been plucked from her fingers and disappeared into thin air before she'd finished the first line.

Sighing, she stared at the paper despairingly. "Can't I keep this one?" she whispered, hoping the letter-stealing magic would take pity on her. Her finger traced over the words she'd never forget.

He called me beautiful.

In her peripheral, she saw something, or *someone,* flicker in and out of existence. She blinked, sure she'd imagined the teenage boy who looked at her over his shoulder before disappearing again, leaving the letter behind.

SIXTEENTH BIRTHDAY

Letter #30

Happy Birthday, Love,
I saw you in the woods with your bow last week. You're
getting better.
Watching you walk through town with my gift strapped
across your back made me feel like everyone knew you were
mine (even if they didn't). It made me want to find something
you could always wear... like a necklace.
I thought one that said MATE, or your name would be
perfect, but Ora said you would hate it. She helped me
choose this one instead.
Wear it for me, little mate.
Yours,
Nick
P.S. I put a sweater in the bag for that little fox of yours.
He looks cold.

❄

Amelia held up the gold necklace and stared at the trout pendant dangling from the chain.

She hated Ora.

"Did she like the necklace?" Rennick asked Finn, eager to hear her reaction.

Finn raised a brow. "I don't wait around to watch her. When she finishes, the letter, I take it and leave."

Rennick threw his hands up. "How am I supposed to know if she liked it or not?" It was the wrong thing to say because Finn looked mad.

No. He looked *furious*.

"I travel through the night to get there before morning, and sometimes I have to wait another couple of hours for her to wake, and you're mad I didn't wait even longer to watch her open a fucking necklace?" Finn shook his head with an incredulous laugh. "Find someone else to do it." He stalked off, and Rennick stared after him in shock.

"Finn, wait," he called after him, jogging to catch up. "I didn't mean to sound ungrateful."

Finn kept walking, his strides heavy. "But you are."

Rennick grabbed his arm and pulled him to a stop. "I'm sorry. I do appreciate what you've been doing, and you know anything you want is yours."

Rennick paid Finn handsomely for his time. He bought him the finest horse and anything else his friend even looked at with longing, but those were material things, and he realized now that he treated Finn like an errand boy instead of his best friend.

"If I could defy the gods and take them myself, I would," Rennick said quietly. "It kills me that I can't." He'd tried crossing the barrier more times than he could count over the last few months. The guards at the barrier gates merely watched him with amusement as he bounced off the invisible wall.

Finn hung his head. "I know." He met Rennick's stare. "I saw what losing your mother did to Callum. I'll do what I can to help you with Amelia, but I have a life, too."

Rennick rolled his lips together to hold back the emotion that swelled up at the mention of his mother. "You're right. If it gets to be too much, you don't have to do it."

His best friend sighed and slapped him on the back. "Stop being a dick and we're good."

ONE YEAR LATER

Rennick watched Amelia through the window of her school as she grinned at a boy with dark blond hair and a stupid smile.

The boy had approached her after class ended and kept her inside for too long. Rennick couldn't visit her often due to increased training back home, but when he could, he didn't want to see a lanky boy, with no right to make Amelia smile, holding her up at school.

Her walks home were Rennick's favorite, especially when she and her friend went to the library, swapping one tall stack of books for another. She always left the library happier than when she'd gone in.

Now that the harsh snowy months were coming to an end, Amelia milled around the village a little longer, looking into shop windows or playing with the tiny fennec fox that followed her everywhere.

If this guy kept her inside too long, Rennick would have Greta gouge his eyes out.

"I'm not doing that," Greta replied, but Rennick ignored her.

When Amelia finally gathered her lunch pail and books,

Greta took flight, already knowing where Rennick wanted to go to see his mate better.

Perched on the rooftop across from the entrance to the school, Rennick stared intently at the door, and when Amelia stepped outside and the sun hit her face, he sighed to himself. He'd not seen her in weeks.

She set down her pail, scooped up the little fox waiting faithfully on the steps, and rubbed his body to warm him up before tucking him into her oversized coat pocket. After securing him safely inside with only his giant ears poking out, she grabbed her pail and picked her way down the front steps.

She forgot to put on his sweater again, Rennick thought crossly. He would send her more.

A small grin graced Rennick's face, but it turned to ash when the lanky boy with the stupid smile appeared and murmured something. When Amelia nodded, he took her hand in his to walk her home.

SEVENTEENTH BIRTHDAY

Letter #47

Happy Birthday, Love,

I hope you like the book bag. I noticed you juggling stacks of books and thought it would be easier if you had a sturdy bag to put them in. Ora said the bag was "cute" and that you would like it. I included one for Clover, too.

Inside the bag is a mold of my hand, so when you feel like holding someone's hand, you can hold mine and not the lanky blond boy's who walked you home.

Seeing your perfect hand in his unworthy one made me murderous, little mate. You are mine, and I will do whatever is necessary to keep you, no matter how unconventional or vicious I have to be.

Always remember that.

Viciously Yours,

Nick

P.S. I wish I knew your favorite color. Mine is red, like blood.

Amelia stared at the white mold of Nick's hand, unable to think of anything other than how large it was. Her fingers traced over his, memorizing the shape of his nails and the grooves of his knuckles. The few times she'd seen Nick fade in and out of sight, he didn't look big enough to have a hand this size, but it'd been a long time since she'd seen him.

"Seeing your perfect hand in his unworthy one made me murderous, little mate."

Amelia blew out a breath. Jacob had asked to walk her home a few times, and once, she'd allowed him to take her hand, but it felt wrong. She wanted a boyfriend like the other girls, but none of the boys gave her butterflies.

As much as she looked forward to Nick's letters, putting her life on hold for him was ludicrous. All of her eggs were in his basket, but what happened if he tired of her or turned out to be someone else entirely? He never said when they would meet, only that they would. The more she thought about it, the more ridiculous it sounded.

The clay hand felt heavy in her own. It was the hand of a fully grown man, not a seventeen-year-old boy. A *thunk* sounded through her tiny room when she set the mold on her desk.

"Here," she said, dropping the letter next to Nick's hand, then watching it disappear into thin air.

EIGHTEENTH BIRTHDAY

Letter #57

Happy Birthday, Love,

You grow more beautiful every day.

Did you know I can feel you touch yourself at night? It took me a few times to realize what you were doing. Do you think about me when you do? Tonight, imagine my tongue trailing across your skin because one day it will. I'll taste every inch of you.

Being away from you is physically painful at times, but each day is one day closer until we meet.

Don't be upset, but a dress was taken from your room while leaving my last letter. I have returned it along with five new ones made in the same style and size. Ora assisted the seamstress in picking out the best fabrics to use.

The chests have been made slightly bigger because I noticed yours seemed tight. If you enjoy your clothing tight, please use the money I've left to have them altered. I want you to be comfortable.

Viciously Yours,

Nick

P.S. There's also a sling. I know they're to carry infants, but I think your fox will fit too.

The garish brown fabric mocked Amelia as she stared at the mirror. It had a hideous floral pattern with mixtures of red, pink, purple, and yellow.

If she ever met Ora, she would choke her with it.

FIVE MONTHS LATER

"Eddy," Amelia chided, straightening the fox's tiny sweater. "What has gotten into you?"

The little rascal weighed all of four pounds soaking wet, but his defiance rivaled that of a teenage boy. Following his arrival shortly after her fifteenth birthday, he'd become her shadow, tagging along wherever she went.

His size made him easy to sneak in and out of the orphanage, but for some reason, he hated sleeping in her room and instead hid under the furniture in the communal areas at night. He never came out from hiding until Amelia was alone, and when she realized she couldn't convince him to stay in her room, she hid blankets under one of the worn cloth settees where she liked to read.

Usually, he enjoyed wearing the sweaters and coats Nick sent for him. Where her mysterious *mate* found small sweaters with arm and leg holes for a fox, she didn't know, but today, Eddy kept trying to tear it off.

Hauling him into her arms, she wrestled with him a little longer before giving up. "You can't be like this today. You have to stay still and quiet in my bag when I get to work."

As if understanding her, he sat quietly and waited for her to

CHAPTER 9   43

pick him up and tuck him into the ugly book bag *Ora* had helped Nick pick out.

Amelia wanted nothing more than to burn the various gifts Ora had assisted in choosing, but she couldn't bring herself to do it because he genuinely thought she'd like them.

He and Ora were probably fucking. The thought made her stomach twist uncomfortably.

She tried not to let her spiraling thoughts dampen her mood, but they did anyway. Nick didn't want Amelia to have anything to do with other boys, but he could gallivant around with another girl, shopping with her.

The bastard.

Throwing open the library door, Amelia quickly schooled her features into a polite smile and approached the desk. "Hello, I'm here for Miss Bea. My name is Amelia."

The guy working the desk looked up, and she sucked in a sharp breath. He was cute, and like with all cute boys, she clammed up. Not because she *liked* him—she didn't know him—but because... well, because...

"Right this way." He straightened and pushed open a door behind the desk that led to a small room with a table, basket of fruit, and shelves filled with plates, napkins, and other various things.

Gesturing for her to sit down, he said, "You can wait here. I'm Michael."

She smiled and shook his hand. "It's nice to meet you."

He pulled out a chair across from her and sat, eyeing her appreciatively. "I've been dying to meet the new daytime librarian my grandmother can't stop talking about. She's excited to have you work here."

Not knowing what to say, she flashed another polite smile. "That's nice of her. I admire her and what she's done with the library." She meant that. When Amelia started coming to the library as a child, the shelves were in disarray, the selection of books was horrible, and most books had worn spines. Miss Bea took over and completely turned the place around. "Do you work here too?" she asked.

He laughed and leaned back. "No. I'm not much of a reader, but I'm helping my grandmother until I leave for the western region. I come back every year during the warmer months."

The western region, also known as the garden region, bordered the fae's Garden Kingdom. Beautiful, plush greenery and different types of colorful flowers and plants covered the entire area. At least, that's what they learned in school. Amelia never left the northern region. All she knew was snow, ice, and freezing winds.

"Are you from there?" she asked, intrigued. Being eighteen, she primarily only interacted with people at the orphanage, school, and a few others here and there. She'd never knowingly met someone from another region.

School finished last month, and she'd be forced to move out of the orphanage soon. Maybe she would save her money and travel somewhere for a holiday.

Not for the first time, she wondered what fae kingdom Nick lived in. He gave her no indication one way or the other, highlighting yet another reason all signs pointed to him stringing her along for fun.

What kind of guy claimed he couldn't meet her "until the time was right," yet delivered things to her and watched her with zero explanation as to how? He only told her his first name and superficial things about himself. Every book she'd read on soulmates made it seem like it was an irresistible pull, a primal need to be with the person. Yet, here they were, five years later, not together.

They were never going to meet.

In his letters, he was witty and thoughtful, a bit stiff, and what she could only describe as *rugged*. As they got older, he became flirtatious, and from time to time he could be possessive and over the top, but she liked knowing someone felt that passionately about her. *Supposedly.* But what good was a one-sided relationship where only one person held the knowledge and power?

It wasn't.

"Amelia?"

Michael's voice startled her out of a daze. "Yes? Sorry. I just dozed off. Dazed off. I was gazing." She wanted to crawl under the table. Taking a deep breath, she met his amused stare. "Sorry. My mind was elsewhere, and I'm nervous for my first day."

Better a lie than the pathetic truth that she was pining away for her supposed fae mate, who was invisible most of the time.

Michael chuckled. "I understand. My grandmother will be here soon. I need to finish sorting through damaged books." He turned to go but paused. "Since our shifts end around the same time, can I walk you home? I'd like to get to know who I'll be spending my days with."

She sat, stunned, and her mind flashed to Nick's weird hand mold that she'd held more times than could be considered sane. Then it flashed to Ora.

"Sure," she replied with a shrug.

He smiled and backed out of the room before turning and leaving her to figure out how to occupy her hands on the way home to keep him from trying to hold them. While she would like an updated version of Nick's hand to see if it'd grown, she'd rather not provoke him on purpose.

Something nudged her leg, and she jumped a foot in the air, then startled again when Eddy made a yipping sound. The pounding in her chest slowed when he cocked his head to the side in question. "Don't look at me like that. Nick can't be mad if someone walks me home."

Eddy knew all about Nick because, sadly, her pet was the only one she could tell. The fox might not understand her words, but he was a good listener who couldn't tell her she was merely a lonely eighteen-year-old girl holding on to the smallest bit of affection thrown her way.

NINETEENTH BIRTHDAY

Letter #67

Happy Birthday, Love,

I hope you like the hats and gloves. I noticed yours was gone again. Finn said ten sets are too many, but he doesn't know how often you lose things like I do.

I had to choose them myself, as Ora was away with her mother for a few weeks, but one of the female warriors assured me they were fine.

Nothing new has changed since my last letter. I still train daily, and I still think of you. I hope you think of me too and not that man who walks you home from work sometimes.

Would you be sad if something happened to him?

I wouldn't.

Viciously Yours,

Nick

P.S. I lie awake some nights when you touch yourself, wondering if you're naked or slipping your hand under your shift. Gods, I hope you're naked. The mental image will be my undoing.

TWENTIETH BIRTHDAY

Letter #74

Happy Birthday, Love,
I didn't think it was possible for you to be any prettier than you already are, but every time I see you, you prove me wrong.
I've left you ribbons that I picked out myself. I think they would look nice against your blonde hair, especially when the sunlight hits it.
Viciously Yours,
Nick
P.S. I love that you still wear your necklace. I imagine you keeping it on at night when you torture me. I'll make sure you keep it on when I torture you.

11

TWENTY-FIRST BIRTHDAY

Letter #80

> *Happy Birthday, Love,*
> *I've left you a new pair of boots. They're lined with wool*
> *to keep your feet warm. Ora said the color was in style.*
> *Viciously Yours,*
> *Nick*

Amelia glared at the tall, leather, wool-lined boots and stomped across her room. Cocking her arm back, she threw the baby-shit-green footwear into the back of her closet as hard as she could.

Not only did she hear from Nick less and less, but his letters grew shorter each time.

And they always mentioned Ora.

"I know what you're doing, princess," Finn said as he approached Ora. The girl was beautiful, but the older they got, the more Finn saw her for what she was: a snake.

Ora rolled her eyes and closed the book she'd been reading. She pilfered through the different books stacked in the empty library Rennick had built for Amelia, separating them into different stacks. She gestured to the piles. "Helping?"

Finn snorted. "Sucking up." Her eyes flared. "I saw the boots you helped Ren pick out for A—Orissa."

Ora sniffed and turned back to the stacks of books. "They're very in style right now."

"The style is," Finn agreed, "but no one in their right minds would wear that color. What is it you're trying to do?" He couldn't make heads or tails of it. Ora might have Ren fooled that she wanted the best for him and his mate, but what she really wanted was him.

What he couldn't figure out was what she thought she'd gain by pissing off his mate.

"How would you know what's in style?" she snapped. "You wear leathers everywhere."

Finn normally didn't stay for Amelia to open her gifts because he needed to get back to training. The rebel attacks were getting worse, and he and Rennick spent their time either training or on scouting missions. Ren would take over as king interim this year, and they'd be even busier. But Amelia's expression when she read Ren's last letter intrigued Finn, and he'd stayed.

The boots were the ugliest color he'd ever seen, but the fact that Amelia didn't look surprised told Finn the gifts she'd previously received were likely equally as bad. He'd never seen her, not in her pajamas, and now he couldn't help but wonder what else Ora had helped Ren pick out. Now he wished he'd stayed to see them all.

"I'm telling Ren to not let you anywhere near her gifts," he told her.

"You're being dramatic," Ora said, but he saw the panic in her eyes. "You've always been jealous of how close Ren and I are."

Finn blinked. She had to be joking, but when he saw the conviction on her face, he burst out laughing.

She marched forward and shoved him, but he barely budged. "Why are you laughing?"

"Because you're insane," he said, trying to hold it together. "Do you really think you and Ren are closer than he and I?"

Now she looked at him like he was the crazy one. "We are!"

Ren stepped into the library and looked between Finn and Ora. "What are you two fighting about now?"

Ora's bright eyes challenged Finn, daring him to say something. In a way, he felt sorry for the girl. She had no other friends other than he and Ren, and while he always suspected she thought she was Ren's mate, it was possible she was worried she'd be pushed out of their circle.

He'd do what he could to ensure she wouldn't interfere anymore. Shaking his head, he looked to Ren and shrugged. "Nothing. Are you ready to go?"

Ren appeared suspicious, but he nodded. "Yes. Father is waiting for us."

Finn smirked at Ora, who glared back. "See you around, princess."

12

EIGHT MONTHS LATER

Rennick wavered in the middle of the celebration as Amelia's emotions stole his breath. They were celebrating the capture of the leader of the rebel faction they'd chased for years, but the celebration halted, and people stopped to stare at Rennick clutching Finn's arm.

Nervous energy zipped through him, and his breaths grew shorter. His brain tried to sort out what he felt. Not fear or pain, but excitement and pleasure tainted with… *obligation* and *guilt* were the best words he could think to describe it.

He knew her self-pleasure like the back of his hand, but this was different than when she touched herself at night. It continued to build, and he was hyperaware of everyone in the ballroom watching him.

Amelia's orgasm brought him to his knees. A moan of pleasure tried to break free, but he slammed his lips shut. There was no choice but to ride it out in the least humiliating way possible.

As his breathing evened out and the tingles subsided, his heart dropped at the realization of what he'd felt.

She gave someone what Rennick thought would be his.

It'd been almost five months since he'd seen her, and six

since he'd written. Over the last few years, the rebel faction had grown bolder, terrorizing the four fae kingdoms with an unfathomable amount of attacks and resulting casualties. Rennick spent most of his time with the warriors, the council, or hunting down those who burned and pillaged villages.

He took over as king interim last year, as is customary in the Mountain Kingdom, adding more stress to his plate. Being one of their top warriors, Finn spent most days training new and established warriors or leading scouting missions, so he couldn't spare time to deliver any letters.

Rennick knew he should have told Amelia his letters might stop for a while, but he hadn't. He laughed humorlessly at the irony of timing. A letter sat on his desk to be delivered tomorrow night, but he was too late.

The stab of fear that she'd fallen in love with someone else in his absence almost brought him to his knees again.

Ignoring everyone's curious stares, he turned to Finn. "Meet me in my rooms at dawn."

He strode toward the ballroom exit, ignoring Ora's voice calling his name as Finn told her to leave him be.

Once in his rooms, Rennick fell into an overstuffed chair in the corner of his sitting room, leaned his head back, and closed his eyes, connecting with Greta.

Another man touched his mate, possibly loved her, and Rennick wouldn't take it lying down.

He didn't blame Amelia—she had needs he wasn't there to fulfill—but he'd not give her the chance to fall in love with someone else. *If she hadn't already.*

As Greta crossed the barrier and wove in and out of the evergreens, his inner turmoil grew, and when Amelia's small village finally came into view, he urged the owl to fly faster.

He felt Greta's unease. *"This is a bad idea."*

"We're only here to see who she's with," he told her.

Greta landed gracefully on a branch outside of the boardinghouse Amelia moved into after graduating school, but Rennick didn't know what to do from there. He weighed his options and decided Greta would have to peck at Amelia's window until she opened it.

Greta bristled. *"I'm not going anywhere near her window."* Even the owl feared finding another man in her room.

He prayed to the gods he was wrong, that he'd misinterpreted her emotions.

Please be home alone.

Time stood still when Amelia's soft laugh floated from across the street, where a man walked her down the cobblestone sidewalk toward the boardinghouse.

Rennick wanted Greta to attack him, but the owl held firm. The man walked Amelia to her porch, kissed her cheek, and waved goodbye.

She smoothed her hair, giving him a smile that men went to war for. A smile Rennick would do far worse for. He drank in everything about her down to the rosy hue of her cheeks until she disappeared inside.

Greta begrudgingly followed the man to a small bookshop one street over from the library, and Rennick watched as the man unlocked the door and disappeared inside. After a few minutes, the glow of a lantern filled a window on the second floor.

He must own the shop and live above it.

Another realization grabbed hold and threatened to drag him into a dark abyss to which there was no return. Amelia hadn't been wearing her necklace.

Greta took to the skies.

Letter # 82

> *Hello, Love,*
> *Forgive me for my prolonged absence. My duties are*
> *more demanding than ever, and I've neglected you. I*
> *shouldn't have left you without notice, and I won't do it*
> *again.*
> *Viciously Yours,*
> *Nick*
> *P.S. I felt you fucking him last night.*

Amelia stared at the letter with a mix of horror and rage.

With every month that passed without a word from Nick, she'd been worried something bad had happened, but then the logical part of her brain recognized that his letters had become increasingly less frequent over the last few years.

She always knew it was only a matter of time before they stopped completely, but the letter in her hand suggested otherwise.

How dare he only write because he felt her with another man? Had she not been with Gilpin, would she have heard from Nick at all?

She sat on her bed in a daze and battled a myriad of emotions.

As pissed off as she was, guilt nibbled at her, just as it had the previous night. How could he feel the difference between her pleasuring herself and another man doing it?

She hadn't been with Gilpin because Nick hurt her. That level of immature pettiness held no appeal. Gilpin stopped by the library often, always able to make her laugh, but she'd kept things platonic because of her sick obsession with a man she'd never met.

A little over four months passed with no word from her so-called mate, and it hurt, but she'd expected it. One day when Gilpin stopped in to chat, she invited him to lunch. That one lunch grew into meals together a few times a week.

When no word came from Nick regarding her time with another man, she'd been certain his interest in her had run its course. For the first time in her life, she allowed herself to be wooed by a man she could see and touch, even if it felt off.

A few lunches a week turned into dinner dates, and last night, she went to his place afterward and forced herself to take the next step for more reasons than one.

A small part of her held out hope that Nick would keep his promise and come for her one day, and if that happened, she wanted to be ready for him and everything he'd promised. The filthy things he'd written in his letters suggested a lot of experience, to which Amelia had none.

It might have been Gilpin's head between her legs, but it was Nick's image in her mind. She often pictured Nick when she pleasured herself, but last night she had the physical sensation too, and it filled her with a wild need she'd not experienced before. She came hard, thinking of Nick's tongue bringing her to release.

When Amelia asked Gilpin how to pleasure him back, she listened studiously, eager to do it correctly because if the time ever came that Nick's cock slid past her lips, she wanted to be ready.

Gilpin was a patient teacher, but before he spilled his seed down Amelia's throat, he laid her back on the bed, claiming he'd not be able to spend himself twice. He waited for her 'okay' and then fucked her for a very uneventful five minutes. It hurt a little, but nothing she couldn't handle.

Amelia blew out a long breath and looked back down at the letter, knowing she wouldn't do it again, even if she had every right. They weren't together. Nick didn't tell her anything about his actual life or who he was. She had no idea if he would come for her.

One year. If she didn't hear from him for one year, she would move on with her life. A weight sat heavy on her chest, because she had a feeling that if he'd not felt her yesterday, she'd have moved on with her life in another six months.

Sighing, she dropped the letter on her desk and watched it disappear.

13

The warm air of the palace dungeon was damp with blood and tears, both belonging to the trembling man huddled against the far wall of his cell. Rennick's footsteps echoed across the stone room, penetrating the silence.

Gilpin.

The man who'd touched Amelia peered through red-rimmed eyes, rightly terrified.

What about him did she like?

Rennick ground his teeth together, fighting against the knowledge of the pleasure this man gave his mate. She was *Rennick's* to please, and no one else's.

Gilpin spoke through sobs as he clutched the place where his dick used to be. "You can't keep me here."

Rennick's lips pulled into an amused smile. "Is that so?" He squatted in front of the man, wondering if his looks pleased Amelia. He had sandy brown hair, light blue eyes, and fair skin. The opposite of Rennick.

"I'm not going to kill you," he said calmly, cocking his head to the side. "But you will stay in this cell until my mate and I marry, and then you will work in our gold mines."

"Y-your mate?" the man asked, bewildered.

Finn stood by quietly, not daring to speak. He didn't agree with Rennick's behavior, but he was loyal.

Rennick wasn't a cruel man; he never had been. He was rational and level-headed, always thinking ten steps ahead, and the ability to rule came naturally to him. Everyone loved him, and he loved his kingdom. But Amelia meant more to him than his kingdom ever would, and if he had to dirty his soul to keep her, so be it.

"I don't know what a mate is, and I've never met a fae before. You have the wrong guy!" Gilpin insisted.

Rennick clucked his tongue. "I saw you with Amelia." His features contorted into ones of hate as he leaned closer. "I *felt* you fucking her."

Gilpin gaped at him, shaking his head frantically as he tried to scoot back. "She's a nice girl, but it wasn't anything serious. She's nothing to m—"

"*She's nothing?*" Hot rage coursed through Rennick's veins, and the man's eyes widened as he shook his head again. "My mate is not *nothing*," Rennick snarled. "She is *everything*." In one swift move, he grabbed his dagger from its sheath at his waist and sliced Gilpin's throat.

Finn cursed as Rennick stood slowly, wiping the blade on his pants. He'd been killing rebels since he was eighteen. Taking a life was nothing new.

Taking an innocent life was, but if it concerned his mate, he didn't care how vicious he needed to be to protect her or their bond.

Turning his now blood-speckled face to his friend, he gestured toward the dead body. "Dispose of him and bring me his clothes."

❄

Letter #83

> *Hello, Love,*
> *I wanted to let you know that your friend Gilpin is not avoiding you. He would come back again and again if I let him, but you are mine, little mate, just as I am yours. Do not ever forget that.*
> *I've left you something as a reminder that I will do whatever it takes to keep you.*
> *Don't worry, it's not my blood.*
> *Viciously Yours,*
> *Nick*
> *P.S. Did you lose your necklace?*

Amelia reached into the bag, closed her hand around crusty fabric, and pulled it out, discarding the bag on her bed.

"What the—?" It looked to be a pair of men's pants covered in dried blood. Realizing what she held, she threw the garment on the ground, frantically wiping her hand on her dress.

After five minutes of trying not to pass out, she spread the pants out with her foot to find a hole cut in the fabric between the legs.

Not cut—*ripped*. Blood saturated the area around it.

"Don't worry. It's not my blood."

She gasped and stumbled backward. *Gilpin.*

He'd not been at the bookstore for a few days, but no flags were raised, and no missing persons reports were made that she knew of. She thought he'd gone on a trip without telling her...

Her throat grew tight.

What did Nick do?

14

TWENTY-SECOND BIRTHDAY

Letter #95

Happy Birthday, Love,

Please don't be angry with me for not giving you a more personable gift, but Finn convinced me to give you money this year instead.

He has been very persistent since last year, and I agreed for no other reason than to shut him up. Please buy yourself something from me.

I've seen women wear lacy breast bands and matching underwear, and all I can think about is what you would look like in one. Do you know what seeing you in a set would do to me? Fuck, I could stroke my cock right now at the thought of a set adorning your soft body.

There is enough money to buy several sets and whatever else you'd like.

Viciously Yours,

Nick

P.S. As soon as I find out what makes you wet, I will drown between your thighs.

Amelia gaped at the exuberant amount of money sitting on her desk. *What in the hell did he do for a living?*

Glancing back at the letter, hot jealousy replaced her shock, slicing through her chest like a freshly sharpened knife.

He expected her to stay celibate, yet he fucked other women and asked her to wear undergarments like theirs? Fury and hurt caught fire within her, and she crumpled the paper into a ball.

"You fucking asshole!" She yelled into the empty room. "You did gods know what to Gilpin, yet you tell me of other women's fucking underwear?"

Snatching the bag of money, she stomped to her window, slammed it open, and cocked her arm back, but before she could cover the snow with paper and coins, something stole the bag from her grasp, along with the ruined letter on the floor, and disappeared.

"Fuck you," she seethed. "Don't come back."

Minutes of silence passed before she dropped to her bed and rested her head in her hands.

Did Ora have a red lacy set she wore especially for him?

Rennick leaned his elbows on his desk and rubbed his eyes. He'd woken that morning with white-hot anger burning bright in his chest, mixed with other things, but the anger was too potent to distinguish the others.

It was only a matter of time before Finn returned, and if he'd not seen anything amiss with Amelia, then Rennick would send Greta. There was no fear, so he knew she was safe, but whatever upset her was big.

"Never once in our lives have I ever thought you were stupid until now," Finn said as he walked into Rennick's study.

Rennick's gaze caught his friend's before trailing to the bag of money and paper ball in his hands.

Finn tossed the bag of money onto Rennick's desk, followed by the paper. "Your mate cried, crushed the letter in her hands, called you an asshole, and tried to throw the money out of the window."

Rennick stood fast enough to knock his chair over. *She was upset with* him? "I told you money was a terrible gift," he barked, already rounding his desk to fetch Ora.

"It wasn't the money, it was your letter," Finn corrected, stopping him. "You told her you saw other women in lacy undergarments."

Rennick stopped and frowned. "I don't understand."

Finn scrubbed a hand down his face and muttered something that sounded like *idiot.* "If she sent you money and asked you to buy undershorts that she saw on another man, what would you do?"

Rennick's frown deepened. "I would kill the man and buy the shorts, if that's what she liked."

Finn waited, and when Rennick didn't continue, he looked disappointed. "Ren, why would you kill the man?"

Oh. "Shit."

Finn shook his head. "She looked hurt, but mainly pissed."

Returning to his desk, Rennick pulled out another piece of paper and sat down, praying to the gods she wouldn't run to another after his foolish words. "I need this delivered immediately."

Finn already had his hand out.

Amelia threw open the door to her room, not caring when it banged loudly against the wall, and stomped inside. Her mood had not improved since that morning, nor did it improve at the sight of a black envelope atop her pillow.

She kicked her door closed, yanked her scarf off, and snatched the envelope off the bed. The pretty black paper ripped as she tore at it to see what Nick had to say for himself. In the past, she'd responded to things in his letters out loud, wondering if he could hear her, but he never acknowledged it.

The closest thing she'd received to a response was when she'd been allowed to keep one of his letters. Her hands shook as she carefully unfolded the paper.

Letter #96

Hello, Love,

I'm afraid I wasn't clear in my last letter. The women I mentioned were not lovers of mine. Fae are not modest, and it is not unusual for people to forgo modesty at certain establishments.

There isn't another woman in all of Eden who could take me from you, little mate, nor is there another man who could take you from me.

I won't allow it.

Please take the money and buy whatever you wish. You could wear a horse's saddle, and I'd still dream of having you in every way possible.

I apologize for making you doubt that.

Viciously Yours,

Nick

P.S. The saddle was a bad example because all I can think about is ripping it off and riding you hard.

Amelia pressed the letter to her chest with wide eyes. Who was this man?

ONE YEAR LATER

Finn winked at Tara, the barmaid at an inn in Friya, and raised his mug. Rennick's obsession with Amelia had become concerning. He sent Finn to deliver letters and random gifts almost every week.

With the rebels neutralized, Finn often opted to travel the day before and make a night of it, sometimes to get Amelia a different gift and chuck whatever stupid thing Ora had convinced Ren to buy, but mostly to enjoy his time with different women in town.

Tara was his favorite, and since Ren sent Amelia harmless chocolates from the Tropical Kingdom, it gave Finn extra time to fuck the pretty barmaid until she covered his back in scratches.

❄

TWENTY-THIRD BIRTHDAY

Letter # 148

> *Happy Birthday, Love,*
> *My days grow dire the longer we're apart, and I cannot see you nearly enough to quench my need to have you here with me.*
> *The sky seems dimmer and the snow colder without you, but our time apart will end soon.*
> *Enjoy the chocolate delicacies from the Tropical Kingdom. Ora went on a trip not long ago and brought them back for you, knowing your birthday was coming up.*
> *Viciously Yours,*
> *Nick*
> *P.S. The number of times you came last night was impressive, but I think we can do better.*

Amelia gagged and spat out the chocolate-covered slug. Her eyes watered as she sputtered and coughed, vowing to poison Ora if ever given the chance.

With her mouth freshly rinsed, she scooted back against her headboard and turned her eyes to the rising sun. Pressing her hand to her chest, she closed her eyes and tried hard to push her thoughts to her mate.

His melancholy words pricked at her heart, and while she didn't know how to send an emotion intentionally, she tried her hardest to send him joy.

This wasn't the first time she'd tried to soothe him when his letters held an air of sadness, nor would it be her last.

TWENTY-FOURTH BIRTHDAY

Letter #200

Happy Birthday, Love,

It's almost time to bring you home.

I fantasize about how your body will respond to me when I take you in my arms. Will you shiver when I say your name? Do your nipples grow hard with a simple touch, or do I need to tug them between my teeth?

I want to bury my face in your cunt and wear your pleasure on my lips for everyone to see.

Your body is my altar, little mate, and I will worship you until the end of our days.

Gods, I can't wait to have you.

Viciously Yours,

Nick

P.S. I don't want to hurt you. Please use the gifts inside the box to prepare for me, but slather them with the oil first. You're going to need it.

❄

Amelia stared slack-jawed at the three dicks laid out before her. They weren't *actual* dicks, but they were as close to the real thing as one could get. Having only seen one in person, she wasn't an expert, but she'd seen drawings in anatomy books.

These were bigger.

She cringed at the memory of Gilpin and briefly wondered where he was. *Probably somewhere hobbling around without a cock.*

The phallic replicas were made of some type of pliable molding clay she'd never seen before and finished with a smooth coating. The bottom of the shafts were covered with different sized bumps and knots, but she didn't know what for.

Her cheeks pinked at the thought of the man she'd seen glimpses of in her room a few times. She looked down at herself and sighed.

Before going to sleep last night, she'd donned a red lace undergarment set, built the fire in the hearth high, and slept atop her blankets in nothing but the very thing he wished to see her in with hopes he would touch her.

If he could.

She didn't know how his magic worked at all. He came into her room but stated he'd not seen her for the first time until she was fifteen.

If he could touch her, he would have already, right? He certainly hadn't last night. No explanation made sense to her, but whether he could touch her or not, she at least gave him a show.

That man had been the subject of her fantasies since the first time she'd caught sight of him leaving her room. Her vision of him transformed as they grew older. Each time she saw him over the years, he'd changed in some way, mainly with age, but the last time she saw him, his normally dark brown hair was blond. She liked blond.

Her body tensed and tingled, and she immediately grabbed

the small jar of oil and the smallest gift he'd so graciously left, knowing she needed to start now to work her way up to the biggest.

She would enjoy the practice.

PART TWO
VICIOUS LOVE

TWENTY-FIFTH BIRTHDAY

Amelia sat on the edge of her bed, staring at the empty spot where a black envelope should be, confused because Nick hadn't missed her birthday in almost twelve years.

Jumping up, she searched the entire room for a letter, gift, or anything suggesting he'd been there.

Against her better judgement, she'd fallen in love with him through his letters. At least she thought she had, but how could you love someone you'd never met?

He made her laugh, made her feel wanted, angry, and even horny to the point of pain. Luckily, his gifts last year helped tremendously, especially since she dared not touch another man after what happened a few years ago.

It was scary to think of what he might have done to the nice man who used to own Amelia's favorite bookstore, but some-how, Nick's possessiveness gave her a thrill. If that meant she was as fucked in the head as he was, then so be it. After all, according to him, their souls were connected.

She was not without possessiveness of her own, especially when it came to Ora. It was laughable to think he and his friend had not slept together. It would explain Ora's need to sabotage Amelia's birthday presents year after year. She could only hope that they'd not slept together recently.

A tryst as teenagers she could handle, but if he'd touched Ora in the last three years, she didn't know what she'd do. Commit a crime of violence, perhaps.

She opened her closet door and glanced at the odd gifts he'd sent over the years. Almost every one neatly lined the back wall, including the doll. Even the books he sent were awful, ranging from war stories to a guide to making soap, but she'd kept them anyway. The only thing she threw away were the chocolate slugs.

She shuddered at the memory.

Her hand strayed to the trout pendant around her neck. As ugly as it was, it meant something to them both. *Take that, Ora.*

"Happy birthday to me," she whispered into the empty room and shivered. The red lace undergarment set she wore did nothing to stave off the cold, but she'd worn it for Nick, knowing he'd bring a letter for her birthday.

Except this year, it seemed.

After getting dressed, she trudged to the kitchen for breakfast and scowled at the empty chair where Clover normally sat. They'd moved into the same boardinghouse after aging out of the orphanage, and just as they had since childhood, they ate breakfast and dinner together and shared a reading lantern at night.

Running back upstairs, she knocked on Clover's door several times with no response. A quick internal pep talk that everything was fine calmed her enough to go back downstairs, grab a banana from the fruit bowl, and hurry toward the door. With her coat in hand, she stepped outside and looked around with a wide smile that promptly dropped at the sight of the empty porch.

Eddy hadn't wanted to stay inside last night, something he

did from time to time, but he almost always waited on the steps for her the next morning. Occasionally, he'd be gone for a few days, but those times were rare. The first time he did it, she'd cried for two days, thinking he'd been hurt. She'd searched the woods for him, nearly freezing to death. Then he showed up on the third day like nothing happened.

"*Eddy*," she called out as she threaded her arms through her coat and tromped down the snow-covered steps. "*Eddy!*"

Her eyes searched for his large ears that were easier to spot than his little body, but the snowy ground remained undisturbed. Her shoulders sagged.

This was officially the worst birthday she'd ever had.

Heaving a sigh, she started toward the library, feeling sorry for herself and hoping for everyone's safety. It was glaringly obvious how few people she had in her life when only *one* of the three most important was a person she could see and touch—the others being a fox and an invisible man.

Her steps slowed as a tingling sense of awareness settled deep within her bones, but a deep, silky voice stopped them completely.

"Hello, Love."

It couldn't be. Heart pounding, she turned around and froze.

Two men stood on the other side of the street wearing leather pants and fitted shirts with fitted leather coats like those the queen's guard wore.

One was severely beautiful with a tall, broad frame and piercing light eyes that stood out against his dark hair and lightly tanned skin. He was the largest man she'd ever seen. The five o'clock shadow did nothing to hide his strong jaw or the dimple in his cheek accompanying his gorgeous smile.

But it was the man beside him who had her eyes widening and the world around her fading away.

Nick.

He was exactly as she'd last seen him. His strong arms were crossed over his chest and his short blond hair stood out against his dark golden-brown skin and eyes. He wasn't as tall as his companion, but he was taller than she was, and that was good enough for her.

Her eyes flicked to the men's pointed ears with surprise. She'd expected fae ears to be long with sharp points, but they weren't much larger than hers, just pointed.

Trying to keep the tremble from her voice, she whispered, "Nick?"

Stunning did not do Amelia justice, and while Rennick had seen her through his *familiar's* eyes, this was different. He'd arrived in Friya as soon as he could, having forced his father to do the king's coronation at midnight.

His mate's eyes lit with recognition, which struck him as odd. Had she figured out who he was despite him giving nothing away?

Protective instinct kicked in when she sprinted toward them across the icy street. He moved toward her, afraid she would slip and fall, but everything dropped from under him when she passed him and threw her arms around Finn, crying into his neck.

Finn's eyes went wide, and he tried to pull out of her grasp, but he wasn't fast enough. Rennick grabbed him by the neck and threw him back with an animalistic snarl. He heard his best friend hit the ground with a grunt, but he didn't care. All he cared about was his mate's terrified scream.

He reached for her, but she jumped away and moved toward Finn.

"*Stay back!*" Finn yelled as he scrambled backward.

"Don't fucking yell at her," Rennick bellowed, taking a menacing step forward.

Finn moved farther away and said to Amelia, "Don't touch me or your mate will rip me in half."

Amelia stopped in her tracks, looking between the two men. "What?" The confusion in her eyes had Rennick advancing toward her, but she held out her hand to ward him off. "Stop," she begged, and he hated the fear in her voice.

She is scared of me. He could feel it through the bond, and the realization gutted him. "I won't hurt you," he said gruffly, unsure why she thought he would.

Her arms went limp, falling to her sides. "*You* are Nick?"

The disappointment in her voice stung. Her hazel eyes slid to Finn again, and a low growl rumbled from Rennick's chest.

"I don't understand," she said, more to herself than them. Shaking her head, she turned to Finn. "I know it was you. *I saw you.*" Her eyes hardened as they moved to Rennick. "You're lying."

Rennick would kill someone today, and at the moment, that person was Finn. Pressing his lips in a flat line, he turned to his friend, who still lay on the ground. "What did you tell her?"

"I never spoke to her," Finn swore. "I don't know how she saw through the glamour."

"What the fuck is going on?" Amelia demanded, as her fear and confusion gave way to anger.

"Finn, take your shirt off," Rennick commanded, removing his own coat.

Finn muttered under his breath as he stood and yanked off his coat and shirt.

Rennick grabbed the collar of his own and ripped it down the middle.

Amelia's brow lowered in confusion as she looked between them. Then realization shuddered across her face when her eyes landed on the tattoo covering half of Rennick's chest and neck.

He smirked when her eyes trailed hungrily over his bare torso with desire.

"Do you like what you see, little mate?" he drawled, closing the distance between them. Ever so slowly, he reached for her, and when she didn't cower from his touch, he gently lifted her chin to run his thumb over her soft bottom lip. "My name is Rennick, and you are mine, love, not his."

18

Amelia swallowed hard as Nick—*Rennick*—dropped his hand. "Are you okay?" The lack of warmth in his voice added to her confusion. He looked and sounded terrifying, like a weapon created to destroy, yet his touch was gentle like his letters.

Well, *some* of his letters.

Taking a closer look, she noted his light green eyes, short, messy hair, and light stubble that begged to be touched. *Her mate.*

Her eyes flicked to the large owl tattoo on his chest again as she recalled a letter he'd sent years ago, telling her about it. *"I hope you don't hate it,"* he'd written. She definitely didn't.

"He brought the letters and gifts?" she asked, pointing at Finn, who looked everywhere but at her.

Rennick's hand went to the small of her back and directed her in the opposite direction of the library. "Yes. Magic bound me to my kingdom until today."

She nodded absent-mindedly, following him without a second's consideration while going over everything she thought she knew. The boy who she'd seen over the years wasn't Nick.

Mortification stopped her in her tracks, and Rennick stiffened and looked down as she stared at Finn's back.

"What's wrong?" he asked, following her line of sight. Grabbing Finn's shoulder, he whipped him around. "What did you do to her?"

Finn tried to shake out of Rennick's hold to no avail. "Nothing!"

Amelia buried her face in her hands and groaned.

Someone hit the ground with a grunt before two large hands gently wrapped around her wrists and lowered them. "What's wrong?"

"I'm fine," she lied.

Rennick stared for a moment. "I can feel your embarrassment."

Great, a walking lie detector. Her throat dried. "I..." Gods, she wanted to die. "I thought he was Nick—*you*—bringing me things, and I..." If ever there was a time for a chasm to open and swallow her whole, now would be it.

He looked from Finn to her, his serious demeanor never wavering. "And what?"

Averting her eyes, she mumbled, "I slept in only my undergarments on top of the blankets sometimes for you." She covered her face again.

The air around them thickened with tension, and when she peeked around her hands, she saw every vein in Rennick's neck straining against his skin as he turned ever so slowly toward Finn.

Finn cursed for the hundredth time and backed up. "I never looked at her like that, Ren."

His words didn't deter the giant angry fae, and Amelia dashed forward, instinctively wrapping her arms around her mate's middle.

He stopped, though his body still vibrated with anger. "You

would defend him?" His tone sent chills skittering across her skin.

"It's not his fault." She sounded more confident than she felt. "He couldn't control what I wore. Be thankful I didn't sleep naked, because I considered it."

"You're making it worse," Finn warned her, still backing away.

Rennick's eyes finally moved to hers, his features transforming into something akin to lust. "You wanted to sleep naked for me, little mate?"

She was all too aware of his bare chest pressed against hers, heating her blood to molten lava. "Yes."

He freed his arms from her hold and grabbed her face gently. "You will."

Finn breathed a sigh of relief. "Thank fuck."

Amelia walked silently beside Rennick, trying and failing to come to terms with the situation.

After putting Finn's face to Nick's letters for years, it was difficult to convince her brain that *Rennick* was Nick, not Finn. When you thought something for so long, you couldn't change it overnight, no matter what your brain knew to be true.

She'd fucked herself to images of Finn countless times, and her desire for Nick was tied to Finn's face. Embarrassment would apparently be her closest companion today.

Rennick stopped abruptly and gently raised her face to look at him. "What's wrong?" he murmured. His eyes searched hers, worry lines etched across his beautiful features.

I want to crawl into a hole indefinitely. "Where are you taking me?" she asked, in lieu of an answer.

He dropped her chin and tilted his own to the north. "Home."

She jerked her thumb over her shoulder. "My home is that way."

He looked past her and furrowed his brow. "Your home is with me now. We're going to my palace in the Mountain Kingdom."

Questions pelted her brain like hail. "You're from the Mountain Kingdom? Why didn't you tell me you were that close?" The ride from Friya to the Mountain Kingdom border wasn't far. To think he'd been that close all along... *wait.* "You live in a palace? Are you a nobleman?" Did noblemen live in palaces? She didn't know, but a worse thought occurred to her, and she backpedaled. "Are you a royal?"

Rennick ran a hand through his hair, mussing it up more. "I couldn't risk telling you anything. There are people who would hurt you because of me."

Amelia stood motionless as her brain slowly caught up to what he'd said and realized she didn't know him at all. She'd been a fool to think she did.

"I'm not going to the Mountain Kingdom." Yesterday she would have gone to the edge of Eden with him, but that was when she thought she knew him. She'd pictured the wrong man and thought he was a warrior who protected his kingdom like other men throughout their world. Not... whatever he was. "You didn't answer my question. Are you a royal?"

Rennick angled his head to the side. "I am the king, and the climate there is no different than here, if that is what you're worried about."

The king? A human mated to a fae king was laughable at best. The fact he thought the weather was her issue showed how little he knew her.

"I don't want to uproot my life here." The lie tasted foul on her tongue, but she needed time to think before being thrust into whatever new life awaited her. "I have friends." *Sort of.* "And Eddy." *Who she couldn't find.* "And I don't know you."

"You know part of me," he said matter-of-factly before his voice dropped dangerously low. "Who is Eddy?"

Her eyes narrowed. "My fox. The one you send sweaters for. Unless that wasn't you either." She glared at Finn, pissed at him as well. They'd tricked her, and what was worse, she'd let them.

There wasn't enough information in his letters to form anything definitive, and the facts never lined up. How many times had she asked herself how he could bring her things but never talk to her? *Godsdammit.* She was a fool.

Rennick's body relaxed, which pissed her off even more. "I will bring you to visit your friends as often as you wish."

How easily he thought she would follow his lead, but she refused to back down. "I wish to stay."

He pursed his lips and turned to Finn. "Head back to ensure everything is ready for our arrival. She and I will retrieve her fox and whatever else she needs."

Had he not heard her? She wasn't going.

"Do I need to send guards with more horses and another carriage?" she heard Finn ask as she turned and walked away.

"I will buy a carriage here and hire a driver," Rennick replied. "No guards are needed. We should be home by nightfall —where are you going, love?"

She walked faster, contemplating if running would be worth the exertion. His long legs would no doubt catch up to her in one stride.

When he appeared at her side without a sound, she screamed, grabbing her chest. "Don't sneak up on me," she snapped.

He smirked but wiped it away when her eyes turned to slits. "Fae are naturally graceful and stealthy."

"Then wear a bell," she grumbled, picking up her pace.

"We will go to the boardinghouse first to gather your things," he said as though she wasn't trying to escape. "I need to know how many trunks you have before buying a cart."

He reached for her hand, but she slapped it away. "For the

last time, I will not leave my life behind because the Mountain King thinks I'm his mate." She was three seconds from losing it. "And if I *did* want to go, I can't just disappear without a trace."

Not that anyone would look for her except Clover and Miss Bea, but Rennick needn't know how pathetic her life was. It occurred to her that as she'd aged, she'd never bothered getting close to anyone because she thought she'd leave with him one day. The thought made her scowl at the man, who stared too intently after her.

He looked amused, and she stomped through the snow like a petulant child. All these years she'd waited for him to come, and now that he was here, she wanted him to leave.

No, you don't, a little voice whispered in the back of her mind.

Fuck you, too, she whispered back.

He'd omitted crucial truths about himself, making her question if anything he said was true.

"Did you mean everything you wrote?" she asked without thinking, praying he couldn't hear the desperation in her voice. *Or feel it.*

He stopped abruptly. "You think I would lie to you?" He didn't sound offended; he sounded hurt, and she wanted to snatch the words back.

She grappled for something to say to reverse what she'd done. "You lied about who you were."

His nostrils flared slightly. "I never lied to you. I couldn't reveal anything about my true identity, but I never lied."

He hadn't lied about coming for her. Her eyes flitted to his fighting leathers and broad, muscular, *bare* chest. It was obvious he trained often, so he hadn't lied about that either. It might be reckless or stupid, but she believed him. What other choice did she have?

"You're ordering me around without asking what I want. I

am not a dog." She crossed her arms defiantly. "In your letters, you were more considerate than this."

Rennick stared at her for the longest time before taking her hand. "We can make a decision together, and if staying here is your wish, then we'll stay."

We'll stay?

Her heart kicked up a beat at his submission. *Can a king live in another kingdom? Doesn't he have duties?*

Nodding dumbly, she squeezed his hand and started toward the boardinghouse.

Rennick ducked his head to step through the doorway of Amelia's small room. He'd seen glimpses of it through her window over the years, but never the entire thing.

A small nightstand sat next to a modest bed tucked into the far corner of the room. Next to her closet on the opposite wall sat a worn dresser adorned with various items, including the mold of his hand. A small overflowing bookshelf stood next to her writing desk near the window, and an old stone hearth took up most of the fourth wall.

It was small, but it was *her*, and he loved everything about it.

"Welcome to my home," she said lamely, chewing on her bottom lip. "I know it's not much."

He smiled and grabbed her desk chair to have a seat. "I love it."

She held out an arm to block his descent. "I don't know if that will hold you."

He frowned down at the chair. "Your furniture is not safe?" Now that he looked at it, the woodwork did look shoddy.

Picking up the repugnant piece of furniture, he debated the best way to break it into a thousand pieces.

Amelia grabbed the other side of the chair. "What are you doing?"

"This doesn't need to be in here if it's unsafe," he said, wondering why she'd want a chair that could kill her. "I'll buy you a new one."

"My chair is fine," she protested, trying to tug it from his grasp. "Just because it won't hold your gigantic body doesn't mean it won't hold mine."

He narrowed his eyes at the piece of furniture. "I would rather not chance it."

"Put my chair down," she said sternly, making him smile.

It creaked when he set it down, earning another glare from him. "Where would you like me to sit?"

She motioned to the bed behind her, and his smile turned wolfish. "Not for that," she huffed. "Sit."

Rennick lowered himself onto the small bed, grabbed her around the waist, and brought her to his lap.

She squeaked, looking at him with wide eyes. "I can sit down on my own."

"I didn't want you to sit in the chair," he half-lied.

Extracting herself from his hold, she stood and turned to face him. "You said if I had questions, you would answer them."

Curiosity was a good sign. "Ask whatever you wish."

She hesitated a moment before crossing to her desk and removing a stack of papers from the top drawer. Rennick tried to read them over her arm, but after picking up the first page, she stuffed the others back inside the old desk.

"I kept a list." She sheepishly held out the paper. "I didn't want to forget anything if you came for me."

"If?" he echoed. "You thought I'd not come?" Had he not been clear in his letters?

She sat down beside him with a half-hearted smile. "Some-times I thought your letters were in my imagination." Her hand gestured toward her closet. "The gifts you sent were the only pieces of tangible evidence I had to prove you were real."

"You kept them all?" His chest swelled with pride. "I was afraid you didn't like some of them because I never saw you use them."

Amelia squirmed, and he could feel the guilt as if it was his own.

"You didn't like them?"

"It's not that," she replied, choosing each word carefully. He didn't miss the fisting of her hands when she said, "Ora and I don't have the same tastes."

Her jealousy pricked at his insides, and he fought a grin. It was nice to know things weren't one sided.

"She is an old friend. Finn and I have known her since we were children." He leaned down and softly kissed the top of her head. "Nothing and no one in this world could compare to you." He tapped his chest. "Can't you feel it?"

She ignored his explanation and peeked over the edge of the paper in his hand. "Question number three."

He scanned the page. *"Why can't I feel your emotions?"*

Setting the paper down, he studied her carefully. She should be able to feel his emotions. A royal and their mate could feel each other's emotions immediately, but then again, a royal had never been mated to someone without magic before.

"Because you don't have magic," he guessed. "When we marry and complete the bond, you should be able to feel what I feel."

"Okay." She exhaled loudly and took the paper from him, reading it over. "Why did your letters disappear?"

"Finn stayed until you read them, and when you were done, he used glamour to take them back."

She blinked a few times before asking, "What is glamour?"

He tried not to grin at the cute line forming between her brows. "It's a magic that fae possess. For normal fae, it only works on humans and animals. It makes them see what the fae want them to see." He held up the paper and used glamour to make her see a cup, then laughed when she blanched. "Royal fae's glamour works on everyone except other royals."

"Royals can glamour other fae, just not other royal fae," she stated slowly, as if memorizing materials for an exam.

"Yes, and their lack of glamour is why humans can't come into the fae kingdoms freely."

At her confused expression, he explained, "There are animals within our forests much more dangerous than those in the Human Kingdom. Fae can hide themselves with glamour when needed. Humans cannot. Before the barrier, many humans died within our forests."

Her eyes almost popped out of her head. "*What?*"

"It's why the gods returned long after creation and created the barrier." He knew the human rulers chose to withhold information regarding the fae, but he hadn't expected it to be the basics.

"You know the gods?" she whispered, her skin turning white as snow.

He threw his head back with a booming laugh, something he hadn't done in a long time. "I'm only twenty-five. The gods have not been in this world since they erected the barrier. All fae children are taught the history of our world in school." He felt her humiliation and pulled her into his lap again. To his satisfaction, she let him. "They filter much from the humans. You had no way of knowing."

"Why do they keep us in the dark?"

"I don't know," he answered honestly. "Your rulers made that decision long ago. If you'd like, I will have a copy of every history book throughout the fae kingdoms made for your personal library."

She perked up. "Personal library?"

His lips twitched at her excitement. "I had one built for you at the palace."

The way her eyes lit up put the moon to shame, and before she could reply, he leaned down and placed a soft kiss on her forehead, vowing to kiss her every chance he had. "Have you made a decision about where you'd like to live, or do you need more time?"

"If I hate the Mountain Kingdom, you'll let me move back?"

Did she think he would deny her anything? "*We* will move back. I will follow you anywhere, little mate, even to hell if that's where you wish to go."

19

Later that afternoon, Rennick waited outside of the library where Amelia worked while she apologized for her absence that morning and ended her employment.

The thought of taking her away from something she loved solidified his decision to build a second home in Friya so they could travel back as often as she desired. They would need a new sturdy carriage, too. He would have construction started immediately and surprise her as a late wedding gift.

His planning shuffled to the back of his mind when the library door opened and Amelia stepped out with slumped shoulders. "All done."

"We don't have to leave." He ran his hands down her arms. "I meant what I said. If you want to live here, we will."

Tears lined her eyes again, but before he could panic, she slipped her hand into his. "I promised Miss Bea we would visit."

Rennick's chest tightened at her willingness to sacrifice her current life to start a new one with him. "Yes, we will. Is there anyone else we need to see before I rent a cart?"

"I need to tell Clover I'm leaving and find Eddy before we go," she said, ticking them off on her fingers.

"Is it unusual for Eddy to be gone this long?" On the days he'd watched her, the little fox was always around.

"He's done this a few times before," she said, tugging Rennick across the street.

He would pay every person in the kingdom to search for Eddy if needed. Leaving without him was not an option. "Did he have on a coat when you saw him last?"

Amelia pressed her lips together, and he noted her attempt to hold in a laugh. "No, but he will be fine."

When they found him, Rennick would see to it that he never stepped outside without one.

"Wait here." She dropped his hand and slipped into a small bakery. It wasn't long before she returned, chewing on the inside of her cheek, deep in thought. "Clover isn't working. Her boss said she took the next few days off to see her family."

"Why do you look like that?" he asked at her cynical expression.

Planting her hands on her hips, she turned back to the bakery. "She doesn't have any family."

Rennick scratched the light scruff on his jaw. "You think they lied to you?"

Amelia shook her head and turned back to him. "I think she lied to them, but I don't know why."

Placing his hand on her lower back, he led her toward the carriage house to buy a storage cart for their journey home. "Perhaps she is at home, taking the day off."

"Maybe," Amelia said distractedly, and allowed him to guide her without protest.

Amelia packed the last of her things into one of the trunks Rennick had delivered to the boardinghouse.

"You don't need to glamour your ears around me," she told

him, trying to sound casual. After a few cross looks from other villagers, he'd glamoured his ears to look human.

Like an apparition, his points appeared, and he shot her a devastating smile over his shoulder. Gods, he was handsome, and she wasn't the only one to think so. Women stared at him wherever they went, glamoured ears or not. If that was the response he received amongst humans, she could only imagine how many fae threw themselves at him daily. She glared at his back. Why couldn't he be average looking?

Sea-glass eyes framed by dark lashes met her own as though he felt her ire. "What has you riled up, little mate?"

"I'm fine," she clipped, slamming the trunk closed. Many things described her state of mind, but fine wasn't one of them. "Everything is packed and ready to go."

"The carriage, cart, and horses will be delivered in the morning," he said, gazing out the window. "We need to find your fox."

"If he's coming home tonight, he'll be on the porch."

Rennick looked uneasy. "If?"

"A few times over the years he's stayed gone for a few days." She opened her bedroom door to head downstairs, worried her furry friend had not eaten all day.

Fennec foxes were native to the eastern desert region, and she didn't know if he could hunt in the snow. With no way of knowing where he went or what he did, she convinced herself he starved each time he left. Amelia hurried to the foyer and threw open the front door, and there, sitting on the top step of the snow-covered porch, sat her little friend, shivering from the cold.

"Get in here," she chided and stepped aside.

Obediently, Eddy pranced through the door without a care in the world and followed her to the kitchen. They both stalled upon seeing the hulking fae king cutting raw steak into tiny bite-sized pieces and placing them onto a small plate.

How did he get in here so fast, and where did he get steak?

At the boardinghouse, meals were included in the weekly rent, but each tenant had their own labeled boxes in the large cold box and another labeled shelf in the pantry.

Amelia didn't have steak in her cold box. "Where did you get that?"

He looked from the steak to her. "The cold box."

"Whose cold box?"

"They're not all yours?" His body went rigid. "Do they withhold food from you here, too?"

Remembering the gigantic food basket from years ago, she raised her hands. "Calm down. I get three meals a day, *as I always have,* but we each have extra we buy ourselves." Looking pointedly at the plate, she said, "I do not buy steak."

His shoulders relaxed. "I will leave money for whoever's it was." He gestured to Eddy. "He needs to eat."

There was nothing more attractive than a scary man cutting up meat for a pocket-sized animal.

She tried to sound as nice as possible, not wanting him to think she wasn't grateful, even though she kind of wanted to strangle him. "It's sweet of you to prepare Eddy food, but can you show me which box?" *What if that was someone else's dinner for tonight?*

After Rennick showed her where the food came from and insisted on giving her the money to replace it, she knocked on her neighbor's door, explained the situation, and handed him enough money to buy twenty steaks.

When she returned to the kitchen, Rennick held Eddy snug against his chest, feeding him like a child. *Did he just coo?*

He looked up with a crooked smile, showcasing a dimple, and her heart stuttered in her chest.

"He likes it," he told her, kissing the top of Eddy's head, and Amelia knew, without a doubt, if this man decided she wasn't what he wanted, she wouldn't survive the fallout.

"We usually eat chicken," she commented, coming around

the island to stand beside him. "Steak is a rare treat." Eddy chomped on another bite while Amelia pet his head. "You need to thank Nick for feeding you like a little king."

Eddy yipped when Rennick's hold tightened. He set Eddy gently on the floor and straightened slowly. With one final lick to each of their legs, the fox scampered off to the common area.

Rennick's eyes flashed when they slid back to Amelia, and her stomach dropped. "I know that's who you've known me as until today, but it's not my name."

Her mouth opened and closed a few times, not knowing what to say.

"Nick is only part of who I am." His tone softened, but his shoulders didn't. "You associated my alias with Finn, and I don't want the ghost of another man between us. There is more to me than I could show you in those letters. Rennick is the man who stands before you, not Nick."

She nodded, understanding completely because she was more than the girl he'd observed over the years. Amelia drummed her fingers on the island and cleared her throat. "I'm sorry. It was a slip of habit."

He released the tension in his shoulders and wandered to the cold boxes. "Which of these is yours?"

Glad for the subject change, she poked her head in behind him and pointed to her box. They'd eaten earlier, but with his size, it wouldn't surprise her if he needed more food. "I learned to make a pretty good roast if you want me to cook you one." Her cheeks burned with the admission when he turned to look at her.

The way he stared made her squirm, but she forced herself not to look away from his unwavering intensity. In one of his many letters, he'd told her a list of his favorite things, and she'd committed a few to memory before Finn took the letter back.

"You learned to make my favorite dish."

It wasn't a question, so she didn't answer. Instead, she busied herself with clearing away Eddy's dishes, and washing and drying them for longer than necessary while Rennick's eyes burned holes into her back.

After wiping her hands on a towel, she swept a hand toward the stairs. "I'll show you the bathroom so you can bathe."

She tried to skirt around him, but his hand caught her arm gently. "You learned to make my favorite dish."

Did he think her a fool for doing what he paid the palace staff to do? "I'm sure it's nothing compared to what you're used to, but—"

He leaned down and brushed his lips over hers, killing whatever she had to say. "Thank you. I'm not hungry, but if you are, *I* will cook for *you*."

She shook her head in a half-stunned state. "I'm fine. We, uh… we should head up if we're going to leave early tomorrow."

He moved out of her way and followed her upstairs. After she showed him where the soaps and towels were in her ensuite bathroom, he retreated to the bedroom and said, "You bathe first. I am unsure how long hot water lasts here."

Her heart flip-flopped at his thoughtfulness. She looked at him then, *really* looked at him, from the dark stubble on his ruggedly handsome face to his large, calloused hands that made a full-sized towel look like a washcloth. He might appear to be a lethal warrior on the exterior, but inside was a kind man who sent tiny sweaters for a fox and worried the hot water would run out before Amelia could shower.

And he was hers.

It might be he who chased her today, imploring her to leave with him, but Amelia knew, deep down, she would follow him to the ends of Eden, whether he wanted her to or not.

20

Rennick stepped out of the bathroom with a towel wrapped around his waist, loathed to put his dirty clothes back on. An overnight stay had not been on his agenda, so he'd brought no other clothes. In the village, he hadn't thought to grab more than a new shirt to replace the one he'd torn.

Amelia looked up, her lips parting as her eyes trailed over every inch of his exposed skin. Her gaze left a trail of heat in its wake, and his cock slowly rose under her perusal. Discretion didn't exist in a room the size of a dinner plate, and he had no choice but to obviously press down on his growing erection.

"I don't have any clean clothes," he explained. "Do you have men's clothes lying around?"

If she did, he would kill every man in the kingdom.

Amelia swallowed hard and dragged her eyes to his. "I don't. Are you going to sleep…" She waved her hand haphazardly, indicating to his naked body.

"Yes." He closed the distance between them. "Or would that make you uncomfortable?"

"It's fine." Rennick bit back a smile as she stumbled over her words and red crept up her neck into her cheeks. He wondered if she flushed when she came, too. "I don't know where you'll sleep," she added, glancing over her shoulder at the small bed in the corner.

"If I hold you, we'll both fit." He didn't need to assess the bed. He would make himself fit on a pea if it meant being next to her. "I won't try to fuck you," he added. "Unless you ask me to."

She straightened and narrowed her eyes when he smirked. "Sleeping *only.*"

Damnit. Whipping off his towel, he sauntered to the bed, relishing in her sharp intake of breath and the mutters that followed.

"I'm only doing this because I feel like I know you," she said defensively, but why she felt the need to defend her actions, she didn't know. They were mates. "I don't jump into bed with men simply because they ask."

He turned to her slowly. "Good. I try to avoid bloodshed when I can."

Eyes wide, she whirled around and snuffed out the candles, then quietly felt her way to the bed.

Amelia sat carefully on the edge and laid back, facing away from him. No matter what she said, he knew his nakedness made her anxious. He draped the towel over his hips to put a small barrier between them.

Gathering the comforter and sheets, he pulled them over their bodies, turned on his side, and laid his arm over her middle. Her body lay stiff against his. "Did you hurt Gilpin?" she whispered.

The mention of her past lover made his teeth grind together. Sitting up, he looked down at her silhouette, shown only by the moonlight filtering through the window. "Does the answer matter?" *Does she still care for him?*

She rolled slightly to meet his gaze. "Yes."

"I killed him." Lying would have eased her fears, but she needed to know him completely. He was a man who would slaughter the masses for her without question. Not even the gods held as much power over him as she did.

Amelia made a strangled sound and tried to scramble out of bed, but he grabbed her hips and yanked her back. "W-why would you *kill* him?" Her voice rose an octave, the tremble more prominent with every word. "He didn't do anything wrong. It was *my* decision."

Amelia's fear penetrating his chest awoke his own. *What if she leaves me?*

As Rennick took in the deathly pallor of her face and her shaking hands, he sighed. "I wasn't going to kill him at first, but he said you were nothing."

She scoffed, and the fear that had invaded Rennick's chest shifted into angry indignation. "It doesn't matter if he called me an ugly bitch. You don't kill an innocent man because of it!"

He sat up, maneuvered her onto her back, and hovered above her, caging her in with his arms.

"Everyone has a moral line they won't cross." His chest heaved, and Amelia braced a trembling hand against his chest. "I don't need a line to know what's considered good or bad, but if I did, there isn't a line I wouldn't cross for you." He lowered himself and brushed his lips against hers. "I will write your name on my chest with the blood of any man who tries to covet what is meant to be ours. Innocent or not."

Amelia stared, slack-jawed, into the eyes of a cold-blooded killer.

My cold-blooded killer. She jolted at her own thoughts. "What is wrong with me?" she whispered, rubbing her eyes. Gilpin was an innocent man.

"You're perfect," Rennick said with so much conviction she almost believed it herself.

"I'm going to hell," she muttered, hating herself for being unnaturally turned on by his words. *Gilpin, please forgive me.*

Rennick moved back to his side of the bed and turned on his side to face her. "If he was a good person, he rests now in an eternal paradise. If he wasn't, he deserved to die anyway."

The words were as simple and pragmatic as they were fucked up. She looked to the gods. "Please let us into the heavens when we die."

Her mate draped his arm across her stomach and pulled her close. "Wherever we go, we go together." He buried his face in her hair and inhaled. "Gods, you smell good."

A small laugh escaped her. "Are you sniffing me?"

"Of course." He did it again, burrowing his face into her neck.

She scrunched her shoulders and rolled sideways to face away from him. He tugged her close, pressing her snuggly against his chest. "Sleep. We have a few hours of travel tomorrow." He buried his nose in her hair again, drawing in another whiff of her scent.

"Stop smelling me," she mumbled and pushed at his large arm. "You're crushing me."

He chuckled and moved his arm to rest on his own leg.

Feeling him against her back made Amelia want to do anything but sleep. She internally scolded herself for insisting they do nothing sexual.

A couple of hours later, when counting the planks on her ceiling didn't help her insomnia and Rennick had long been asleep, she trailed her hand down her body toward the apex of her thighs. If she didn't get relief soon, sleep would evade her all night.

Their towel barrier was long gone, and his semi-hard dick pressed against her ass was too much to bear. Would getting up to go to the bathroom wake him? She didn't want to chance it. Staying in bed with slow and silent movements might be safer.

Snails moved faster than the hem of her shift slid to her waist. Once the fabric rested on her stomach, she dipped her hand into her underwear.

The tips of her fingers skimmed past her clit and delved slightly into her entrance, wetting them enough to glide smoothly across her skin. She remained hyperaware of Rennick behind her and tried not to pulse her hips as her fingers moved in gentle circles on her clit.

His filthy promises resurfaced, and she wondered if he would make good on them. She bit her lip to hold back the moan summoned by the thought of his handsome face buried between her legs.

A large hand covered hers over the top of her underwear, and Rennick's deep voice rumbled, "If you don't like me smelling your neck, you will hate what I smell next if you keep that up."

"I thought you were asleep," she choked out, slightly mortified, but mainly aroused by his large hand so close to where her body wanted it. The feeling only intensified when he lightly stroked the back of her hand through the thin cloth.

Her head dipped when he slid his arm from under her pillow and pressed himself closer to the wall, guiding her body from her side to her back. He propped himself on his elbow, his eyes never leaving hers as he moved his hand down to caress the inside of her thighs.

"Couldn't sleep?" he asked, his voice cavalier like her hand wasn't inside of her pussy.

She shook her head, unsure what to do, but when his fingers trailed up the sensitive skin of her inner thighs and over her hand again with the slightest pressure, her hips moved on their own accord.

His hand continued its ascent, moving over her bunched up shift to her breasts. The friction of the silk moving over her nipples made her whimper and close her eyes.

"Eyes on me, love."

Her lashes fluttered open, and a light sheen of cold sweat broke out on her forehead from the anticipation.

"Do you know how many times I thought about you touching yourself?" He trailed his eyes down her body, stopping them where her hand disappeared into her underwear. He sat up to position himself between her legs. "Millions."

His face stopped inches from her lace-covered pussy, and when he looked up at her, she gave a subtle nod. His teeth were on the white cloth in an instant, biting the fabric. His large hands lifted her hips, and her legs flailed a little. With her underwear still between his teeth, he moved them down her thighs, stopping at her knees to remove them the rest of the way with one of his hands.

It was the most erotic thing she'd ever seen, and arousal coated her fingers. He grasped her wrist and brought her hand to his face. His tongue ran the length of her fingers until the tips were at his lips. "I knew you'd taste divine," he said before sucking her fingers into his mouth.

All she could do was stare with fascination. "Get up," he commanded. She scrambled out of bed and waited expectantly. He laid back and beckoned her closer before grabbing her waist and hoisting her over to him. "Bring that perfect cunt to my face, love."

High winds didn't shake trees as much as his words made her body vibrate with need. She positioned her knees on either side of his head, holding her shift up to see him.

He stared at her pussy and licked his lips. "I have waited for this moment since I knew what it meant to eat." He looked at her face. "Grab the headboard and sit down."

A boldness she didn't normally possess overcame her, and she moved down his chest, or tried to. He grabbed her hips with a growl. "Where do you think you're going?"

"To do this," she said as seductively as she could and leaned forward, pressing her mouth to his. A large hand cupped the back of her head, holding her in place. His tongue licked her lips, and she met it with her own, tangling them together in a sensual dance.

She moaned against his mouth and rocked her hips against his stomach. He broke away, panting. "Move your pussy to my face or I'll move it for you."

She shifted her body up, but before she could lower her hips, he tugged her down, impaling her with his tongue. She cried out, bracing one hand on the wall and the other on the headboard.

Breathing must have been impossible for him, but it didn't stop him from licking every inch of her. She tried to raise her body, but he held her firm, his tongue moving between the valleys of her sensitive skin, circling her clit, and driving her mad.

His movements switched between frenzied and languid, the drag of his tongue creating a sensation like no other. He'd push into her entrance, only to trace his way to her clit and suck until she screamed.

She was a mess, unable to stop the unintelligible sounds escaping her as she rode his talented mouth. Her hips moved faster, and he moaned against her as his fingers dug into the soft flesh of her hips.

He said something, the sound muffled by her body, and when his tongue flicked over her clit at rapid speed, she came harder than she ever had with his name on her lips. As she rode out her release, her thighs seized and squeezed his head.

Once the twitching stopped, he moved her down his body, resting her on his hips. The shine to his lips made her already warm cheeks hotter, and he smiled lazily. "Beautiful."

They stared at each other for what felt like forever. Realizing his dick strained against her ass, Amelia lifted to her knees to align herself with the head of his cock, but he stopped her.

"Not tonight." He sat up, running his hand down her spine.

"The first time I have you, I want to take my time, and we have an early morning tomorrow."

Disappointment surged forward, accompanied by her insecurities.

"Don't do that," he said, forcing her to look at him. "I want nothing more than to bury myself in your perfect little cunt, but not tonight." He kissed her softly and laid back. "Lift up."

Confused, she did as he said, and he slid his hand under her, lifting his first three fingers. "Sit down, love."

Understanding dawned on her, and she tentatively lowered herself. He focused on where their bodies would connect to guide his fingers inside.

A gasp caught in her throat as he filled her, and once fully seated, she rested her hands on his chest. Before she could say anything, he said one word.

"Ride."

He didn't have to tell her twice. She rolled her hips once, testing out the new position.

Rennick's eyes trailed over every inch of her, like he couldn't decide where to focus his attention. "Look how pretty you are riding my hand." His gaze locked on where she moved against his palm. "So fucking beautiful."

His fingers flicked in a steady rhythm inside her, making her dizzy as her senses zeroed in on the feeling. She didn't know how long she rode his hand—it could have been seconds, minutes, or hours as the euphoria took over.

His free hand traced up her side to cup her breast, his thumb grazing over her nipple. He sat forward and hooked the same hand around her back to shift her body from his pelvis to his thighs.

With every roll of her hips, he thrust his large fingers harder. They filled her completely as his palm ground against her clit. "Your cunt can't get enough." He groaned. "My fingers are fucking soaked." He thrust them harder, and she cried out. Her tits bounced with the harsh rhythm, but his eyes were on hers. "Hold on to my shoulders, love."

Her arms wrapped around his neck, and his hand released the support from her back. It appeared before her mouth and he pushed his middle finger inside. On instinct, she sucked him in and swirled her tongue around.

He groaned again, extracted his finger from her mouth, and moved his hand to her ass. Her body tensed as the tip of his finger teased her back entrance, but he shushed her. "Relax, love. Keep riding and let me take care of you."

She could only nod, but her movements slowed, afraid of the pain. The pressure of his finger remained gentle as it pushed in slowly. Her body resisted, but when his mouth found her neck, she moaned and writhed against him.

He hummed against her neck, and his finger slipped deeper inside. "Good girl. Hold on."

What?

His hand, palming her ass with his finger pressed in her tight hole, squeezed her flesh and pushed her hips against his other hand buried in her pussy, creating a bruising pace.

"Oh, fuck," she gasped. She didn't know what to focus on— his tongue on her skin, her nipples scraping against his chest, his palm rubbing against her clit, his fingers flicking against the sensitive spot inside her pussy, or his finger filling her from behind.

The myriad of sensations overwhelmed her, and she tumbled over the edge. "*Rennick.*"

His cock hardened between them as he continued to move her body, and when she twitched with the last of her orgasm, he slowed down until she sat, breathing hard, in his lap, with his fingers still inside her.

His chest heaved in time with hers. "I could come from just watching you."

She whined when he extracted his hands, and when he held

up the fingers covered in her cum, he rubbed them with his thumb.

She covered her face with her hands at the sight of her release stringing between his fingers. "Gods."

"Embarrassed is the last thing you should be, love." She lowered her hands to see a mischievous grin painted across his face. He stuck his glistening fingers into his mouth and sucked them clean, rolling his eyes back. "Fuck, I will never get enough of your taste."

Unsure what to do, Amelia made to get up. "I need to clean myself."

Large hands captured her hips, holding her in place. "Let me." He gently placed her on the bed and disappeared into the bathroom, returning with a damp washcloth. "Spread for me."

Her legs opened, and the warm cloth trailed over her skin until there was nothing left. He tossed the cloth back in the bathroom, picked her up, and laid back on the bed. "Straddle me."

Grinning, she threw her leg over his pelvis, but instead of fucking her, he pulled her against his chest and ran a hand down her back. "Sleep, love."

21

Fingers played with Amelia's hair, stirring her from a deep sleep. She came to quickly, hyperaware that both of them were naked from the waist down in a very compromising position, with her body still straddling Rennick's hips and her chest pressed to his.

"Good morning, love," his gravelly morning voice rumbled, vibrating his chest.

She waited for embarrassment to come but felt nothing other than giddy excitement. Everything she'd waited for, *for years,* lay beneath her. "Good morning," she giggled, then mentally slapped herself. *Giggles? What am I, twelve?*

His heart beat steady against her ear with every rise of his chest. "What are you thinking about, love?"

If I come on to you, will you turn me down again?

"Don't even think about it," he warned. "I doubt you want to be sore while traveling in a bouncing carriage."

If he meant to dampen her lust, he'd failed miserably. His hand snaked around the back of her thigh and skimmed over her pussy. "Fuck. We need to go now, or I won't be able to hold back."

She finally lifted her head from his chest with a coy smile. "Then don't."

He was up from the bed in three seconds flat and placing her on her feet. "Get dressed. The men and carriage will be here soon." His dick jutted out, long and proud, and she thanked the gods she'd used the fake ones he sent because in no other world would he be able to fit inside of her otherwise.

"Stop looking at me like that," he told her, pushing down his erection. "I will dress you myself if I have to."

"Don't tempt me," she teased before disappearing into the bathroom to relieve herself and get ready for the long day ahead.

The ride to the Mountain Kingdom wasn't as long as Amelia initially thought, though Rennick claimed it took longer because of the extra weight of the cart. It wasn't even lunch time yet when they approached the barrier. Amelia peeked her head through the window of the carriage and gasped. She could *feel* the magic radiating toward her.

Her eyes darted toward the human and fae guards standing at the gate. "I don't have a permit."

Rennick pulled a slip of paper from his pocket and handed it to the guard approaching their window. "Yes, you do."

She stared at the paper as the guard read it, straightened, and handed it back. "Have a safe trip, Your Majesty." He stepped back and signaled for the other guards to let them through.

Amelia took the permit from Rennick and scanned it over. "When did you get this?" She'd run into him fairly early in the morning, then they had spent the entire day together. When had he found the time?

"Finn and I rode through the night to see the queen."

Imagine being able to see the queen whenever you wished?

Ignoring the authority this man held, she changed the subject before she chickened out and demanded to go back home. She wasn't worthy of him, and she knew it. Everyone would know it when they saw her. "Tell me about the fae."

The carriage drove through a forest with trees unlike any Amelia had ever seen. Pine needles and leaves of all different colors adorned them. With snow capping the colorful foliage, they reminded her of candy dipped in sugar.

"All fae are faster and stronger than humans," Rennick said, leaning back against the plush cushioned seat, "and they can glamour. That's the extent of non-royal fae magic."

She lifted a brow. "And what of royal fae?"

He grinned, deepening the dimples she loved so much. "We have the same magic, but stronger. I can glamour an entire king-dom's population at once, while other fae can glamour them-selves and maybe one or two others. Royals are faster and stronger than non-royals. We have mate bonds." He tapped the left side of his chest. "And we have *familiars*."

"Non-royals don't have mates?"

He shook his head. "Not unless they're a royal's fated mate."

She considered the new information, wishing she'd waited until she had a piece of paper to write it all down. "And what's a *familiar*?" She glanced at the wing tattoo poking out of the top of his shirt.

After he explained *familiars* and told her about Greta, she stared out the window, lost in thought. *What would it be like to see through the eyes of a wild animal?* Glancing down at Eddy in her lap, she smiled. *What would I see through your eyes?*

The tiny fox nuzzled into her legs as if reading her thoughts.

"How did you know where to find me?" she mused, turning her attention back to Rennick. "You couldn't leave your king-dom." She'd peppered him with questions about his life the entire ride, and when he'd told her about why he couldn't retrieve her sooner, she felt a pang of guilt at the irritation she'd harbored for his absence.

He thought for too long, and she wondered if he considered lying to her. "When royal fae turn thirteen, the gods whisper the name of their fated mate for only them to hear." His eyes softened. "The first time I heard your name, I thought it was the prettiest name I'd ever heard."

She bit back a smile that quickly turned to a scream when she glanced out of the window and saw a giant beast. It looked like a wolf, but it was the size of a horse and had red eyes and long teeth that extended past its bottom jaw. It was menacing at best.

The monstrous creature didn't faze the driver. He must bring people across the barrier often, but how did one get used to a brush with death?

The beast itself ignored their presence, but she didn't care and practically jumped across the seat into Rennick's lap, clutching a miffed Eddy to her chest.

Rennick held her tight as she squeezed her eyes shut, wrapped her free arm around him, and smashed her face against his chest. He ran a soothing hand down her hair and rested his chin on the top of her head. "He cannot see us."

Glamour.

For the one-hundredth time since meeting her mate, she felt stupid. "Sorry," she mumbled against his shirt and pulled back. She glanced at her seat, reluctant to leave the safe haven of his arms.

He re-situated her to a more comfortable position and said, "You'll stay here."

Eddy huffed and jumped onto the seat beside them. Amelia burrowed deeper into Rennick's chest and swore she felt him smile.

Unsure how to broach a subject she'd been curious about for years, she ran a hand down his chest, playing with the edge of his jacket. "Will you tell me about your mother?" It was a delicate subject, but if they were to be married, she wanted to know everything about him. "I used to talk to her in the stars," she added quietly.

A long pause followed her admission, and she feared she'd gone too far until his arms tightened around her, and he took a deep breath. "Every time you show me more of yourself, I thank the gods for you."

She didn't know how to respond to his admission, so she said, "Tell me about her."

After a long pause, Rennick spoke, his voice carrying a carrying fond notes of nostalgia. "Everything excited her," he divulged. "She never met a stranger, and the staff loved her, especially the gardeners. She grew up in the Garden Kingdom, and my father said no one was more determined to make something grow in the snow than she was."

"And did she?" Not much vegetation survived in the northern region of the Human Kingdom. Only the green of the evergreen trees.

"She did." His eyes glittered as he chuckled. "After my father built her a hot house. I'll show you once you're settled in."

She feared how he would react to her next question. "How did she die?"

Rennick's chest stopped moving, and Amelia held her breath, too. "A group of rebels killed her while she was gardening."

Amelia's breath hitched. "Rebels?"

"Groups of fae who wish to overthrow the royals," he explained. "Here in the Mountain Kingdom, we treat our people well. They always have food and adequate lodging regardless of their financial status, as well as access to medical attention when needed."

Her mouth turned down. "Then why are the rebels unhappy?"

"There will always be those who think they would do a better job or who think it's unfair that the throne is inherited through bloodlines." He shifted beneath her. "They forget that our bloodlines are blessed by the gods. We can protect the people in a way they cannot. I could glamour every citizen in our kingdom. Non-royal fae can't."

"What about the royal fae who don't rule the kingdoms?" He'd told her in an old letter that he was an only child, but what if he'd had siblings?

After a beat, he responded, "Royals usually only have one child."

She lifted a skeptical brow. *"Usually?"*

"Anything is possible," he said cryptically.

"But what if an heir or the ruling king and queen die before they have a child?"

He sighed, but his voice was patient. "That's never happened, but if it did, either the gods will fix it, or they won't. We don't know much about them other than they're in the heavens and Orcus, the devil himself, is in hell. The gods created us, gave the first fae and humans decrees to follow, then left. With the exception of coming back to create the barrier thousands of years ago, no one has heard from them since." He brushed a piece of hair from her face. "The world is the way it is because it just is, and if something abnormal happens that we've never seen before, either the gods will grace us with their presence, or we'll find a way to deal with it ourselves."

Amelia stared, wide-eyed, at the enormous palace built from white stone with ornate golden accents adorning its tall towers. It was bigger than anything she'd ever seen.

Rennick's lips grazed her ear. "Welcome home."

Home. This kingdom didn't feel like home, but *he* did.

Which was insane because they just met. Kind of.

Did his correspondence over the years make her feel that

way, or was it the bond? Her heart dropped at the thought of him only wanting her because of something he had no choice in.

Without it, she knew he wouldn't spare her a second glance. She wasn't beautiful like some women. It wasn't a woe-is-me mentality; it was a fact. She wasn't ugly, nor did she feel lesser than, but she wasn't naïve either. In her experience, someone who looked like him didn't want plain when they could have exquisite.

Rennick gripped Amelia's chin and lifted her face toward his. "What's wrong?" Noticing her confusion, he added, "I can feel you."

Annoyance at the lack of privacy within her own mind had her wrenching herself from his grip. "Stop reading my emotions. Can you cut off the connection?

His body froze. Statues moved more than he did in that moment. "You don't want the mate bond?"

Shit. "That's not what I meant," she said quickly. "I don't like you knowing what I'm feeling. Is there any way to stop that part of the bond?"

He relaxed against the seat. "Not to my knowledge, but we can look into it." His fingers ran through the ends of her hair, something he had done often since meeting her. "I like knowing when something affects you enough to travel down the bond. When you're overjoyed, so am I, and when you hurt, I will destroy whatever caused you to feel that way."

"That's not healthy." She leaned into him, staring out the window. "You shouldn't sacrifice your happiness for mine. I want you to do what makes you happy, and if it makes me unhappy, I'll let you know."

He tugged on the ends of her hair, and she tilted her head back. "Your happiness is not the only thing that makes me happy, but make no mistake, if a sacrifice is required, I will do it. Nothing is more important to me than you, little mate. Never forget that."

❄

A group of men waiting to unload the cart stared openly at Amelia as she and Rennick exited the carriage.

Ever the protective mate, Rennick wrapped his arm around Amelia's shoulders and tucked her into his side. "You have nothing to be afraid of," he whispered. "No one knows who you are and your human ears are covered by your hair."

"You didn't tell them you were bringing your mate home?" She didn't know why, but the knowledge that he'd not told anyone they were mates hurt a little. Did Ora really know who she was to him, or did she think Amelia was someone else, like a friend or a cousin?

Remembering the catty gifts, she knew Ora had at least an inkling of who Amelia was to him.

"You have no magic," he replied, as though that was answer enough. "If someone tries to hurt you, you'll be powerless against them, but when we marry, you will be as powerful as I am."

"Will I have a *familiar*?" The thought excited her. How would Eddy handle another animal? On cue, the fox started thrashing around until she put him down.

He licked her leg and trotted off, slipping through the palace gates, and then disappearing around the corner. She trusted he'd find his way back, even though they were in an unfamiliar area. While she considered him a pet, he was still a wild animal, and she had to remember that.

Rennick scratched at his jaw. "I'm not sure. Usually only those of royal blood get them. You might."

There was that word again. *Usually.*

"I'll get your other abilities even though I'm human?"

"I'm not sure," he admitted, "but I believe so. You're the first magicless mate of any fae that I know of."

"If you aren't sure, wouldn't it have been smarter to leave me in the Human Kingdom instead of bringing me to a kingdom full of fae?"

He ran a hand through his dark hair. "If you remain mostly human after we marry, you will have the protection of the royal guards when I'm not around. You'll have it now as well, but once you are queen, they will be bound to you as they are to me."

She balked. "Bound?" *How many bonds would she have?*

He chuckled. "Not by magic, by an oath. They swore an oath to the royal family, and once you marry into it, they are bound to you by duty."

"That would have been good information to offer when I asked about fae," she grumbled.

Palace staff members stared as they walked by, and she offered them friendly smiles. Some returned the gesture, but others turned away and whispered amongst themselves. They must know what she was despite her hidden ears. "Do fae not like humans?" she asked quietly.

"It's not a dislike," he said carefully, "more of a disinterest. They think humans are a weak liability."

Her steps faltered. "Then why marry me? Just because I'm your mate doesn't mean they'll accept me as their queen." Panic tried to claw its way through her. "Will I have a target on my back? They'll try to kill me for weakening the royal bloodline!"

Rennick stopped and grabbed both sides of her face, forcing her to look at him. "No one will harm a hair on your head or speak ill of you, and if they try, I will mount their heads on the front gate."

"Stop threatening to kill people," she whisper-yelled, calming slightly at his touch. "You can't murder someone for not liking me. You would likely have no kingdom left."

He straightened and shrugged. "It would be easier to manage."

22

Amelia's trepidation made Rennick's own multiply. He would be lying if he said he wasn't worried about how the citizens of the fae kingdoms would receive her. Being his mate should extinguish all wariness, but if not, the marriage would, because if it didn't, he would become the star of their nightmares.

He and his father theorized the fully accepted bond would strengthen her, possibly turn her back into a fae, but they couldn't be sure.

He meant what he had said to her. If anyone disrespected her, or worse, tried to hurt her, they wouldn't live to right their wrongs.

Rennick's father never forgave himself for his wife's death. He was there inside the hot house, speaking with the gardener, while she was outside tending to a rose bush she was determined to grow. The rebels had climbed the impossibly tall palace walls, and when they recognized Rennick's mother, they'd gutted her before the guards could save her.

Rennick and his father tracked down the rebels who'd managed to escape over the course of several years, delivering the slow deaths they deserved.

Since then, his father had tall spikes added to the top of the palace walls, rendering it impossible to climb without being impaled, and more guards were stationed around the palace perimeter.

Rennick stopped Amelia at the foot of the stairs. "Do you want a late lunch?"

Her eyes darted to every person who passed. "I'm too nervous to eat."

"Ren," a familiar voice said, making him turn.

He squeezed Amelia's hand and released it, shooting Ora a broad smile. "Hello, princess."

Ora rolled her eyes with a teasing smile. "Don't call me that."

It was a nickname he and Finn gave her when they were teenagers because of her obsession with all things royalty, including the fashion. She adorned herself with jewels and head-bands that resembled small tiaras.

Amelia moved back, putting too much distance between him and her for his liking, but he refrained from commenting on it. Ora didn't know Rennick had retrieved his mate; no one save for a select few did, and he needed to keep it that way until they married.

He trusted Ora, but not enough to gamble Amelia's life.

Ora's blue eyes fell on Amelia, and her smile tightened. "I don't believe we've met." She reached out her hand and widened her smile. "I'm Ora."

Amelia stepped around Rennick and shook the other woman's hand. "Amelia."

"What brings you to our palace?" Ora asked politely, folding her hands in front of her.

If Rennick was the type of man to roll his eyes, he would. She'd always called the palace *hers* since she was here daily with her father.

"She's a friend," he answered coolly, noticing Amelia's

hands clenched behind her back. A dark emotion that was not his own bloomed in his chest.

"A friend?" Ora eyed Amelia up and down. "You've never brought any of your *friends* to the palace before."

He didn't miss the insinuation in her tone, but he hadn't the time or patience to deal with her now. "If you'll excuse us, I need to show Amelia to her rooms."

Without waiting for a reply, he held his arm out, indicating for his mate to climb the stairs.

Ora gave him an incredulous look that he countered with one warning her to choose her next words carefully. "I'll see you at dinner tonight," she said, glancing at Amelia before she bound down the stairs.

"Yes, *we* will see you then," he replied, climbing the steps two at a time to catch up with his mate.

When he and Amelia crested the top of the staircase, that dark feeling was gone, and he wondered if he'd imagined it.

He led her up another set of stairs, and asked, "Did Ora make you uncomfortable?"

Amelia smoothed her skirts and looked straight ahead. "No. I'm nervous."

He didn't believe her, but he owed her his trust anyway. Accusing her of lying would do him no favors.

Once outside his—*their*—rooms, he opened the door and stood aside.

Amelia walked past him and surveyed the rooms with child-like wonder, leaving whatever worries she had in the hallway. "This is incredible," she breathed, floating between the sitting room, bedroom, dressing room, and bathroom.

"Are these mine?"

"Ours," he corrected.

She turned slowly. "Ours?"

He took measured steps toward her, clasping his hands

behind his back to keep from touching her. "If you'd rather not share a bed, I will have another prepared for you." *Please stay.*

She rubbed her chest mindlessly, deep in thought. Nervousness was not an emotion Rennick felt often, but his own overcame him now.

Her brows furrowed before she dropped her arm and moved her pretty eyes to his. "Is it safe?"

Every muscle in his body tensed. "You don't feel safe with me?"

Her eyes flared. "I do, but you said no one knows who I am to you, and you told Ora I was a friend." She motioned around her. "Staying in your rooms might raise red flags."

"Only a select few of the staff are allowed in the royal rooms, and before we left, they were informed I would have a guest returning with me. They needn't know anything else."

"Okay." Her smile was small but seemed genuine. "I'll stay."

Rennick couldn't stop his own smile from spreading across his face. "I'll show you where your things are." With his hand on her lower back, he led her to their dressing room. "Would you like to take a bath before dinner?"

She sighed happily, like he'd offered her a mosquito net in the middle of the Tropical Kingdom. "Yes, please."

He leaned down and kissed her lips, unable to go another second without her affections. "I'll run your water."

Amelia grabbed clean undergarments to put on after her bath and forcefully pushed down the jealousy trying to bubble to the surface since the damned bond would alert Rennick if she couldn't get herself under control.

The way Ora sneered the word *friend* after he introduced them made Amelia feel like shit, and the way he'd called that vile woman *princess* made her feel worse. One thing she learned today was that Ora would be a problem, and if Amelia had to fight dirty for her mate, she would.

She didn't doubt his loyalty now that they were together, but Ora seemed the type to sabotage their relationship any way she could.

Dismissing all thoughts of Ora, Amelia squared her shoulders, determined to seduce her mate today. She'd waited for years after stacks of letters. She would fuck him tonight if it was the last thing she did. What better time than in the bath? He'd run her water, and now he stood in the bathroom, waiting for her.

"Do you need help, love?" he called through the door.

With a steadying breath, she stepped into the bathroom with what she hoped was a seductive smile. "I'm ready."

Rennick held his hand under the water, adjusted one of the knobs, and pointed to a ceramic tray holding various soaps. "This is for your face, body, and hair," he said, tapping each bar. "I made them myself."

He made them himself? She didn't have time to dwell on the surprising information right now.

You can do this, she told herself, *just ask him.* If he said no, she would run away and start a new life somewhere warm. "Would you like to bathe with me?" She spoke fast, and the words ran together in the most unattractive way possible. Her nerves made no sense after last night, but meeting Ora had shaken her.

Rennick had been halfway through the door and halted mid-step. He turned and their eyes met, his darkening by the second. "More than anything."

As he prowled across the room, he removed his shirt with quick, graceful movements. After toeing off his boots, he stood in front of her in nothing but his pants, and his large hand wasted no time trailing from her cheek to the top of her breasts. "Is this your favorite dress?"

She looked down at her clothes. "No?"

"Good," he all but growled, grabbing the front with both hands and ripping it down the middle. He wet his lips and trailed his eyes over every inch of her exposed skin.

Only her red lacey breast band and matching underwear remained. She refused to squirm or hide herself, even though she wanted to after seeing Ora. *Stop it.*

He took the clean undergarments from her hands and tossed them aside, never removing his eyes from her body. Her dress fell effortlessly to the ground when he pushed it off her shoulders, and as he reached for her breast band, she stopped his hand.

Wetting her dry lips, she blew out a shaky breath. "I don't know what I'm doing. I tried to learn with Gilpin, but we barely did anything."

"Don't bring his memory in here with us," Rennick said darkly. "I don't care what you did with him; I only care that you're here, with me, letting me touch you."

"No." She squeezed his wrist lightly. "I need to tell you this." His jaw tensed, but she pushed on. "I did things with him to get more experience. I didn't know you would be able to tell the difference between that and what I did at night. You'd not written in months, and I wasn't sure you'd ever come for me, but if you did, I wanted to be ready." Silence filled the room as he stared at her with an indiscernible look. "I'm sorry," she whispered. "I didn't want to be inexperienced because you're," she waved her hand over his body, "you. I'm not blaming you for my decision." She stopped and squared her shoulders. "But it wasn't fair that I was expected to remain celibate while you were not."

How had she gone from apologizing to chastising him? That wasn't how apologies worked. It didn't matter; she meant every word, because it *wasn't* fair.

He recoiled. "You think I would touch another woman?"

What? All the blood drained from her body.

"I'm not upset with you," he said, moving his hand to grab the side of her neck. "You had needs. If I said anything in my letters to make you believe I was bedding someone else, I'm sorry, but I have never touched another."

Amelia blinked, too stunned to speak at first, then shook her head. "But the things you said, the things you did last night... how did you know how if you've never been with anyone?"

He released her neck and reached around to unclasp her breast band. "We have places where I could watch and learn."

The thought of him watching other women made her ill, but she had no right to be.

"When I watched a man bury his face in a woman's cunt, feasting until she screamed, I imagined how much sweeter your cries would be, and I watched closely to ensure I would hear them."

His thumbs trailed lightly over her nipples, and goosebumps covered her entire body.

"As he bounced her on his dick, taking her breasts into his mouth, I imagined tugging your pert nipples between my teeth while your pussy choked my cock and covered it in cum."

The water level reached the edge of the porcelain tub, and he leaned over to turn it off. Moving his attention back to her, he slid her underwear down her legs and helped her step out of them. Without breaking eye contact, he brought them to his mouth and licked the damp slip of the fabric. His mouth curled into a satisfied smirk. "Wet for me already, little mate?"

Fire couldn't make her skin hotter than he did.

Rennick picked her up, lowered her into the warm water, and climbed in behind her. Liquid splashed over the sides of the tub, creating a small lake on the marble floor.

His hardness pressed against her lower back, and she leaned closer. Large, calloused hands ran slowly up her thighs and through her folds, eliciting a long moan from her.

He lightened his touch, skimming over her sensitive skin. The gentle brush of his fingers grazing past her opening and back to her clit made her hips move involuntarily.

She needed more.

He chuckled against her neck. "Open wider, love."

She hooked her legs over his, offering herself to him, and two of his fingers pressed inside her, causing her hips to buck at the intrusion.

"Mmm," he hummed against her skin. "You have a needy cunt, don't you?"

His palm rubbed over her clit as he moved in and out, and when his other hand snaked up her stomach toward her breasts, she moaned, arching her back. Water sloshed against them like a rising tide, but she didn't care.

"Fuck," Rennick said, nuzzling his face into the crook of her neck. "I will bury myself in you time and again, if only to hear the sounds you make." Rolling her nipples between his fingers, he ran his nose up the column of her neck. "I love you, little mate."

Her breath hitched at his admission. He'd never said it before.

"Tell me," he murmured, "when you fucked yourself with a replica of my dick, did you think of my body covering yours as I made you mine?" One hand grabbed her chin and tilted her face back. "Or did I bend you over and bruise your hips?"

"Nick," she breathed as her inner walls clenched around his fingers, and when she rolled her hips on instinct, tingles erupted all over seconds before she came, crying out with her release.

The man behind her hadn't moved a muscle or said a word as she rode his hand, and after she came down from the high and he pulled his fingers away, she wasn't prepared for his next question in her post-orgasm haze.

She wished she had been, because when he asked, "It wasn't me you saw as Nick, was it?" she could only stare.

23

Rennick stood and stepped out of the water without a word.

Finn. Amelia thought Nick was Finn all those years, and it was *Nick* she'd cried out for today, even though he'd asked her not to call him that and explained why.

All those times he stroked himself to her building pleasure, she'd pictured another man. She had no way of knowing what he looked like, but to picture his best friend, or worse, Gilpin, was a punch to his heart and pride.

Water sloshed around with Amelia's movements as she tried to scramble out of the bath. "I'm sorry. It wasn't him; I swear."

"Stop," he rasped from the doorway.

The blame wasn't hers—how could it be? But the last thing he wanted to hear after confessing his love was a name she associated with another man's image.

Her gaze burned into his back, but he couldn't face her. Not now. This felt worse than when she'd fucked another man.

People said things in the heat of the moment, and he couldn't fault her for that, no matter how much it hurt, but he needed a moment alone.

Silently, he pulled on his training gear, laced up his boots, and left, trying to ignore the fact that she didn't stop him.

An insurmountable pile of guilt pressed down on Amelia like a lead blanket. He'd asked her not to use his alias. So even though to her Nick *was* Rennick now, and it was an honest slip up, the look on his face told her intent didn't matter.

The impact had devastated him.

He'd told her he loved her, and she broke his heart and let him walk away.

There had to be a way to make it right.

An hour of wearing a hole in the rug of the sitting room had her shoulders tight with stress, and a knock at the door made her heart leap into her throat.

Rennick?

She sprinted across the room and threw open the door to find a pair of startled brown eyes staring back at her. A young maid stood beside a cart of food, and Amelia moved aside to let her in with a disappointed smile.

Dinner, she realized, remembering Ora's words from earlier. *"I'll see you at dinner tonight."*

Had Rennick met Ora for dinner without her? If he had, she would return to the Human Kingdom. Amelia would not fight another woman for her mate's attention.

The thought of being by herself made her feel worse, so when the maid tried to leave, Amelia blocked her path. "Will you stay?"

"Yes, Miss," the maid replied instantly with a small curtsey.

Amelia scrunched her nose. "Don't do that. I'm not royalty."

The girl seemed to war with herself for a moment. "We were instructed to treat you as we would a noble guest, Miss."

"I'm Amelia," she said, waving off Rennick's orders. "Stop calling me Miss and please don't curtsey again."

The maid took Amelia's outstretched hand. "I'm Fawn."

"You don't *have* to stay," Amelia amended, realizing her request may have come off as an order. "I won't be offended."

Fawn shrugged and plopped down at the table across from where Amelia took a seat. "This was my last stop of the day." Her eyes lingered on Amelia's now exposed ears.

"I'm from the winter region of the Human Kingdom," Amelia told her with a wry smile. "Bet you feel silly for curtsying now."

Fawn pushed her hair behind her own human ear and smiled back when Amelia's eyes rounded. "I'm half fae. My mother fell in love with a fae man from here."

"How did they meet?" There were plenty of romance books about humans and fae, star-crossed lovers who beat the odds. She wanted to know how it played out in real life. For her own sake, she hoped well.

"My mother's family owned a farm, and my grandfather delivered fresh produce to the Mountain Kingdom. My father owned a produce stand here, and one day, my mother accompanied my grandfather on a delivery." Fawn fiddled with the tablecloth, her eyes distant. "I was born in the Human Kingdom, but right before I turned fourteen, they decided to raise me here. My ears are round, and for all intents and purposes, I was human."

Amelia leaned forward, intrigued. "Was?"

"When I was twelve, I came to stay with my grandparents in the Mountain Kingdom for a few weeks while my parents traveled on an anniversary trip. Ever since then, I've had weak fae magic." She chuckled. "About a year or so later, I was at school and had wished I could knock a boy's teeth out for teasing me, and everyone started screaming when he smiled. I didn't get it because he looked fine to me, but apparently, I'd glamoured him to be toothless."

Amelia clapped as she laughed. She'd have given anything to see that. "Did they realize it was you?"

Fawn's grin faded. "Yes. The teachers were nice about it, but my parents moved us here the next week. They didn't want anyone fearing me. My father said fear makes people danger-ous." The faraway look in Fawn's eyes vanished, and a mask of indifference slipped into place. "My parents were killed in a rebel attack a month later."

Amelia recalled Rennick's mentions of rebels. "Are there a lot of rebel attacks?"

"The attack that killed my parents had a lot of casualties, but it was a rare occurrence at the time. About five or so years ago, they'd become commonplace." She smoothed her skirt and lifted a slim shoulder. "The last attack was three years ago, then the king and his father killed or captured them all... that we know of."

Fawn hid her emotions better than anyone Amelia had ever met. She'd delivered the information with a convincing air of nonchalance.

"Don't," Fawn said sharply when Amelia opened her mouth to give her condolences. "I don't need pity or to be treated like I'll break."

Amelia sat back in her chair. "I don't pity you, but I do understand what it's like to have no parents." Fawn gave her a questioning look. "I grew up in an orphanage, and I didn't have to go through the pain of loving them and losing them like you did, but I am familiar with the pitying stares. I assure you, pitying you is not on my agenda," she leaned forward again, "but I do empathize."

Fawn laughed humorlessly. "Who'd have thought two orphans with human ears would be dining in a fae king's rooms?"

Amelia snorted. "I'm dining. You're staring at me." She

waved her fork at the cart. "Eat before I order you to." She tilted her head thoughtfully. "Can I order people around?"

Rolling her eyes, Fawn reached for a plate and filled it with steamed vegetables and a giant turkey leg bigger than her head. "Yes, *Miss*."

Amelia smiled and ripped off a piece of roll to dunk into her gravy. "Are you married?"

Fawn choked, spewing her water across the table and misting the pretty candles that flickered between them. "I'm only twenty-six!"

"In the Human Kingdom, you've been an adult since you were eighteen," Amelia pointed out. "Are the laws the same here?"

"Yes, but I don't want to settle down yet, if ever. Men are worthless." Fawn's knuckles turned white around her fork.

Amelia cocked an eyebrow. "Spill it. What asshole broke your heart?"

The poor carrots on Fawn's plate didn't stand a chance against her stabbing assault. "We've had enough sob stories for today. Tell me why you're really in the palace," she gestured around them, "staying in the king's rooms."

Setting her silverware down, Amelia leaned her elbows on the table. "What does everyone think I'm doing here?" The vegetable assault halted. "Say it."

"Some think you're the king's whore, but a few think you're his mate, since he's never brought another woman to the palace," Fawn answered carefully. "No one knows you're human, though. That was a surprise."

Wrinkling her nose, Amelia aggressively ripped off another piece of bread. "Why would they think I'm his whore if he's never brought anyone to the palace?"

"Those who don't believe Ora is his mate think he's given up on finding her since he's not yet married."

"They think Ora is his mate?" The thundercloud following her around turned positively black.

"Only because they have the same birthday and she leads everyone to believe she is."

They have the same birthday? What did that have to do with anything?

Amelia sighed, touching her ear lightly. "I'm not allowed to tell anyone who I am." She held up two fingers on each hand, bending them as she said, "For my protection." Something told her Fawn was trustworthy, so she added, "If you tell anyone this, Rennick will kill you without hesitation, and I'd rather not lose the only person who's been nice to me thus far." The maid looked amused, not scared, and Amelia liked her even more. "I'm his mate."

Fawn's jaw dropped. "How?"

Amelia gasped and pointed at her. "You thought I was his whore!"

"I thought you were his mate," Fawn replied defensively. "Until I saw your ears. I didn't know it was possible for a fae to have human mates, especially not a royal."

"I don't know how it's possible," Amelia said, deciding not to be offended, "but he's written me letters since we were thirteen. His friend, Finn, delivered them."

"And you're positive there was no mix up?" Fawn asked.

Amelia decided she was offended, after all. "He can feel my emotions, even when I lived in the Human Kingdom."

"This is the best news I've heard in a while." Amusement bounced in Fawn's almond-shaped eyes. "The thought of Miss Ora as queen makes me want to move. She is horrid."

"I think so too," Amelia grumbled. "Rennick sent me gifts, and Ora helped him pick them out. They were awful." She jumped up and dashed to the dressing room, retrieved the baby-shit-green boots, and rushed back, holding them up. "Look at these!"

Fawn's hand slapped over her mouth to suppress her laughter, but the crinkling beside her eyes gave her away.

Amelia deposited the boots on the floor and sat down with a groan. "You should see the dresses. I knew she couldn't be as wonderful as he made her out to be."

"She treats the staff like servants when the king isn't around," Fawn informed bitterly. "Yet, if he is present, she's so sweet you'd think she shits cupcakes. Everyone hates her, but no one dares say a word about the king's best friend."

"Best friend?" Amelia clenched her fists. "I thought Finn was his best friend."

Fawn pressed her lips together, her face full of sympathy. "They both are."

Amelia pushed down the emotion building in her throat. "He called her princess and told her I was just a friend."

Fawn looked indignant on her behalf. "Why?"

Amelia sagged against the back of her chair, but Fawn's hand clasped hers on the table with a reassuring squeeze. "If he brought you here, she is no threat to you. The king I've seen is not a deceptive one. He is a good ruler who treats everyone as equals, even his staff. He ensures his people are fed, housed, and supplied with everything they need, despite their financial status."

Amelia's heart warmed to hear Rennick's people speak highly of him, but memories from earlier doused it with ice. "He might have changed his mind about me since this morning."

Gods, to think she'd traveled to the Mountain Kingdom, met Ora, possibly ruined her relationship with Rennick, and ate dinner with Fawn in just a day.

Fawn stood and gathered their mostly empty plates. "I doubt it. You're his mate."

"We were being intimate earlier," she began, halting Fawn mid stride. "He told me he loved me, and I ruined it."

Fawn set down the dishes on the cart and looked her way. "You do not love him?"

"I think I do." Amelia rubbed her forehead, trying to find the right words. "I told myself I couldn't love someone through letters alone, having never met them." She sighed. "But in person, he's the same but more, in the best way."

Saying it out loud sounded worse.

After Fawn wiped down the table, she took a seat and leaned back. "I don't think so. You said he's the same as his letters, and if you fell in love with his letters, it stands to reason you fell in love with the man, too. The more is merely a bonus." She paused in thought for a moment. "How far would you go to make him happy?"

Without hesitation, Amelia responded, "As far as it takes."

"Most people don't do whatever it takes for someone they don't love," Fawn said with a tinge of sadness. "You're thinking too hard about what you *should* feel instead of what you *do* feel."

Amelia nodded, her thoughts eating at her. Her heart physically hurt, and whenever she thought of him, it became hard to breathe. "I hate that he's somewhere hurting because of me, and I don't know where to find him to make it right."

"He'll be back once he cools off," Fawn assured her. "It will give you time to think of a plan to make it up to him."

Amelia hoped she was right.

The next morning, Amelia paced the length of their sitting room, having not heard from Rennick since last night. What if it was too late to fix her mistake?

The green boots mocked her when she stepped into their dressing room. Had he run to Ora yesterday? He'd saved his virginity for Amelia, but what if she'd driven him into another woman's arms?

"No," she spoke into the empty room. The man she knew wasn't so fickle as to run to another woman that quickly.

Pushing her pride aside, she donned the ugly boots, wanting him to see her wear something he gave her, and switched out her current dress for one of the nightmarish ones.

Various trunks lined the open walls, and she opened each one until she procured her bow set. The thought of hunting made her queasy, and while she'd practiced shooting the bow in hopes of impressing him if they ever met, she'd never intended to shoot a living animal.

That would change today. He liked to hunt, and she would ask him to go. She strapped the bow and quiver across her back. *Do not puke.*

She set off down the hallway in search of someone to help her find Rennick, but after taking what felt like ten turns down various massive hallways, she vowed to obtain a map of the palace as soon as possible. She'd been walking for an hour and had seen no one, as if the floor was completely deserted.

After another turn, she resigned herself to the fact that she'd die of old age in one of these hallways. Thankfully, an older maid with light brown skin and a tight grey bun hurried up a set of stairs Amelia had not seen.

"Excuse me!"

The maid looked up, freezing when she saw Amelia. "Yes, Miss?"

Amelia approached her with a friendly smile and glanced at the stack of linens in the maid's arms. "I'm sorry to ask because I know you're busy working, but have you seen King Rennick?"

The woman's lips pinched together when she took stock of Amelia's attire. "He is usually in his study in the mornings."

"I'm afraid I don't know my way around," Amelia explained sheepishly. "Would you mind taking me?"

"Of course, Miss. It's on the main floor."

Amelia followed the woman through winding halls and down two flights of stairs, asking her questions about herself to pass the time. She went by Birdie, a nickname her father gave her, and she was sixty-four with three children. Her husband worked as a groundskeeper at the palace, and they'd been married for thirty-three years.

By the time they rounded the final corner, Amelia held half of the linens, and they were laughing like old friends. Birdie tipped her head to an open door down the hall. "He's in there, Miss."

"I told you to call me Amelia and thank you."

Her heart raced at the sound of Rennick's deep voice, even if she couldn't make out his words. Since their carriage ride in, she'd been trying to suppress her emotions, and she prayed he didn't feel her anxiety. *Calm yourself.*

Birdie smiled when Amelia turned to bid her goodbye, but they both stopped when a melodic voice floated down the hall.

The unknown voice said with a giggle, "You're terrible, Ren."

Rennick's deep laugh followed. "No worse than you. Do you have any plans today?"

The linens in Amelia's hands fell to the ground, and Birdie's brow lowered, looking between Amelia and the study.

"Are you okay?" the older woman whispered low enough for only them to hear.

"Who is the woman with him?" Amelia whispered back, already knowing the answer.

"That's Miss Ora." The sympathy in Birdie's voice was too much. Did she think Ora was his mate and Amelia was his mistress?

Amelia's heart that beat nervously moments before shattered, joining the crumpled sheets on the floor. She wanted to disap-

pear, to go home, to do anything but stand in the hall and listen
to him with her.

Birdie jumped back, looking around frantically. "What in the
world?" Her hand reached out, bumping into Amelia's shoulder.
"Where did you go?"

"What do you mean?" she asked the woman, still staring at
the office.

"You're a royal," Birdie breathed in awe.

More laughter sounded from Rennick's study, and Amelia
didn't have time to decipher the maid's odd claim because everything in her broke. *Everything*.

A deep grunt sounded from the room, followed by Ora's
sweet voice. "Ren, are you okay?"

Amelia ran.

24

The pain lancing Rennick's chest stole his breath. His heart hurt and throbbed with the aching desire to throw itself from the tallest tower.

He clutched at the shirt covering his chest as Ora leaned over him, rubbing soothing circles over his back. "Ren, talk to me."

Heart attacks were rare, but they did happen, though it was usually in the elderly. As he homed in on the feeling, he realized it wasn't physical pain; it wasn't his pain at all.

Amelia.

Ora called after him as he ran from the room and skidded to a halt in the hall. A maid gathered linens from the floor with concern etched in her features as she glanced behind her.

When her eyes snagged on Rennick, she gathered the sheets faster.

"Should I call the healer?" Ora asked, surveying where he'd fisted his shirt.

"I need to find Amelia."

"She was here, Your Majesty," the maid said. "She just left." With the sheets piled haphazardly in her arms, she turned on her heel to leave.

"Stop," Rennick commanded. The maid froze. "Which way did she go?"

The woman motioned down the hall leading away from Rennick's study, where her gaze had previously wandered with worry. "That way, Your Majesty."

He swerved around her as he ran, throwing a "thank you" over his shoulder and praying his mate was okay.

A stray arrow on the ground snagged Rennick's attention. *One of Amelia's,* he surmised, recognizing the craftmanship from all those years ago.

"Ren!" Ora's footsteps moved closer as she jogged after him. "Tell me what's going on."

Bending down, he swiped the arrow off the ground and rolled it between his fingers. *What was she doing and why does my chest feel like someone ripped it wide open?*

"Ren," Ora snapped.

He turned to face her. "What?" he snapped back with a glare.

She reared back, her blue eyes going wide before they slid behind him. Moving toward him, she touched his arm and leaned in, lowering her voice. "What has gotten into you?"

Anguish exploded within him, followed by a sob behind him. Spinning around, he saw Amelia at the opposite end of the hall.

He ran to her side, vowing to kill whoever had upset her. "What's wrong, love?" He reached for her, but she backed away.

"I can't find Eddy." *Well, I can't kill him.*

Even though the reason for her ire made sense, it didn't feel right. In the past, she barely blinked when the fox disappeared for a day. "We'll find him."

Ora approached, and Amelia backed farther away, her red-rimmed eyes hardening.

"I don't want to interrupt," his mate snipped and did an about face to leave, but Rennick reached out to stop her.

"I'm coming with you."

"I'll wait for you in your study," Ora murmured.

Amelia snatched her arm from his grasp and left without looking back.

Frustration made his skin itch, and he turned to Ora. He'd planned to show Amelia her library and needed Ora to explain a few things to him since she'd helped design it, but the woman was insane if she thought he would continue their conversation while his mate was hurting.

"Find Finn and tell him to find Eddy." Ora's mouth turned down. "Now," he added forcefully. She wisely kept her mouth shut and stormed off in the opposite direction.

Cursing, he followed after Amelia, who kept glancing down different hallways, muttering to herself, before taking the closest stairway to the next floor. If he didn't get to the bottom of her pain, it would drive him mad. "What's wrong, love?" Silence stretched between them. "Don't shut me out."

She scoffed and practically ran up the next set of stairs toward the royal quarters. "You left me alone all afternoon and night in an unfamiliar place, so don't talk to me about shutting someone out." The venom in her voice took him aback.

"I needed time to think."

At the top of the stairs, she looked both ways several times.

"This way." He guided her toward their room.

"You don't run when I upset you," she seethed, opening their door. He wanted to point out that she literally ran from him just now, but decided against it. "Leaving me alone was bad, but running to Ora was unforgivable. I'm leaving."

She stomped toward the dressing room with him on her heels, and when he stepped through the door and saw her trunks open, he saw red.

Did she already pack her things?

A quick survey of the room showed her clothing hung neatly across from his, squashing his fears. He grabbed her around the waist and hauled her against him. "You're not going anywhere."

He never saw the elbow coming until it jabbed him in the

gut. If she hadn't threatened to leave him, her feistiness would have turned him on.

"Let me go right now," she shouted, trying to wiggle out of his hold. "You said if I decided to leave, I could leave."

He fought to differentiate his emotions from hers as everything spiraled out of control. "*We* will leave. If you leave, I leave, so if you're trying to leave *me*, that won't work."

With a huff, she stopped struggling. "Let me go, please." Defeat colored her words, and it hit harder than her elbow.

After releasing her, he spun her around and held her in place by the shoulders. "Please, tell me what's wrong. If me leaving yesterday upset you this much, I will never leave your side again."

"Stop that." She swatted at his hands. "Yes, I'm angry you left, but you left because I upset you." A tear ran down her cheek. "I can't control how you react, but I also can't fix anything if you're not here. I was careless with my words, and I'm sorry." She blew out a long breath. "I'm asking for a little grace. I thought you were someone else for years."

If this was her idea of fixing things, she was terrible at it, because all he wanted to do was break Finn's neck.

"But it was *you* I wanted," she whispered through her tears. "*Your* letters; he was only a face. I don't care about him. I care about the man who wrote to me for years, whose loyalty never wavered, the man who I considered sneaking through the barrier to search every kingdom for, consequences be damned."

He could feel her honesty laced with sadness, but her words made his protectiveness flare up. Had she tried to sneak into the fae kingdoms, she could have died by a number of things.

"Imagine my surprise when I came to tell you those things and found you with another woman." Daggers would cut less than her eyes. "I can handle your silence, but not you running to someone else."

Quick as lightning, she yanked dresses from their hangers

and dropped them into an open trunk with him staring in stunned silence.

He removed the dresses from the trunk and dumped them on the floor. "You're accusing me of running to another woman?"

She freed another dress from its hanger, but he slammed the trunk shut before she could throw it in.

"I went in search of you to apologize and invite you hunting because I know you love it." Tears lined her eyes again, and her cute chin wobbled. "I heard you laughing with Ora in your study. While I fretted over where you were, what you were thinking, and if you were okay all night, you were having a great time with your *best friend.*"

He frowned. "Finn is my best friend."

Her eyes flashed as she took a step toward him. "She touched your arm like a lover, a familiarity we can't have in public, and *you let her.*"

He digested her words and stabbed a hand through his hair, deciding which part to tackle first, but her eyes were wild.

"I left my home and my kingdom for you! You *asshole!*"

"Stop accusing me of bedding other women," he said in a low voice, trying not to yell. "I have never touched another woman, nor will I ever. I asked you if Ora bothered you, and you said no."

"I shouldn't have to ask you not to let other women touch you when you murdered an innocent man for fucking me before we even met!" She waved her hands wildly. "Should I have lied and said I was fine? No. That was childish of me, and I know I was wrong, but you can't hold me to a standard you don't practice yourself."

She was right. If a man touched her arm in such a manner, he would no longer have a hand. Rennick removed his shirt, tossing it to the ground. "Where did she touch me?"

Amelia faltered, a bit of her anger giving way to confusion. "What?"

"Where did she touch me?" he repeated, punctuating every word as he held out his arms. "I was distracted. Show me exactly where."

Her eyes turned to slits. "This isn't a fucking joke, Rennick."

"I'm not laughing, love."

Annoyance pulled at her mouth. "Your right arm."

"Where on my right arm?"

She stared for a moment and touched his upper arm lightly. "Here."

Leaning down, he removed a dagger from his boot, held it against his skin, and sliced downward, flicking his wrist outward to remove a thin layer of skin.

Amelia screamed, and ran forward, babbling incoherently as she grabbed a dress from the floor to press against his arm. "Are you insane!" Her face paled when she looked from his bloody arm to the bloody spot on the floor.

Green replaced the pale pallor of her skin, and she dry heaved.

His arm burned, but not enough to regret his actions. Taking the dress from her hands, he ripped it into strips, wrapped his arm tightly to stop the bleeding, and assisted Amelia to the sitting room while she continued to heave and mumble about his mental state.

After depositing her into a chair, he walked to the door and pulled on the bell cord to summon someone while worrying over the sweat gathering on his mate's brow.

He grabbed a wet cloth from the bathroom and held it against Amelia's forehead, but she pushed his hand away and stood on shaky legs. "You mutilated yourself!"

The blood-soaked cloth tied around his arm made the wound look worse than it was. "It was only the skin."

She bent over and put her hands on her knees, gagging again.

When she'd finally regained control of herself, she straightened. "Why in the seven rings of hell would you do that?"

Rennick stepped into her space and wrapped his hand around her nape. "There is no longer any part of my body she has touched." He kissed her forehead and felt her fury and jealousy dissolve.

"You were wearing long sleeves," she croaked. "She didn't touch your skin."

He shrugged. "I'll burn the shirt, too."

"Why is that attractive?" she muttered quietly, eliciting a wide smile from him.

"I will kill her and serve you her head on a silver platter."

She blanched. "You cannot threaten to kill everyone who upsets one of us!"

"I was being facetious." *Not really.* "Ora will no longer be allowed in our palace." He needed to rid their relationship of the other woman. "Tomorrow, we'll tell her together. I wish you'd told me sooner."

Her eyes lit up. "I get to be there?"

He laughed, loving his mate's possessive streak. "You can be the one to tell her." Caressing her jaw, he forced her eyes to his, relishing in the happiness radiating from her. "If you'd like to stake your claim, I'll bend you over my desk and fuck you while you tell her."

His cock hardened at the pretty blush blooming across her skin as she pulled from his grasp and flitted from trunk to trunk.

The contents of the last trunk rattled as she dug around. "Ah ha!" Straightening, she held out a stack of papers to him. "I wanted to stake my claim on whomever wrote those letters long ago, and if I'd been able to deliver these to you, you'd never question that."

Rennick loathed to leave, but Amelia, with a still green face, insisted he visit the infirmary without her. A maid showed up to answer his earlier summons, and he sent for the warriors-in-training to clean the area of the dressing room floor covered in blood.

Seeing his mate almost pass out reminded him that not everyone was comfortable around blood, and he didn't want any of the in-house staff to faint. The trainees were accustomed to blood and wounds alike, so removing a bloody rug wouldn't faze them in the least.

Amelia wanted to see her friend Fawn while he tended to his arm, and once the girl showed up, he kissed his mate goodbye and left.

An hour and a fresh bandage later, Rennick headed to his study, removing the folded stack of papers from his back pocket.

He crossed his study to the corner near the dark floor-to-ceiling bookcases, lit the table lamp, dropped into a plush over-stuffed chair, placed the stack of papers on the side table, and picked up the first page.

Scanning the paper, he barked out a laugh.

Dear Nick,
Screw you.
Not Sincerely,
Amelia
P.S. I'm sorry about your mom.

He grinned at young Amelia's loopy handwriting, punctuated with a snark he'd not known she possessed until meeting her in person.

Time ceased to exist as he traveled back in time through the letters Amelia had written him throughout the years. He chuckled at her wit and honesty, loving her humor and soaking in every detail she gave about her life.

A black envelope he recognized well hid amongst the stack.

How does she still have this?

The paper inside had worn creases from years of being opened and re-folded, and when he opened the letter, he sat forward.

> *Hello, Love,*
> *My imagination did not do you justice.*
> *You are beautiful.*
> *Always Yours,*
> *Nick*
> *P.S. Are the other girls at the orphanage taking your food? I've included a basket of things for you to keep in your room, just in case.*

The words took him back in time to when he'd first laid eyes on Amelia. It was an experience unlike any other to finally put a face to the girl he'd dreamed about. Love at first sight was thought to be a fairytale written in books, but Rennick knew it to be true.

It was strange—the feeling he had that day that had nothing to do with their bond and everything to do with her. Over the years, Finn and Ora called it infatuation that later turned to obsession, and they were right, but there was love, too.

He didn't give a fuck what anyone else thought. He knew what he felt.

Folding the paper, he slid it carefully into the envelope and dropped it on the stack of already read letters to continue with the others. Each letter left him hungry for more of her thoughts, and he couldn't devour them fast enough.

One letter from a few years ago made him stop, his hands squeezing into fists and crinkling the paper. A glutton for punishment, he read it again.

Dear Nick,

I saw you last night. It's not the first time, but I was afraid to tell you because I didn't want you to stop coming (not that you read these anyway).

I'm only telling you now to let you know that I liked your hair brown, but I love it blond. What made you want to color it?

How did you color it? Do fae have magic to do it, or do you have hair shops like humans? (I've always loved blond hair on men)

I sound pathetic, but I'm lonely here without you.

Wish you were here.

Pathetically Yours,

Amelia

P.S. You once asked if I wonder about you, and I do. Every day.

Fucking Finn, that handsome bastard. Rennick wanted to find the hair shop Finn used to dye his hair blond and torch it to the ground. A loud knock sounded from the other side of the door. "Come in."

Ora peeked her head in, her long black hair swinging like a silk curtain. "Is it okay if I come in?"

"No," he replied, placing Amelia's letter on the stack.

She laughed lightly and strutted in anyway. "You've been testy since yesterday. Is your *friend* not performing well?"

He didn't respond right away, because if he did, it would be with violence. More than anything, he wanted to tell her to leave his palace and never return, but he'd promised Amelia the pleasure of doing so, and he'd not take that from her. "Her name is Amelia, and I told you to leave."

Ora's blue eyes rounded. He abandoned Amelia's letters and clasped his hands over his stomach. "Why are you still here?"

She pressed her hand against her chest. "Why are you treating me this way? Is she turning you against me when I was nothing but nice to her?"

He recalled Ora's behavior, how she'd looked over Rennick's shoulder and stepped closer to grab his arm. *Staking a claim that was not hers.*

"You forget your place," he replied dangerously. "You touched me earlier when you had no right. That right belongs to my mate and no one else."

Her cheeks flushed scarlet, and he watched with fascination as something in her snapped. "This is ridiculous. *I* am your mate, and you know that as well as I do. Drop this silly pretense and admit it."

She could have showed him a dog tail growing out of her neck and it would have surprised him less than her declaration. Ora's words struck him speechless.

Did she really believe that?

"Think about it," she went on, "We have the same birthday, our personalities are perfect together, and you think you heard *Orissa*? Really, Ren? It never occurred to you that it was Ora you heard?"

Her expression held a delusional sincerity, and he knew not telling her Amelia's true identity was the right call.

"If we were mates, we would feel each other's emotions," he replied carefully, trying to rationalize with her. Standing to his full six-foot-five height, he tapped his chest. "I can feel my mate here, and you are not her."

Ora's hands balled into tight fists. "Why are you denying our bond? I feel everything you feel. Have I not been able to anticipate everything you needed our entire lives?"

"No," he deadpanned. "If you had been able to read my emotions, you would've known that when I looked at you, I felt nothing but platonic friendship. No part of me has ever desired you in a romantic or sexual way. Release whatever fantasy you're holding on to."

Big drops slithered down her cheeks, her mouth open as she stared at him. "You don't mean that."

He lifted a brow and crossed his arms. "I assure you, I do. Leave and be back tomorrow afternoon at four o'clock after my council meeting."

The devastation on her face morphed into happiness, and he cringed at the delusional hope in her eyes. "We can figure this out," she said, beaming at him. "I know we can."

"Leave," he replied and sat back down.

"I'll see you at four." She left with a bounce in her step that had him gaping after her.

Has she always been this deranged?

No sooner had she shut the door did it opened again, and Finn walked through. "Ora looked delighted."

Rennick eyed Finn's blond hair and scowled. He opened the side table drawer and grabbed a blank piece of paper, ink pot, and quill. Placing the blank paper on top of Amelia's letters, he unscrewed the ink well lid, dipped his quill, and began to write as he said, "I told her to remember her place and keep her hands to herself."

Finn took a seat in the other reading chair. "She's convinced you two are mates."

Rennick's hand jerked, almost spilling the ink. "You knew?"

"Everyone knows but you. Personally, I don't see the

appeal," Finn joked, crossing his leg. "You've been so blinded by Amelia and the rebel attacks that you missed out on her longing looks and attempts to sway you."

Rennick pursed his lips. "If what you say is true, keep her away from me or I will separate her head from her body."

Finn snorted, then blanched when Rennick lifted his head and leveled him with a look. "You're serious."

Rennick put down his quill and read over the document. "Have this decree announced throughout the kingdom." He stood and held out the paper. "Send warriors to ensure it's followed. Anyone who refuses to comply of their own will be forced."

Finn took the paper, read it, and scoffed. "You can't be serious."

Rennick walked to the door and looked over his shoulder. "I want it done as soon as possible."

25

Amelia smiled nervously at the guards as she walked through the palace gates toward the training arena. It was a large structure that looked miles away, but it couldn't be that far.

Hopefully.

Not two steps outside of the walls, something bumped against her leg. She jumped and looked down to find the cutest thing she'd ever seen. A fluffy light brown lynx with white paws and black sprigs of fur sprouting from its ears stared up at her expectantly.

It struck her then that lynx were a type of wild mountain cat, and she scooted away, but with every step she took, it followed.

"Uh, hello." She leaned to the side and glanced between its legs. "Little guy."

It sat down, and she looked around. "Are you someone's pet?"

She swore to the gods the thing shook its head. "Can you understand me?" It stared at her like she was stupid. "Guess not."

She stood in a stare off with the cat, not knowing what to do. "Are you going to bite me?" The lynx looked bored, and she reached down, knowing she might lose a finger, and pet the cat's head. To her astonishment, it purred. "Well," she said finally, "if you're coming with me, let's go."

The lynx trotted happily beside her across the large field toward the training arena, earning a few looks from passersby, including the guards at the entrance. Fawn wasn't kidding when she said everyone was instructed to treat her like royalty, because the guard at the gate tipped his head and granted her entry when she told him her name. He glanced wearily at the lynx, but said nothing.

Amelia stayed close to the edge of the arena and warriors paused their training as she passed them, staring openly until she found a hiding place between a group of weapons racks. The lynx planted its butt on the muddy slush beside her and, together, they watched the warriors and young trainees with rapt fascination.

She'd come out here to keep her mind off Eddy and her growing concern he'd ventured back to the Human Kingdom looking for her, but her new furry sidekick only reminded her of him more. Fawn had a lot to do today, so here Amelia stood, with a cat she was fairly certain ate other animals, watching sweaty fae try to kill each other.

There must have been hundreds of warriors in the arena, and she wondered if they were all from the Mountain Kingdom capital or if some traveled from smaller villages. It was a testament to the size of the structure because they had ample room to fight and move about.

Finn walked into the arena with a group of people behind him and whistled loudly. Everyone stopped and fell into rows of regimented lines, backs straight, facing forward. Their discipline was impressive.

"Every male presenting fae with blond hair, line up on the right side of the arena," Finn yelled, pointing in Amelia's direction. She shrank back further into the shadows. "All others, gather your weapons and move to the left side."

Confused looks passed between the guards while an impressive number of blond soldiers moved to one side.

Finn joined them and called for their attention. "A decree has been issued by the king that all male presenting citizens of the Mountain Kingdom with blond hair must shave their heads until after he and his chosen mate are wed."

Wed? Amelia's mind worked overtime, trying to make sense of it all.

Everyone started talking at once, and Finn whistled again. "The king has treated his people well since taking over as interim king. He has fought tirelessly at our sides to defeat rebels, some of whom took your loved ones away. You *will* do this for him voluntarily, or it will be done to you by force." He motioned for the people who'd accompanied him to step forward. "I will go first."

The warriors quieted. Why would Rennick force the blonds to shave their heads? It didn't make sense.

Amelia watched as warrior after warrior took their turns, their blond hair sprinkling the muddy snow, and briefly she wondered how they would clean it all up.

"Do you have any idea why your mate is doing this?" Finn asked from the other side of the weapons rack, startling her.

Covering her pounding heart, she stepped out of the shadows, squinting from the sun. "He's insane?"

Finn walked around the racks to stand in front of her. "He isn't, except for when it comes to you." His brows raised when he spotted the lynx at her feet, and he glanced quickly at her chest. He looked confused, but she was too offended to care.

"I didn't ask him to do this."

"I know you didn't, but I'd bet every piece of coin I have that something involving you prompted this."

He sounded curious, not mad, and her mind raced as she

sifted through her interactions with Rennick that day, slightly gagging at their time in the dressing room. Blond men never came up. After the dressing room, she'd given him the letters, and... Her wide eyes lifted to Finn's bare head.

"Oh, no." Her eyes raked over the soldiers; her hand rose to cover her mouth. "I wrote him letters too," she began. "Over the years, I'd kept them all, and I gave them to him today and..." She pressed her fists into her eyes. "Gods, this is humiliating."

Finn took a wide stance and folded his arms across his chest. "And?"

"And after you dyed your hair blond, I wrote that I liked men with blond hair," she confessed, refusing to look at him.

Finn groaned and ran a hand over his freshly shaved head. "I'm lucky he didn't kill me. Ren is dangerous when it comes to you."

"I'm sorry," she said with a gulp. "Will he always be like this?"

He hung his hands on his hips with a thoughtful look on his face. "I think once you marry, his jealousy will subside. Until then, the bond can still be broken."

The new information made her uneasy. "How? I thought mate bonds were strong?"

He nodded. "They are, but if one of the mates marries another person before their mate bond is completed through marriage, the bond breaks."

Oh. She chewed on her lip, feeling guilty for what he'd done to these fae because of her. *Does Rennick think I would consider marrying someone else?* The thought made more guilt slam into her. If he was that insecure in their relationship, she was a terrible mate.

"Do you know where he is?" she asked.

"The last I saw him, he was leaving his study. Check your rooms. The only other place he would be is here."

Her skirts twisted around her legs as she skirted around Finn and ran toward one of the exits with her new shadow on her heels. She had to calm his insecurities before he burned the entire world to ash.

Amelia stopped a guard in a hallway of the palace for directions to her rooms. He was hesitant at first, but when she told him her name, he instructed her to follow him. Like everyone else she passed, he balked at the lynx trailing behind her but said nothing.

She thanked him at the door of their rooms and burst inside without a plan, a fact she realized when Rennick glanced up from the book in his hand. He lounged in an oversized chair in the corner of their sitting room, looking like a wet dream.

"You like to read?" she asked, trying to see the title.

Placing a bookmark between the pages, he snapped the book closed and set it on the side table. "I do."

She peeked at the cover and made a sound somewhere between a laugh and a curse. "You gave me that book."

He nodded. "I did. Normally I wouldn't read a book on the birthing techniques of mountain lions, but if it interests you, I'd like to know a little." His smile was brilliant, warming her from the inside out.

The odd book blasted her rational thoughts to bits.

"I love you," she blurted, cringing at her botched delivery.

The grace with which he stood and prowled across the room was impressive for such a large man, but her heart hammered too loudly against her ribcage to comment. With his attention locked on her, he wrapped his hands around the sides of her neck and tilted her head back.

"You love me."

She licked her suddenly dry lips. "Yes. I wanted to tell you in a grand way," *that I hadn't thought of yet,* "but my mouth decided it couldn't wait."

He lowered his face, hovering his lips above hers. "Mine can't either."

Closing the distance between them, he claimed her mouth with his own. His tongue glided across her lips, and she gladly opened for him, greedy for more. Hearing that he was afraid she would break their bond had cracked something inside of her, and all she wanted was to show him love in every way possible.

It had always been him; the boy whose letters kept her warm when the icy shards of loneliness crept in, who'd deemed her beautiful when no one else had. The man who showed her his stunningly charcoaled soul time and again, whether through sending sweaters for a tiny fox or death threats to anyone who threatened what he knew they would have.

Bit by bit over the years, Rennick laid a sturdy path for love to cross from her heart to his. Some of his methods were fucked up and wrong, but she no longer cared. Loneliness was a cold feeling, like being buried alive in the snow, crushed and paralyzed, but love was a raging inferno, incinerating its victims from the inside out. They'd answer for their sins at Death's gate, and should he look upon them and damn them to hell, they would burn together as they always had.

Breaking their kiss, he pressed his forehead to hers and closed his eyes. "I love you too, little mate. I always have."

26

She loves me, Rennick thought, his heart soaring. "Lift your dress, love."

Without question, she gathered the fabric in her hands. He grabbed her thighs to hoist her into his arms. Her long legs wound around his middle, pressing their bodies closer together, yet not close enough.

"I think I can feel you," she whispered with a touch of uncertainty and awe. "There's a feeling in my chest that matches what I feel, but it's not mine."

Interesting. He assumed her fae abilities would manifest when they wed, but possibly being on fae land started the process early.

"Get used to that feeling, love," he murmured while silently praying to the gods that he lasted more than three minutes when he felt her warmth encompass his cock.

Finn told him the first time would be quick, and he loathed to know he couldn't stay buried inside her for hours at a time. Something hitting his leg interrupted his thoughts.

Looking down, a snow lynx similar to the stuffed one he'd had as a child stared up at him. He set Amelia down and pushed her behind him. Lynx were small creatures, coming in at about knee height, but they could be vicious.

The lynx made a sound and knocked its body into his leg again.

"Stop," Amelia chastised, stepping around him.

Rennick stared at her incredulously. "That's a wild lynx."

"I think he's someone's pet and lost," she replied. "He's been following me all morning."

Could it be...

He grabbed the edge of the bodice of her dress and tried to pull it aside, but she grabbed his wrist. "What are you doing?"

"Seeing if you have a *familiar* mark."

She gasped and ran to a mirror, but her shoulders slumped. "There's nothing there."

Rennick's eyes narrowed on the lynx, and he swore the cat glared at him. Maybe the magic drew the cat to her, and she'd get her mark later.

"What's his name?"

Amelia joined him in the sitting room and jokingly said, "He didn't tell me."

"You should name him."

"And keep him like Eddy?" she asked, bending down to pet the lynx. "What if Eddy doesn't like him?"

Lynx aren't domesticated. He had to be her *familiar*. Rennick smiled. "Something tells me they'll get along fine. Keep him."

He felt her excitement that mirrored the look on her face, and his grew, too.

She squatted in front of the cat. "Charlie," she said with finality. The lynx purred. "You don't have to stay, but if you do, I promise you'll have a good life."

"He has to find something to do for a while, though," Rennick tacked on. He needed to fuck his mate after her declaration of love. Charlie made a rumbling sound. "Unless he wants to see my bare ass."

The cat chuffed and headed to the door.

"They'll try to throw him out," Amelia protested.

She was right. Rennick rang the bell near the door. "I'll give him an escort."

"You're already getting the royal treatment," Amelia cooed, petting Charlie's head.

Rennick smiled down at her. "You took to a wild animal quickly." She must feel the connection.

She shrugged. "Eddy is a wild animal. Maybe I'm an animal whisperer."

"Do not go near another wild animal," Rennick said sharply. "They might hurt you."

She started to say something with an ornery look on her face, but a knock at the door cut her off.

Rennick opened the door to an expectant maid, and he summoned her into the room. She squeaked at the sight of the lynx and backed up.

"He's harmless," Amelia assured her. "He's mine. Can you escort him wherever he wants to go? I don't want anyone to throw him out." An incredulous look affixed to the maid's face.

"Tell every staff and guard you pass that this lynx is as welcome in the palace as Reyna." The maid snapped her gaze to Amelia. "He's not a familiar," Rennick added quickly, not wanting anyone to get any ideas, "but he is a domesticated pet."

Charlie glared at Rennick again, and he fought a laugh. Definitely her familiar. He wondered when her mark and their bond would appear.

The maid nodded. "Yes, Your Majesty."

"His name is Charlie," Amelia added. The maid simply nodded and led Charlie from the room with a nervous smile.

Once the door shut, Rennick scooped Amelia up and threw her on the bed. A grin split his face when she laughed—the sound was his favorite in all of Eden. The joy and desire he felt from her was pure ecstasy, an addiction he would do anything to feed time and again. Gone was the shy woman he'd watched for years, and in her place, a goddess had come to life.

Reaching down, he grabbed her ankles and yanked her to the edge of the bed.

"Rennick!" she squealed with another laugh as her dress bunched around her legs.

He glared at her skirts. "There are too many layers between us."

"I'm not fond of this dress," she teased. "Or these boots."

He frowned slightly at the dress and boots he'd gifted her. *Did she not like them?*

Pushing the thought aside, he crawled over her and leaned down, licking her neck, wanting nothing more than to sink his teeth into her delicate flesh.

The thought of his teeth marks on her flesh made his dick harden to the point of pain, threatening to spill too soon. Unable to take anymore, he sank down, kneeling at her feet to remove her shoes.

Amelia propped herself up on her elbows with an eager glint in her eye. "Hurry."

"Patience, love," he tsked, freeing her foot. The skin of her calf felt like silk beneath his lips when he placed a gentle kiss there, and within minutes, he'd tossed both boots behind him and stood.

As he reached for the bodice of her dress to rip it to shreds, she held out her hand. "Wait." He stilled midair. "I was kidding. I do like this dress. Don't rip it."

Pride swelled in his chest. He leaned down to peck her lips, then he helped her stand and quickly undid the three buttons at the top of her back and untied the back of her skirts. Turning to face him, she lifted her arms in the air, and he gathered the heavy fabric to slide it over her head.

How do women get these off without help? He would see to it that Amelia had a lady's maid to help her dress.

Random freckles dotted her skin, and more than anything, he wanted to kiss every one, but there was no time. He needed her now. He reached out and ran a thumb over the nipple visible through her lace breast band. Once he had her back on the bed, he laid her down before leaning over and latching onto her breast, wetting the lace.

Amelia's hands raked through his hair, her whispered sounds of pleasure egging him on. His teeth closed around the rough lace and pulled to release her breasts from their confinement. They bounced lightly, and he groaned. "You're stunning."

Rennick ran his tongue along the valley of her chest, biting the side of her soft flesh hard enough to leave a mark. She cried out and jerked beneath him.

As he traveled down her body, he hooked his fingers around the band and slid it off, along with her underwear.

She tried to press her knees together, but he caught them and shook his head. "None of that. Open up."

Her knees fell apart, exposing every inch of perfection for him to admire.

Kneeling, he pulled her closer and kissed the inside of her thigh. Her lower lips clenched before she relaxed on the bed with a contented sigh. Slowly, he ran his tongue the length of her pussy, swearing when her taste hit his tongue.

Like a man starved, he feasted on her delicate flesh, licking every inch of slick skin he could. His tongue ventured between her soft folds and circled her clit, sucking it into his mouth. *Fuck.* She bucked and clawed at the bed, crying his name and squeezing her thighs around his head. When he laid on his deathbed, he wanted this to be his final meal.

Her hips were soft when he gripped them and forced her body against his face to fuck her harder with his tongue. No matter how many times she came, he would never be sated. He flattened his tongue and licked slowly from bottom to top, lapping up everything she had to offer. The more he moved, the more she gave him to taste, and it urged him to eat faster.

She screamed and, knowing she was close, he moved his mouth back to her clit and pressed two fingers into her, curling them toward her stomach. They pumped in tandem with his mouth, and her body lifted, knees drawing up as her walls fluttered around his fingers and coated them with cum. Her climax rocked through him as well, and he moaned with her. The euphoric feeling of her release would never get old.

"Rennick," she panted, reaching for him.

He stood, never moving his eyes from hers, and sucked his fingers clean.

She licked her lips as he swiped his fingers against her entrance again to ensure nothing was left.

The glazed look in her eyes mirrored his own, and he took his time removing his clothes, watching her eye-fuck him with drunken lust. He tossed his pants aside. "I like it when you look at me like that. I can't promise this will last long, and it might hurt."

"I've been using the gifts you left me for my twenty-fourth birthday." She turned a pretty shade of red, rendering his restraint a thing of the past.

Rennick aligned himself with her entrance and met her gaze. She nodded once, and he pushed into her, stopping after a few inches with a hiss. "I—fuck," he swore.

Nothing in the world could have prepared him for this.

"More," she moaned, struggling to move her body down, but he held her firm.

"Not yet," he rasped with a glance at where their bodies connected. "I wish you could see how your pussy looks around me." Moving his hips back, he slid out, stopping with only the head left inside before pushing in more. "So red and swollen," he murmured. "Swallowing my dick like a godsdamn dream."

He kept his thrusts shallow until he could seat himself

without hurting her, and when he filled her to the hilt, they both gasped. Every ounce of his pleasure was heightened by hers pulsing through him, too.

"Faster," she begged, lifting her hips, and he felt her wild need.

"If I go too fast, I'll cum."

Her eyes met his, and a mischievous smile spread across her face. "Good."

The effect her words had on him was unmatched, and when he rolled his hips faster, it took four thrusts until a tightness started in his balls, sending a tingling sensation throughout his body.

Black dots spotted his vision as he came with another strangled moan, panting as his cock twitched inside his mate and his movements slowed. Breathing hard, he dropped his head into the crook of Amelia's neck. "I'm sorry, love."

She grasped the side of his neck to bring his face to hers. "Don't be sorry," she murmured before gently pressing her lips to his. "I'm not. And... I felt a bit of your pleasure, too, I think. It was hard to tell."

Gods, I love this woman.

"I'm going to take care of you," he promised, before slipping out of her with a groan. "I'll be right back."

Amelia couldn't put her finger on it, but something inside her had changed. Sex with Rennick was better than anything she could have imagined, and thoughts of how it would be when he stopped restraining himself had her worked up all over again.

For a man who had never had sex before, he moved his hips like a professional, and had he lasted a little longer, she would have come a second time.

There was something to be said about being a man's first and knowing no other woman had touched him intimately before her. A possessiveness she'd not known reared its ugly head, and an understanding of her mate's behavior settled in her soul.

He was hers, and she couldn't wait to tell Ora to get the fuck out of their home tomorrow.

Maybe I will *let him fuck me while the princess watches.*

Her brows pinched together at the absurdity of her last thought. Amelia had never been a vindictive person, but the situation with Ora turned her into someone else. She was still herself in all other aspects, just not where Rennick's childhood friend was concerned.

Amelia no longer questioned Rennick's loyalty, but that didn't mean she would sit back while another woman disrespected her and her relationship. He was *her* mate, not Ora's, and it was time to make that abundantly clear.

Rennick walked into the bedroom in all his naked glory, carrying the largest of the fake dicks he'd sent her last year. Never looking away from her, he spit into his hand and wet the shaft. Her eyes snapped to his in question, but instead of answering, he set the toy on the bedside table.

"Did you think I would leave you wanting, love?"

Her chest heaved as she looked from his real dick to the fake one to his expectant face. "What are you going to do?"

"Stand up," he instructed, ignoring her question.

Cum dripped down her legs when she stood, making her squeeze her thighs together to stop it.

Moving behind her, Rennick sat on the edge of the bed and tapped the top of his muscular thighs. "Sit down."

She made to straddle him, but he stopped her, flipping her around to sit with her back pressed to his front and grabbing each of her legs to hook over his own. The position left her exposed, and she shivered from the cool air caressing her most intimate parts.

He pressed her close to his body and leaned over to grab the toy from the side table. It glistened with his spit, and her body coiled tight.

Using his free hand, he moved her hair to one side and brought his lips to her ear. "Keep your thighs spread, love, and watch yourself take everything I give you."

Amelia's eyes remained glued to the large cock in his hand, the textured base covered with knots to tease her.

Rennick swiped the tip of the toy through the sticky cum coating her thighs, gathering as much on the tip as possible. The head of the cock moved gently over her pussy, grazing her clit and entrance.

What he intended to do was the most erotic thing she'd ever done, and the anticipation building within her made sitting still seem impossible. Rennick's chuckle vibrated down her back. "Stop squirming or it might slip somewhere you aren't ready for, little mate."

She almost knocked his nose with her head when she whipped around to look at him. "You wouldn't dare."

"Not until you're ready." Smirks shouldn't be that attractive, but his was.

Any further retorts died on her tongue, replaced with a decidedly unattractive squeak at the feel of the slick rod pushing into her. The need for him to fill her had her hips canting forward of their own accord, eager for more.

Rennick slid his free hand to palm her breast with a light squeeze. "Look how beautifully you take it."

Amelia couldn't take her eyes off his large hand wrapped around the base of the clay cock, pulsing the toy lightly as it slid in a little at a time. Again, she tried to push her hips forward, needing the fullness. *And the knots.*

Rennick's hand left her breast and snaked up her chest to grab her throat. "Lay your head back." Soft lips brushed against her neck as she rested her head on his broad shoulder.

The toy filled her completely in one swift move and retreated just as fast. A cry burst from her lips. "*Rennick.*"

Again, he pushed it all the way in, but this time he twisted it, stealing her breath. Had he not been pinning her by the neck, she would have fallen off his lap from the shock of it. He pushed and pulled faster, twisting each time the knots reached her skin.

Overwhelming pleasure and need controlled her body; every part of her chased the promise of release. Rennick released her neck and replaced his hand with his tongue and teeth, lightly nibbling on her sensitive flesh.

"I can feel how much you like it." His voice was tight, as if her building release was his own. Oh, how she couldn't wait to experience that fully once they were married.

She was in sensory overload, whining like a bitch in heat, begging to be mounted. Her hips moved faster, her back bent away from his body, and when her pussy started to spasm, teeth sank into her neck.

A scream tore from her throat from both pain and pleasure as her orgasm ripped through her, at odds with the throbbing pain his teeth had created.

Rennick licked and sucked at the spot he'd bitten, purring against her skin, "Such a good mate."

His praise paired with her already sensitive nerves sent an aftershock through her. A small whimper escaped when he removed the toy, but when she felt something wet against her mouth, her eyes flew open. He rubbed the tip over her lips, leaving behind a trail of their mixed pleasure.

"Lick your lips," he said with an authority only a king could possess.

The slick on her lips didn't taste like much. A little salty, but nothing more.

"Look at me."

Another command she couldn't resist.

Her mouth fell open at the sight of his red-tinged lips, and when he winked and smiled, running his tongue over his bloody teeth, she got light-headed.

She reached for her neck. "What did you do?"

"There isn't a part of you I won't taste before this life is over," he promised. Unpleasant images came to her, but she assumed he hadn't meant that literally. Though, happily licking her blood did toe the line of insanity.

Why is that oddly attractive? She shook the thoughts from her head and jumped off his lap on wobbly legs. "You bit me."

He rose to his feet, his wide body dwarfing hers.

"And I'll do it again." He brushed his thumb over the wound. "I now understand why animals mark their territory."

She slapped at his hand and left the room to clean up, throwing over her shoulder, "Don't bite me again."

Rennick followed her into the bathroom with a smile that said he *would* bite her again, and she narrowed her eyes at him. He maneuvered her to stand in front of the mirror, wet a washcloth, and tenderly cleaned her broken flesh. "I can't wear my necklace now," she complained, inspecting the set of perfect teeth marks blemishing her skin.

He frowned and glared at the bite mark like it wasn't his doing. "I can buy you a matching bracelet."

"No, that's okay," she rushed, then cleared her throat, aiming for a more casual demeanor when she said, "I can wear it when this heals."

A yelp escaped her as he lifted her off the ground, carried her to the massive bath, and lowered her feet to the bottom of the porcelain tub before turning on the water. The water warmed quickly, and he ran the wet rag over the inside of her thighs.

"I can clean myself," she protested weakly.

He rinsed the cloth and tilted his head to look at her. "I can either clean you with this cloth or with my tongue, but either way, I will clean you."

"The cloth is fine," she muttered, knowing if she chose the latter, they'd never leave their rooms again.

As he washed her legs, she had a sudden realization of how surreal her life was. She could remember his first letter like it was yesterday. To think she'd thought the strange note was a joke.

"What are you thinking about, love?"

Her lips twisted to the side to prevent herself from laughing at the memory of a thirteen-year-old boy trying to woo a girl he didn't know. "Do you remember the different pet names you tried out in your first letters? You always marked them out, but I could read them, anyway."

"Yes." He laughed lightly. "I was nervous because I wanted it to be perfect."

"It was." She paused before asking him, "What made you decide on 'love?'"

Depositing the cloth into a nearby pail used for dirty linens, he grabbed a fresh towel and held it out for her. "It's what my father called my mother when I was young." He cleared his throat and shrugged a shoulder. "I wanted a relationship like theirs. It felt right."

A ball of emotion clogged Amelia's throat. "I love it."

27

Rennick clapped one of his generals on the shoulder and wove his way through the tables in the massive dining hall. Staff and warriors were welcome to enjoy free meals at the palace if they desired, something his mother had started years ago.

The tables for royals and other high-ranking officials sat at the back of the room on a podium overlooking the others. He approached the head table and pulled out the chair next to his for Amelia, who chatted with an older maid as they set the tables.

Charlie sat faithfully at her heels, earning a few astonished looks from the staff, but those looks turned curious after other staff members leaned toward them and whispered something, likely informing them of the earlier announcement that Charlie was her pet.

Amelia and the maid laughed like old friends, even though Amelia had only been at the palace for two days. Every interaction she had with their staff put him more at ease that his people would accept her without much pushback. Everyone loved her.

"What's on the menu this evening?" an unfortunately familiar voice queried from the bottom of the podium.

Finn shot Rennick a knowing look and glanced between Ora

and Amelia with a taunting smile. "Roast," he told her, offering nothing else. Her lip curled slightly at his tone.

Amelia's eyes turned to slits from the far side of the table where she still stood with the maid. "Hello again," she greeted Ora with a tight smile. "I didn't expect to see you tonight. Do you live here as part of the staff?"

One of the warriors nearby choked, and the room fell silent.

Ora stiffened and narrowed her eyes briefly before gliding across the podium with a fake laugh. "My father is a council member, but sometimes it feels like I live here." Her hand went to her silver necklace, one Rennick recognized well. It was a gift he'd given her for her eighteenth birthday as a thank you for helping him with Amelia's gifts. "But I do have my own rooms for the nights we stay up too late."

She winked at Rennick, and he wanted to rip her eyelids off.

Finn stopped chewing and glanced quickly at Amelia. Rennick felt his mate struggle to keep her anger in check, and he made to move toward her, but stopped when Ora gasped.

"Oh no!" She looked pitifully down at the necklace in her hands. Her face was the picture of distraught when she turned to him and said, "It caught on my finger and broke."

More like she broke it on purpose. *Oh, fuck,* he thought when her intention clicked.

Before he could stop her, she said to Amelia, "The necklace was a gift from Ren for my eighteenth birthday." Ora smiled fondly. "He said it made him think of me."

He heard a few murmurs from the room and hated that so many bore witness to the scene, but his options were limited to hauling Amelia away, killing Ora, or forcefully removing the latter. "It was a thank you for your help," he amended through gritted teeth.

Ora ignored him and lifted the necklace—a silver chain holding a heart with an arrow through it. "Isn't it pretty?"

She'd picked the damned thing out herself, but he'd been a

stupid boy, not realizing it could be construed another way. He realized it now. He corrected her again, with a warning in his tone. "You picked it out."

Amelia's hand touched the base of her throat where her trout necklace usually lay, and Rennick could feel her anger building. He readied himself for her to flee or turn her hard eyes on him, but she did neither. Instead, a sigh escaped her, and her eyes filled with false pity.

"Silver *is* a cheap metal." She turned to Rennick and shook her head. "She deserved better than a weak silver chain for all the help she gave you in picking out my gifts." She pushed her hair over her shoulder, exposing his bite mark to everyone, and Rennick covered his mouth to hide his smile.

The whispers around the room grew as Amelia stared at Ora with a silent challenge. A feeling of sly satisfaction flowed from Amelia to him as she walked closer, with Charlie at her side. If the lynx decided to rip Ora's throat out, Rennick would let him.

His mate touched his arm over his still healing scab. A claim. Even if no one else knew, they did. "Shame on you," she chided him, biting back a coy smile.

Rennick leaned down and kissed the top of her head, not caring if everyone saw. He would marry her in secret as soon as possible to ensure her safety.

He'd wanted her to adjust to the fae world first, but he couldn't wait any longer. A guard he trusted would be assigned to her when he wasn't around to prevent anyone from trying to touch her.

"I'm sorry, love," he said loudly. "I didn't give it much thought."

The chair he'd pulled out for Amelia moved beneath his hand, startling him. Breaking his attention on Amelia, he turned to find Ora beaming up at him from the chair.

"Sit," she said, nodding toward his chair and looking at the rest of those on the podium. "Everyone eat up before the food gets cold."

She addressed the others like a queen, and he'd not stand for it. People around the room exchanged nervous glances, but did as she said, which pissed Rennick off more. *How did I not notice her antics until now?*

"That's Amelia's seat," he said coolly, deciding not to kill her in front of everyone. He'd do that out of sight of prying eyes.

Ora leaned forward and looked around him at Amelia. "I've always sat here. You don't mind, do you?"

Another challenge. Everyone knew the queen sat on the king's right. It's true she'd always sat there, but he thought it was so she could talk with him and Finn during meals.

His mate bared her teeth in a dangerous smile but kept her voice pleasant. "Not at all."

His face darkened, ready to rip Ora out of the chair, but Amelia subtly squeezed his arm.

He raised a brow at her. *What are you planning, little mate?*

She gestured for him to sit down. With growing curiosity over her intentions, he obeyed. Amelia stopped him from scooting his chair under the table and lowered herself onto his lap, giving Ora her back with her legs pointed at Finn.

A few people in the room laughed, including Finn, who tried to cover it with a cough.

Rennick banded an arm around Amelia's middle and tugged her snugly against him to brush a kiss against her cheek.

Completely ignoring the daggers Ora threw her way, Amelia smiled at the older maid, who placed a plate in front of her. "Thank you, Birdie."

Birdie smirked, and the two traded a knowing look. "You're welcome, dear." She shot Ora a look of loathing and walked off.

Amelia filled Rennick's plate, not bothering to ask what he liked, but he knew it was a power move. Even if he hated what she'd served, which he didn't, he would eat with a smile on his face.

Ora looked ready to spit nails and diverted her attention to Finn. "What happened to your hair?"

A few murmurs from the crowd didn't escape Rennick's attention, nor did the perturbed looks from a few of the bald fae.

"Our friend decided blond hair was offensive," he replied before tucking more potatoes into his mouth.

Amelia side-eyed Rennick but said nothing, and Ora's eyes gleamed as they scanned Amelia's blonde braid. "That makes sense. Rennick used to say he hoped his mate had dark hair."

Gods. He wanted to tell Ora to leave right then, but he knew his mate wanted to prove a point, something he would fuck her for later.

"Is that so?" Amelia asked, rotating her body to look at the other woman.

"Oh, yes," Ora went on smugly. "He tried to imagine what she looked like. Do you remember what you said, Ren?"

He did, and he wished he could take the words back and shove them down her throat.

"Ora," Finn warned, but she was like a dog with a bone.

"He wanted someone with dark hair and light eyes." She twisted her own dark hair around her finger and batted her light blue eyes at him. "And short." She giggled and pointedly scanned Amelia's tall form. "He wanted her short enough to carry on his shoulders. Isn't that adorable?"

"We were fourteen," Finn interjected with a level of venom that surprised Rennick. "He thought a tall girl would kick his balls. If he mated a short girl now, he'd look like an inchworm trying to kiss her."

Amelia's hand clapped over her mouth to stifle a laugh, and Rennick was so thankful that he almost felt bad for making Finn shave his head.

Almost.

Amelia reached for the glass of wine on the table and took a long drink. "That's all very cute," she agreed, followed by the fakest yawn Rennick had ever seen in his life. Her hazel eyes, his new favorite color, slipped to his. "Can we go back to our rooms? I'm exhausted from earlier." She gave him a flirtatious smile that couldn't be interpreted as anything other than the insinuation it was.

Ora's silverware clanged against her plate, but he ignored her. "Of course, love. Birdie," he called the maid serving their table, "please have our food delivered to our rooms."

"*Your* rooms?" Ora asked in disbelief. "Ren, you can't be serious! What about your mate?"

The mood in the room shifted, and every person paused, waiting for his answer.

He turned eerily slow to look at the woman he'd considered a friend for most of his life. "Yes. *Our* rooms. Now, if everyone would excuse us."

He tipped his head to the room and the others on the podium as Amelia slid off his lap so he could stand.

With his hands on Amelia's shoulders, Rennick moved her toward the wall at the back of the podium, her back facing everyone in the room.

"Hold the front of your skirts above your waist," he whispered in her ear. She flashed him a curious smile and leaned over to gather the long fabric. He moved in front of her and squatted down, with his back to her and one knee on the floor. "Get on, love."

Laughter bubbled out of her. "What?"

"Grab one of my hands and place the other on my head to climb onto my shoulders."

Directly behind him, a chair scraped loudly, followed by the echo of angry stomps down the podium steps. Finn muttered something under his breath, but all Rennick focused on was Amelia hoisting herself up and tossing one leg over his shoulder.

He helped maneuver her other leg in place and secured her thighs on either side of his head.

Standing with ease, he looked up at her as she looked down. "I'm going to let go of your hands to grab your legs. Hold on to my hair if you need to."

They turned, and the room stared unabashedly as he carefully descended from the podium and left the dining hall, with Charlie trailing behind.

Their laughter bounced off the palace walls as he carried her the long way back to their rooms to show her just how much he loved blonde hair, hazel eyes, and long legs more than anything else in the world.

Rennick lowered Amelia to the ground outside of their rooms and opened the door to usher her inside while telling Charlie to find something else to do. A cart with their dinner sat near the small breakfast table, but she knew they wouldn't be eating anytime soon.

At least not food.

"You like dark hair, huh?" she teased.

His hand reached around and fisted her hair, yanking her head back. "Blonde looks better around my hand," he replied roughly. His other hand slid down the front of her dress to cup her pussy. "And around my cock." *Oh.*

The words heated her from the inside out. "What color are my lips?"

His brows bent slightly. "Which ones?"

Her breath hitched, and she wordlessly tapped her mouth.

"I don't know what the color is called." He focused on her lips and ran his thumb softly across them. "They're slightly darker than your skin. A little pink, too."

She tilted her head slightly and bit her lip with a smile. "Does that color look good around your cock?"

If she couldn't hear his heart beating wildly in his chest, she would've thought him a corpse with how stiff he went. Wild green eyes met hers. "The only color that looks prettier around my cock than your barely pink lips is your red, swollen pussy."

A shiver of pleasure ran down her spine, lighting every nerve she had on fire. "I think we need to compare before we make that decision," she taunted breathlessly and reached for his pants.

Clothes went flying. Sinking to her knees, Amelia caught Rennick's eye and licked her hand to wrap around the base of his shaft.

She sank her nails into the flesh of his backside and slid her mouth over the head of his cock. Rennick groaned like a tortured soul, his hands twitching at his sides. As she worked her hand and mouth together, he lost the fight and threaded a hand into her hair, pushing her head down farther.

"Let me hear you gag." He thrust his hips forward. It wasn't hard, and she could have easily pulled back, but she didn't.

She prayed she wouldn't puke when she gagged, but if she did, it was his fault for shoving himself to the back of her throat. He eased back for her to catch her breath, then pushed his cock down her throat again.

Suddenly, he pulled out and hauled her over his shoulder, getting to their bedroom in record time. He set her on her feet facing the end of the bed, moved her hands to the bedpost, and said, "Bend over and hold on, love."

She obliged, wondering what tricks he'd learned over the years, and squirmed when his fingers swiped through her arousal. "If I'd known my cock between your lips made you this wet, I would have fucked your mouth our first night together."

And then his mouth was on her.

She moaned and pushed back against his face as he ravaged

her relentlessly with his tongue. "You're perfect," he said, pushing a finger inside of her.

Her legs shook, and when her inner walls spasmed, he removed his finger and stood.

Amelia cried out in protest, but the feel of his dick nudging her entrance made her swallow her words. Without warning, he slammed into her, and she understood why he'd told her to hold on, because without the bedpost, she would have tumbled head-first onto the mattress.

He set a bruising pace, and she was already sensitive from his teasing. His fingers brushed against her clit, sending her over the edge. They both moaned and, seconds later, he pumped strings of cum inside of her for what felt like forever.

"I knew the first time I felt you come on my cock would be exquisite," he murmured, kissing her back.

Cum dripped down her legs when he pulled out of her, and she bowed them, peering down. Waddling wasn't the sexiest thing in the world, but she didn't want to get cum on the expensive rug. She clamped her thighs together and shuffled toward the bare stone floor.

Strong arms scooped her up and lifted her to rest against a warm chest. "Where are you going, little mate?"

"I was trying to move off of the rug, so I didn't ruin it with your bodily fluids."

He threw his head back with a booming laugh. "I don't think so." Laying her on the plush rug, he moved his hand to her pussy and swiped through the cum on her legs to push it back inside of her. "Your cunt will soak in every bit of me."

Oh my.

Once he was satisfied, he crawled over her and latched on to her nipple, sucking it into his mouth. "I have something I'd like to try," he murmured. "If you're okay with it."

She lifted her head to look at him. "What?"

He stood. "Don't move."

Rennick disappeared into the bathroom and returned with a wooden box. He flipped the lid open and pulled something out. It was made of the same material as her fake cocks, but this possessed a pointed tip, bulbous middle, and a wide, flat base.

"What is that for?"

"I want to fill every hole you have." His gaze trailed to her spread legs. "These are to help prepare you."

Her eyes flared. "These?"

He opened the box again and showed her the contents. It contained similar objects to the one in his hand, but in different sizes. "It will feel odd at first, but you'll get used to them, and once you're ready, your ass will take my cock as well as your greedy little cunt."

She gaped at him, but intrigue kept her from objecting. "What if it hurts?"

"That's the purpose of these." He gestured to the box. "I would never hurt you."

"On purpose," she countered.

"Ever." He bent down next to her. "Anyone who says they're scared of hurting you on purpose is warning you." After setting the box down, he pulled a small jar of oil out and slathered in on the plug in his hand. "I know I won't, accident or not."

She nodded and waited expectantly.

"Get on your hands and knees, love."

Once in position, she looked over her shoulder at him, but he was staring at her backside, biting his lip. "Fuck. Every inch of you is stunning."

He ran an oiled finger over the area he'd later fill, pressing the tip of it against her tightness. "I know it's difficult, but relax."

"I don't know how." She was nervous.

"Close your eyes and breathe in deep, then focus on loosening your body as you release it."

She tried, gods, she tried, but her anticipation kept her drawn up tight.

His other hand found her clit and moved in lazy circles. "Oh," she whimpered, dropping her head forward.

"Keep breathing," he encouraged softly. "I won't hurt you." With every breath and stroke, she felt her muscles loosen. "Bear down as if using the latrine."

"What?" She turned to him. "You can't mean…" Embarrassment colored her face.

His mouth twitched. "Never be embarrassed around me. Everyone does it. It will help."

He cannot be serious. "What if I *go?*" she sputtered.

He shrugged. "I will wash you, and we'll try again."

"Oh, my gods."

His fingers still worked her clit, and the other caressed her backside lovingly. "Please?"

Closing her eyes, she nodded. "Okay."

She did as he asked, focusing on staying loose, and to her surprise, his finger slipped inside. "Good girl." He continued to push inside and moved his finger in a circular motion. She jerked at the new sensation. "You're doing great, love."

Her breathing grew heavy when he slipped his thumb into her pussy, while his other finger still worked on her clit. There was a lot going on down there, and everything spiraled. He pulled out his finger from her backside but maintained a steady rhythm with his other hand.

"Bear down, love."

She breathed too hard to answer, but tried to do as he said. The tip of the plug pressed against her, and Rennick wiggled it gently. Eventually, her body accepted it with a soft pop, and the fullness took her by surprise, sending her into an intense climax.

Her cries echoed around their bedroom, and Rennick's lips found her supple cheek. She rocked back against his hand with the intensity of her orgasm until the sensations ebbed.

He removed his hand and held her hips. "Come here."

Pushing up to her knees, she allowed him to pull her into his lap and laid her head against his shoulder.

"I love you," he murmured. "Thank you for doing this."

"I love you too, and I have a feeling I'll enjoy it as much as you." She pressed a kiss to his chest. "How long do I need to wear it?"

His hand stroked her stomach. "A few hours to start."

She balked. *Hours? To* start?

"Let me wash you, and then we'll eat," Rennick proposed.

She nodded, feeling the exhaustion, and spoke against his neck. "Only if I can wash you, too."

Later that night, as they lay in bed with Amelia tucked snuggly under Rennick's arm, he brought up the one name she'd rather never hear again. "We need to talk about Ora."

Her irritation rose at the thought. "I'm not sorry for how I acted."

"You shouldn't be. I would have forced her out of the palace already, but I didn't want to take that opportunity away from you."

On the one hand, Amelia appreciated him honoring their agreement about telling Ora together, but on the other hand, it would have been intoxicating to see her disgraced in front of the entire dining hall after her thinly veiled attempts to usurp her.

Amelia tipped her head up to see Rennick's face. "We're meeting her tomorrow at four, correct?"

"Yes, after my meetings. Do you know what you want to say?"

"I thought 'Get the fuck out of our home' would suffice." She craned her neck more to gauge his reaction and grinned when he laughed with abandon.

His fingers ran a soothing path down the length of her arm, leaving goosebumps in their wake. "Let me know where you'll be tomorrow, and I'll walk you to my study when my meetings are over."

It was cute, seeing a hulking fae king who killed people because he felt like it want to walk her somewhere like a teenage schoolboy. An unexpected pang soured her stomach at everything they'd missed out on because she was human.

"If I were fae and grew up in one of the fae kingdoms, would we have met sooner?"

For the longest time, he said nothing, and she worried she'd asked a stupid question. Finally, he exhaled loudly. "When a royal hears their mate's name, they locate them and, if they are from a different kingdom, the mate and their family move to the royal's kingdom, but not always."

"It doesn't seem fair to ask them to uproot their lives when they can't marry until they're twenty-five, anyway."

"Twenty-two," he corrected. "Most royals marry their mates when they turn twenty-two."

Another hit. "Either way, asking someone to leave their friends and other family isn't fair."

"It's not," he agreed, "but it's for their own safety and the preservation of the royal bloodlines."

Right. Because royal mates possessed a strong magical bond needed to create stronger heirs.

So much had happened in one day, which made her realize it'd only been a handful of days since meeting Rennick in person. She didn't even know what his father looked like. She didn't feel the bond, yet she loved him from years of letters and the days they'd spent together since. But he'd had no way of falling in love with her as a person over the years. Watching her sometimes didn't give him insight into anything about her other than her looks and daily routine.

He tugged lightly on her hair. "What's wrong?"

She swallowed, not wanting to sound pathetic. What sane person complained that a beautiful fae king was obsessed with them, magic or not? "I hate that we missed out on being together for the last twelve years."

Soft lips brushed against hers. "We have plenty of time to make up for it. Tell me about your friend, Clover," he said, switching the subject fast enough to be suspicious, but she didn't want to think too hard about why.

Maybe he'd liked not having her breathing down his neck during his teenage years.

"What do you want to know?"

He adjusted them into a more comfortable position and ran his fingers through her hair. "Did you two grow up together?"

"No." A memory of the first day she met Clover surfaced. "She didn't come to the orphanage until after I turned thirteen. I remember thinking how pretty she was and hoping she wasn't terrible, like Ana and Farrah."

"Who are Ana and Farrah?"

"Two girls who don't matter, but Clover is nothing like them. She's painfully shy and quiet. I thought she didn't like me at first." A smile spread across her face. "I wore her down." The night Clover showed her the paragraph had turned the tide of their friendship, and she would always treasure it. "You might not remember this, but in one of your first letters, you said you felt me laugh."

"I do," he murmured. "I'd been eating dinner when I felt it. I remember laughing too, as though I was in on the joke."

"It was Clover. I didn't have any friends then." She plucked at a string on the comforter. "Most of my schoolmates were nice, but when I was younger, I preferred to keep to myself." She shrugged. "But Clover liked to hide away and read too. That night you felt me. She'd showed me that she wanted a friend too."

"You said Clover had no family?"

"That's right, and no other friends that I knew of." Amelia

frowned. "I don't know why she lied to her boss or where she really went."

"I can send for her." Rennick shifted. "She can live in the palace, or in a house of her choosing here in the Mountain Kingdom if she'd like."

Amelia sat up and twisted to look down at him with stinging eyes over how readily he jumped at the chance to make her happy without a second thought. "I don't deserve you."

"You're right." Her stomach plummeted. "You deserve better, and I'll try to be that for you."

"Are you joking?" She couldn't tell.

"I don't joke," he replied with a straight face, his voice void of humor.

She laughed at his serious expression, but the laugh died quickly. "You deserve more than I can give you. Look at you." She swept her hand over his body. "You should be with a powerful fae who can fight alongside you and support you in every way.

"I can train until I'm blue in the face and I still wouldn't be as strong as the weakest fae. Half of the fae, if not more, won't respect a human queen. You and I both know it. If it weren't for the bond, you wouldn't have looked at me twice."

He sat up so fast that she fell back with a squeak. She'd only felt his emotions once, but she felt them now, and he was *pissed*. "You are everything I need and better than anything I ever wanted." Words escaped her at the fierceness in his declaration. "You think I give a fuck that you're physically weak?"

She frowned. She didn't say she was weak, just weak*er* than fae.

"I couldn't care less what shape your ears are or what kingdom you're from. You are good and kind and everything I'm not." She opened her mouth to protest, but he cut her off. "I once watched you set your pile of books in the snow to open a door for a woman juggling three children. You took in a pet fox, for fuck's sake." With each word, her mouth opened more until she stared at him slack-jawed, like the trout on her necklace. "You thought I might not come for you, yet you learned to cook my favorite dish, anyway."

Hearing the conviction in his words took her breath away.

"If we weren't mates, I'd pray our paths never crossed." She flinched, his words inflicting physical pain. "My fated mate wouldn't have stood a chance. No bond could compare to how you make me feel. Don't ever question my loyalty and love for you again."

"I'm sorry," she whispered. Her eyes blurred with tears, overwhelmed with gratitude. She didn't see herself the way he did, and no one in her life knew her well enough to see her that way, either.

Warmth encircled her waist, and he dragged her into his lap. "Don't be sorry, love, but don't doubt me again."

Tears trickled down her cheeks. "I won't, I promise." She finally met his gaze. "I know I'm not the best at showing it, but I love you, and I don't want you to doubt that either."

"Marry me," he murmured, staring at her with more intensity than she'd ever seen from him.

"I thought that was the plan," she joked, loving the way his mouth tugged into a crooked smile.

"We were to wed at the coronation celebration in six days' time for everyone to bear witness to the blood exchange, but I don't want to wait. I want to marry you sooner."

"What coronation celebration? Blood exchange?" She felt woozy.

He smirked. "Which answer would you like first?"

Neither. "The blood exchange."

"When fae marry, they do the holy blood exchange. After agreeing to the marriage, the royal officiant spreads holy oil on your skin here." His finger skimmed over the side of her neck.

"We'll take turns making a small cut over the oil on each other's skin and then lick it clean."

The room spun, and Amelia grasped Rennick's arm tightly. "Is there another way? I can't *lick* your blood."

"You must ingest the other's blood, love, but it will be quick."

She licked her lips and swallowed the saliva collecting in her mouth. "Okay." Closing her eyes, she blew out a long breath. "Tell me about the celebration." Anything to get her mind off consuming someone's blood.

"The coronation celebration is a big party to celebrate my becoming king with the other royal families and council members. I've acted in my father's stead for years, but I wasn't officially crowned until a few days ago, upon our twenty-fifth birthday. My father and I decided to postpone the celebration until after I brought you home."

The blood drained from her face. "All of the royal families are coming for our wedding in six days?"

"They think they're only coming to celebrate my corona-tion." He smoothed her hair back lovingly. "No one knows I've found my mate."

"You said royals hear the name of their mates."

He looked amused. "We do."

"Then what excuse did you give when you didn't marry yours when you turned twenty-two?"

"My father gave excuses to no one other than his closest advisors and swore them to secrecy. The other kingdoms' rulers likely think I'm an asshole who refused to marry my mate or that my mate died." He shrugged like people thinking less of him was nothing.

"What are the coronations and weddings like?"

"I couldn't leave my kingdom until I turned twenty-five and took the throne," he reminded her. "I've never been to one, but even if I could leave, none of the other three heirs have married yet, either."

"Are they all young?"

He shook his head, and her lips pinched together. "The Desert King is twenty-five, and the Garden King is twenty-six. The Tropical King is twenty-four."

"I thought they had to marry when they were twenty-two?"

"They don't have to, but it's tradition."

"That doesn't seem suspicious to you? What are the odds that none of the heirs have married?"

Rennick thought for a moment. "All four heirs not marrying at twenty-two is unheard of." He held on to her and laid them back against the pillows. "The Tropical King is too young to leave his kingdom, but the Garden King and Desert King will be here for my coronation celebration. You can ask them yourself."

She blanched. "I'm not going to ask a stranger why they're not married!"

He laughed, rolled them over, and hovered above her. "Marry me. I can't wait another week."

She leaned up and kissed him softly. "I'd love to."

28

The next morning, Amelia stood in the middle of her library in awe. Everything in the Mountain Kingdom took her breath away, but this was something else all together.

The circular room boasted the tallest bookshelves she'd ever seen. They covered every inch of the wall with sliding ladders attached. Even the door was a bookshelf, which blended seamlessly into the wall when shut, save for the door handle.

The shelves were a dark cherry wood that went well with the overstuffed leather furniture and matching wooden side tables. A gold desk sat in the middle of the large room, accented by the gold reading lanterns adorning each table. It was unreal.

A disturbance at the border needed Rennick's attention, and after she'd convinced him that she didn't need to be locked in their rooms all day to stay safe, he'd assigned a guard to accompany her wherever she wished to go until he returned.

Echo stood guard at the door, a permanent scowl pinned to their face. They had a slim build and dark, collar-length hair that contrasted starkly against their ivory skin.

After an hour of perusing the shelves, Amelia decided to find Fawn.

"Do you know Fawn?" she asked Echo, who lifted a brow.

"The maid?" Echo frowned down at Charlie, who rubbed against their leg.

Amelia crossed to the door, but jumped back when Echo blocked her way. "I'll leave first." She stepped back, knowing the guard was only doing their job. Echo walked into the hall and looked both ways before saying, "If Fawn works today, she'll either be in the laundry room or cleaning rooms."

Drat. She didn't want to keep interrupting Fawn's work. "Actually, can we walk through the gardens? I need fresh air."

Echo glanced at her as the two of them meandered down the hall. "Have you seen them yet?"

Amelia shook her head. "No. Rennick promised to show me, but we haven't had time."

"There's my future daughter-in-law," a larger-than-life voice said, cutting off their conversation.

Echo snapped their back straight with an about face and bowed slightly to a large man with a handsome face and salt and pepper hair. "Your Majesty."

The man waved a hand dismissively. "Call me Callum. Your Majesty is my son."

It was Amelia's turn to straighten and look at Echo for help. The traitor moved back to give Callum room when he approached. She took in his strong, stubble-sprinkled jaw, broad shoulders, and straight nose. Rennick was a spitting image of his father, and it took her slightly off guard.

A large, white snow leopard prowled beside him, and when Amelia's brain caught up enough to notice, she screamed like a banshee and jumped behind Echo. It wasn't a normal snow leopard. It was huge, with solid black eyes and the sharpest teeth she'd ever seen. It also possessed a surprisingly fluffy tail.

Charlie walked forward and stared at the leopard like he stood a chance of winning a fight with the beast.

Alarm coated Callum's face. Then he realized what had frightened Amelia and roared with laughter. Echo's shoulders shook lightly, and Amelia poked them in the back. "What's so funny?" she hissed at her guard.

"It's alright. My girl, Reyna, won't hurt you," Callum assured with a hearty laugh. "She's my *familiar*."

"Did the big cat tell you to say that?" she mumbled under her breath. The leopard chuffed, earning itself another wary glance from Amelia.

Inching around Echo's other side, far away from Reyna, she held out her hand to Rennick's father. "Hello. You will have to excuse me. I'm not used to seeing the *interesting* animals of the fae kingdom."

Callum's large hand engulfed hers, and he glanced at the lynx at Amelia's feet with interest before flicking his gaze to her chest. "He's not my familiar," she said. "Rennick said I could keep him, though."

Callum stared at Charlie a bit longer before releasing Amelia's hand. "I've been waiting to meet you for twelve years, Amelia."

A male guard ran down the hall, shouting, "*Rebel attack on the south wall! Everyone to safe rooms!*"

The few staff members in the hall scrambled in different directions, and Callum cursed. "Get her somewhere safe," he ordered Echo. "Protect your queen."

Echo grabbed Amelia's wrist, tugged her toward a nearby door, and shuffled her inside. When Amelia flipped around, she bumped into a large, furry head.

"Oh, my gods!" she shrieked, trying to move backward, only to be met by a wall.

"Shh," Echo whispered. "Reyna won't hurt you. The former king can see and hear through her to check on you." The shouting in the hall died down after a bit, but Echo made no move to leave. "If something happens and we are separated, stay with Reyna."

"What do you mean, '*if we are separated*?'" Amelia whisper-yelled. Charlie moved against her, and she had the feeling he was trying to provide comfort. "You can't leave me here."

"I would never willingly leave you," Echo replied vehemently. "But if someone comes through that door or I have to move you to a different location, things might happen."

Amelia reached out to steady herself on the wall but was met with fabric and air that sent her tumbling to the ground.

Echo blindly reached for her in the dark. "Are you okay?"

Amelia felt a wet furry nose nudge her head. "I'm fine." She jerked back when Charlie's warm breath hit her square in the face. "Are we in a big closet?" It must be huge to fit two people, a lynx, and an oversized leopard, but she wouldn't know because it was pitch black except for a small sliver of light under the door.

"Yes. It's one of dozens around the palace."

"Whose clothes are these?"

She heard Echo shift. "An older guard once told me that King Rennick had them added into the walls and filled with different types of women's coats and blankets when he was a teenager."

Amelia fingered the fabric above her. "Are they for the staff?"

Her question was met with silence at first, and she wondered if Echo was shaking or nodding their head. "No, but the maids must keep them dust free. No one knows why."

How would someone pick out a coat in the dark? Bringing in a lantern might be dangerous with this much fabric jammed into one closet. Her mate was so peculiar.

Rennick. Amelia climbed to her feet and reached for Echo's arm, grabbing a fistful of fluffy tail instead. Yanking her hand back, she said, "We have to find Rennick or get a message to him that I'm safe."

Echo choked or scoffed. Amelia couldn't tell. "I will not take you anywhere while rebels are trying to get through the palace walls."

"You don't understand." Amelia felt panic filling her chest and worked to tamp it down. "Rebels killed his mother, and if he finds out they're near the palace, he will kill everyone in his path to get to me." *Or get himself killed.*

"Then let him. Either way, someone will die, and I'd rather it not be you."

Damnit.

"Then I need something to write with." She felt around in the dark, finding only blankets and coats. "How close are we to a room that might have something to write with? It sounds quiet out there."

Silence followed, and she imagined Echo wished they were fighting rebels instead of stuck in a closet with her. "Why?" they eventually asked.

"I can attach a letter to Reyna and have her take it to Rennick. That way he—oof!" Amelia glared at Reyna's silhouette in the dark. "Did you head-butt me?" Charlie stood at her feet and growled at the other cat.

Echo made a blowing sound like one did when trying to hold back a laugh, and Reyna released a growl of her own that was somehow not menacing, but a warning all the same.

"Fine," Amelia conceded, "but when half of the palace staff are slaughtered for not moving out of his way fast enough, don't say I didn't try to warn you."

Echo's voice softened. "It's admirable that you're worried about the safety of your staff, but they're all barricaded in safe rooms."

A bit of Amelia's tension loosened, having forgotten the

earlier guard yelled about safe rooms as he ran down the hall. "Good."

Sometime later, the door handle rattled, and Echo drew their sword while Reyna pushed Amelia back and Charlie pressed against her leg.

"Stay with Reyna," Echo whispered.

Icy fear gripped Amelia like a vise.

"Open this door," a commanding voice yelled to someone outside. "I want to see every room until she's found."

The doorknob rattled again. "It's locked, Your Highness."

Your Highness?

"Move," the first voice barked, and seconds later, the door was ripped from its hinges.

A towering man with blond hair and skin slightly darker than Amelia's stood like a murderous angel, holding the door with one hand. Reyna ran forward, slammed her paws into his chest, and... licked him. Amelia and Echo both gaped at the deserter.

Seeing Reyna, the man dropped the door with a loud crash and petted her head, relief evident on his face. The leopard dropped to the ground and stepped around him, leaving Amelia and Echo to the mercy of a man who could rip locked doors off hinges with one hand.

Echo, gods bless them, still had their sword up, ready to fight.

The torchlights in the halls weren't bright enough to light the back of the closet, and Amelia tried to make herself as small as possible.

The man held his hands up. "I'm not going to hurt her."

"Pardon me, sir, but I don't know that," Echo shot back.

"I appreciate you protecting Amelia, but I will see her one way or another. Lower your weapon."

The man knew her name.

Echo tightened their grip on the sword. "Not until someone I trust gives the order."

Amelia, not wanting Echo's death on her hands, stepped forward. "I'm fine."

"Get back," Echo demanded, stepping in front of her.

A small bark drew their attention to the man's feet, and there, looking healthy and happy, was a tiny fennec fox. "Eddy!" Amelia cried and tried to move forward.

Echo blocked her again. "Get back."

"You told me to stay with Reyna." Amelia pointed to the snow leopard. "If you weren't here, Reyna would let me see him."

Echo considered her words and turned to the giant cat sitting quietly in the hall. "If he hurts her, I will use your fur as a rug."

The man looked at Echo appreciatively. "If you ever move to the Desert Kingdom, you will have a job as my guard."

"Who are you?" Amelia demanded with more valor than she felt.

Eyes the same color as her own landed on her. "My name is Amos."

She waited for him to elaborate and when he didn't, she looked at the warriors barricading each end of the hall. "It's nice to meet you." *I think.*

The guards parted, drawing her attention, and there, at the end of the hall, stood a mountain of a man, covered in blood, looking like Death himself.

Rennick's chest heaved, and Amelia hadn't realized how worried she'd been until that moment. A relieved cry tore from her throat, and she ran toward him, jumping into his arms, not caring that the blood covering him smeared all over her dress. He buried his head into the crook of her neck and held her tight, whispering soothing words and assuring her she was okay.

"I worried you were hurt, and Reyna wouldn't take you a note to let you know I was safe," she mumbled against his shoulder.

He pulled back to look at her. "I would never leave you

unless I knew you were safe. Echo is the best warrior we have, even more so than Finn."

Amelia looked at Echo, who shrugged like it was no big deal.

"Amos," Rennick said, tipping his head. "Thank you for finding her."

Amos stalked toward them, motioning for his guards to leave. "I thought the rebel situation was taken care of in the Mountain Kingdom."

"I did too," Rennick replied grimly, tightening his hold on Amelia. "But they never truly go away."

She dropped her legs and patted his shoulder until he reluctantly let her down. "Why does he know my name?"

Rennick sighed. "We'll explain everything soon, love." His attention snagged on Eddy sitting at Amos's feet. "Where is his coat?"

Amos rolled his eyes, and Amelia bit back a laugh. "I'll put it on him when we get back to the room," she promised.

Amos stepped slightly in front of Eddy. "That won't be necessary. He'll be going home with me."

Eddy whined and Amelia bristled. "You can't steal my fox."

"He is my *familiar*," Amos said quietly. "It's been difficult being away from him for the last ten years, and he isn't made for the cold."

What is he talking about? Amelia looked at Rennick, and the expression on his face confirmed Amos' words. The realization punched her square in the chest.

Rennick took notice and moved in front of her, his voice terrifying. "I will kill you if you don't let her keep him."

Eddy looked between the two men, and Amelia lightly popped Rennick's side. "Stop threatening to kill people. You've explained *familiars* to me, and I understand how important they are to their owners." Reyna growled at Amelia's words, and Charlie growled back. The little lynx was brave. She'd give him that. "Or whatever you are to them," Amelia amended.

She knew Eddy needed to be with Amos, but she hated it. "Can I visit him?"

Eddy made a barking sound and Amos reached down to pick him up. "As often as you'd like."

Rennick shut his study door behind Amos and Amelia and offered the Desert King a seat in front of the desk. Rennick wanted his mate beside him at all times, especially after today, and dragged another chair to sit next to his own.

The disturbance at the south-west border of Vale, near the Desert Kingdom border, had been a ploy to distract from the other rebels sneaking in from the northern wilderness to attack the palace. Amos and his men were traveling to Vale early for the coronation ceremony and intercepted the faction just outside of the capital's border by the time Rennick had arrived.

Upon their return to the palace, Rennick and Amos found pure chaos. The Desert King agreed to find Amelia while Rennick eliminated the lingering threat.

Rennick had become a killing machine, ending every rebel in sight. Taking hostages for questioning wasn't an option, and when his father fought alongside him, doing the same, he knew they both remembered the night his mother died.

Protecting Amelia was their number one priority. The rebels never made it inside the palace walls, nor would any ever again.

He knew she was safe between Echo, Reyna, and Amos, but he took no chances with his mate's life.

No one knew how to start what was sure to be a shocking conversation for Amelia, and Rennick worried about how she'd react. He'd kept the truth from her out of respect for Amos, but she might perceive it as a betrayal.

Amelia lowered herself into the chair and clasped her hands in her lap. "Explain."

Jumping right in, then.

Amos drew in a deep breath. "There's no easy way to say this," he began, "but you're my sister and second in line to the Desert Kingdom throne."

Amos and Rennick waited with bated breath, and both men were taken aback when Amelia burst out laughing. "Very funny."

"It's true, love," Rennick said softly.

Amelia's laughter died down, and she motioned to Amos. "He's fae." She pushed her hair behind her ear and pointed to it. "I'm a human."

"Your ears were clipped when you were born to hide your heritage," Amos explained, his voice cautious.

She made an intelligible sound. "Come again? Because it sounded like you insinuated that someone cut off part of my ears as a baby."

Amos raked a hand through his short blond hair, and the longer Rennick looked at him, the more he saw the similarities between the two. Their coloring was the same as were their mouths. Amos had a sharp jawline, where Amelia had a rounded face, but other than that, the resemblance was uncanny.

"When our mother was pregnant with us—"

"Us?" she parroted.

Amos nodded. "We're twins." She scanned his face, and Rennick saw the moment she realized what he said was true. "Our father wasn't a good man," Amos continued. "I could go on for hours about the horrors he inflicted on his family and people, but that's a conversation for another day."

Amelia looked as though she'd seen a ghost, and Rennick reached for her hand. She squeezed it with impressive strength. He wouldn't be able to feel his fingers by the end of this conversation.

"He believed women shouldn't hold positions of power." Amos' voice held a hint of nervousness. "There were no female warriors like there are in other kingdoms, no female council members, and more importantly, no female heirs."

Amelia looked like she might say something, but only silence filled the room.

"Our grandfather was the same way, and when his wife bore him twins, the firstborn of which was a girl, he changed the babe's name and sent her away the day after she was born, but later in life, she found out her heritage and tried to overthrow our father not long after he took the throne." Amos cleared his throat and leaned his elbows on his knees. "He killed her and vowed that if he had a daughter, he would kill her immediately to prevent history from repeating itself. That's what he told our mother."

Amelia held up a hand. "Royals only have one child." Her hazel eyes met Rennick's. "Unless you lied."

Rennick sat forward. "I wouldn't lie to you, love. *Usually,* they only have one. No one knew your father had a twin or that Amos does."

"I wouldn't have known if not for our mother," Amos added.

Amelia wavered, and Rennick extracted himself from her death grip to lay a steadying hand on her back.

"Our mother didn't know it yet, but she was already pregnant with us when our father told her about his sister. When the midwife told her there were two heartbeats, she begged the woman not to tell anyone until she had a plan for what to do if one or both of the babes were girls." He smiled fondly. "The midwife agreed without hesitation. The staff adored our mother and would have done whatever she asked." Amos' lips tilted into a half smile. "You're a lot like her."

"How do you know what I'm like?" Amelia cut him off. "We've never met, and I grew up in an orphanage with no family."

He scrubbed a hand over his face, sat back, and motioned to Eddy. "I checked in on you periodically through Roland."

Rennick felt the moment Amelia's patience snapped. "His name is *Eddy*. You sent him to me when I was fifteen. That's when you get your *familiar*, no?"

Amos pressed his lips into a grim line. "It is."

"Then he is more mine than yours." She lifted her chin. "He has lived with me for almost ten years. His fucking name is Eddy."

Eddy whined and jumped into her lap, earning a look of betrayal from Amos. Charlie moved closer too, the two animals banding together against the Desert King. "He is my *familiar*, Amelia. I'm sorry, but he belongs with me."

She leveled her brother with a stare that Rennick never wanted to be on the receiving end of. "I didn't say otherwise, but his name is Eddy. You wouldn't call a child by one name most of their lives and change it ten years later, would you?"

Rennick knew she spoke from a place of hurt, but he would make sure the fox's name remained Eddy. He didn't know how, but he would find a way.

Amos hung his head in defeat. "Fine. Do you want to hear the rest of the story or not?"

"Watch your tone," Rennick warned.

Amelia motioned for Amos to continue.

"Our mother met Charlotte, the human queen, at a diplomat meeting, and they kept in touch over the years. Mom would visit the Human Kingdom often, and when she found out she was pregnant, Charlotte agreed to help her if she had a daughter.

Charlotte hated our father more than anyone because he condescended to her in their meetings.

"Because Mom carried twins, the midwife said she'd likely deliver early. Our father didn't know there were two babies and thought she had at least two more months to go when our mother asked if she could visit Charlotte one last time before giving birth. He said yes.

"She stayed with Charlotte, and when she went into labor, she gave birth to me." Amos looked pained. "And then you."

Amelia looked away. "How disappointed she must have been."

"She was, but not because she didn't want a girl, because she knew she'd never see you again until I took the throne." The somberness in his tone tugged at Rennick's chest. "She gave Father an excuse to stay another month with Charlotte to give herself time with you."

Tears raced down Amelia's cheeks, and Rennick felt her grief, a feeling he knew all too well.

Amos took a moment to collect himself. "She left you in the Human Kingdom with Charlotte and crossed back into the Desert Kingdom with me. She told Father she'd only just had me so that our births were recorded a few weeks apart." He chuckled humorlessly. "I never understood why she decided to change my birthday and not yours, but it worked out in my favor in the end."

"Heirs can't cross the barrier," Amelia argued, looking to Rennick for confirmation. The hazel eyes he loved so much pleaded with him to make everything better, but he couldn't. Her confusion, anger, pain, and grief swirled within him like a hurricane, almost taking his breath away. Damnit, if he didn't feel like the most helpless man in the world.

He did the only thing he could and attempted to push reassurance and tranquility through the bond. It might be futile, but he had to try.

"They can't *leave* their kingdom," Amos corrected. "But I wasn't leaving, I was entering. There is no magic in the human lands to tie an heir there."

"If she left me with the human queen, how did I end up in an orphanage?"

"They couldn't chance anyone knowing who you were. They hid you until your ears healed, then left you where they knew you'd be safe. The queen monitored who ran the orphanage and had extra patrols stationed in your village."

"Why couldn't I leave with Rennick?" she asked. "We could have married when we turned twenty-two." She turned to Rennick then, and he saw the hurt in her eyes, *felt* it clawing at his chest. "Why didn't you send for me sooner? I had no one. I thought I had no family, and the entire time you knew."

If his mate hated him for this, he would kill Amos. "We tried, love, I swear it. The human queen wouldn't let you leave until I took the throne."

"Why?"

"Because until you married him, you were considered an heir to the Desert Kingdom," Amos said softly. "One look at you, and our father would have known you were his." He gestured between them. "We look just like him. If you married another king, you'd no longer be in line for the throne because you'd already rule another kingdom."

Her forehead wrinkled. "How do you know that sitting on one throne prevents you from taking another?"

Rennick noticed the dark circles under Amos' eyes when he looked listlessly at his sister. "A treaty signed between the five kingdoms over a thousand years ago states that no one person can rule two kingdoms."

"Rennick would've kept me safe," she argued weakly, her shoulders slumping with defeat.

Amos shook his head. "It wasn't worth the risk."

"Where are our parents now?" Her voice sounded bone tired. "Did our mother not want to meet me?"

Amos's eyes filled with unshed tears, and Rennick knew this was hard for him, too. "She fell ill when we were twelve. She'd been so full of life one minute, and the next she puked for hours, and her mouth filled with sores as if burned." He stared at his feet for a moment. "I think she was poisoned, possibly by mistake, but there's no way to know for sure. There were many people in our kingdom who wanted our father dead." He sniffed. "When she realized she was dying, she told me everything and begged me to make sure our father never knew of your existence.

"I was a child, but I swore to her I would take care of you. The following year, the Mountain King came looking for his son's mate—a girl named Amelia born on my real birthday. I knew in my gut it was you, and I thought Callum could protect you. I managed to get him alone before he left and told him everything."

Silence sat heavy between them.

Amelia shuddered out a sob, breaking Rennick's heart into a million pieces. Amos stood and rounded the desk to kneel beside her chair, but Charlie wouldn't let him.

Amos stared at the lynx and raised his brow, then glanced at Rennick, who subtly shook his head. *We'll discuss it later.*

Amos looked unsure of himself as he awkwardly laid a hand on Amelia's shoulder. "You were always loved, and I came for you as soon as I could."

Face in her hands, she nodded, unable to speak through her cries. Eddy whined and pushed his body into hers.

Amos backed away and motioned to the door. "I'll find towels."

Rennick nodded as the Desert King left, then wrapped his hand around Amelia's wrist. "Come here, love."

Eddy hopped down from her lap, and she crawled into Rennick's, laying her head against his shoulder. "You could have told me when you came for me." Her chest shuddered. "Why didn't you?"

He rested his cheek against the top of her head. "Amos wanted to be the one to tell you, and were it not for him, I would have never found you. I owed him that much."

Amos returned with two towels, one dry and one wet, and held them out to his sister. Amelia cleaned her face and blew her nose repeatedly until her tears finally subsided. "What if your father still tries to kill me?"

"I'll kill him," Rennick said, knowing he'd kill him anyway.

He watched Amos' demeanor transform into one of cold indifference. "I already did."

Amelia sucked in a sharp breath. "You didn't have to do that for me."

His expression remained blank. "Our father was a monster. He received the death he deserved."

Rennick saw the way his mate assessed her brother and squeezed her side lightly. It was clearly not something Amos wanted to discuss with them. She chewed the corner of her lip and changed the subject. "If I'm fae, why don't I have magic?"

Rennick and his father had talked extensively on the subject and came up with one answer. "You never crossed into fae lands."

Understanding lit up her face. "You said that's why royal heirs can't leave their lands; they need the land for their magic to develop to its full strength."

He nodded. "We hope you'll gain at least some of your magic when we marry."

She sat up straighter. "Birdie."

Rennick adjusted her in his lap to see her face better. "The maid?"

"Yes. She called me a royal."

Rennick and Amos both swore. "What do you mean? Who is this woman?" Amos demanded.

Amelia waved her hands. "I think I made myself disappear." They stared at her, and Rennick wondered if the shock had affected her more than he'd realized. "When you were in your study with Ora, Birdie and I stood in the hall, and I wanted to disappear. I hadn't meant literally, but Birdie looked scared and asked where I was. She reached out and bumped my shoulder. I looked at her to see what was wrong, and she appeared startled, then called me a royal. She never brought it up again, and I didn't think anything of it."

Rennick's mind raced. If the woman mentioned the occurrence to anyone, there's no telling what would happen. "Why didn't you tell me? We need to find this maid."

"Rennick, if you do anything to hurt her, I will not marry you." The air whooshed out of him, and he ran through ways to force the marriage. Amelia wouldn't leave him. "She's my friend."

"Fine," he reluctantly agreed. "But I'd still like to speak to her."

"*We* will speak to her. I don't trust you not to scare her."

Smart girl.

Amos crossed his arms and widened his stance. "I'd like to speak to her too."

Amelia glowered at him, and Rennick looked away to keep from smiling at how easily the twins fell into their natural sibling roles.

"Thank you for telling me," she said to her brother with a weak smile. "Please, don't take this the wrong way, but I'd like to go to my rooms."

What the fuck?

Amelia walked silently beside Rennick to their rooms, thankful to have someone to lean on for once. She could feel his worry, and he had enough things on his plate without her familial crisis weighing him down.

"What was the point in telling me?" she wondered aloud. "I would have been none the wiser."

Rennick opened the door to their rooms and waited for her to cross the threshold. "He wants to know you. He watched you grow up without him."

Guilt slammed into her. She'd been so worried about herself that she'd not taken a moment to think of how it might have affected Amos. "I'm a terrible person."

"You're in shock, love." Rennick led her to the bathroom, started a bath, and stood behind her to undo her dress. "He understands."

After he helped her bathe and get ready for bed, they climbed under the covers and faced each other. She noticed the lines etched into his young face and reached up to smooth them away. It'd been a long day for them both, and it wasn't even dinner time yet.

"Are you okay?" she asked quietly.

He smiled wryly. "I'm not the one who had their world tipped upside down today."

She scooted closer and stroked the dark stubble on his jaw. "Did rebels attacking the walls remind you of your mother?"

He covered her hand with his and leaned into her palm. "It did. I remember watching my father run with her limp body in his arms, and when I saw our men fighting outside of the walls, I —what if you'd been outside and one had slipped in somehow?"

Seeing the mighty King of the Mountain Kingdom fight back tears, feeling his despair, was heart-wrenching. "You left me with Echo, and your father left his murderous house cat, too."

Rennick's chest shook with laughter, the tight lines around his eyes loosening. "Don't let Reyna hear you say that."

"How did she know Amos? Echo wanted to run a sword through his heart, but Reyna licked him."

"My father traveled to the Desert Kingdom often to check on Amos. He didn't want your father's ideals to rub off on him."

That surprised her. "Why did it matter?"

"Amos knew everything about you. My father would have gone to the human queen and demanded you be moved if he felt your brother had become a threat." Rennick mindlessly stroked the back of her hand. "And I think he saw a little boy with a cruel father and no mother who needed someone to love him. Over the years, they bonded. My father talks about Amos as though he is his own son."

Amelia's throat tightened at what Callum did for her brother. "The Desert King wasn't suspicious of your father visiting often?" She found that hard to believe. If what they'd spoken was true, the two kings' personalities were vastly different.

Rennick's smile was small, but pride shone in his eyes. "My father made friends with the man, even though he despised everything the former Desert King stood for. He didn't care what others thought. Our people know he is good, and that was all that mattered. He did what he had to do for you and your brother."

She trailed her hand down Rennick's neck, watching the skin raise under her touch, willing herself not to cry again. "The people know you're good, too." Her eyes met his. "I'll do everything I can to make them accept me."

He cuffed her wrist and rubbed her pulse with his thumb. "I'm a good king, but I am not my father. I am not *good*. My soul is not beautiful or bright or even a shade of grey. It is an unforgiving inferno, and if our people refuse to accept you as their queen, they will burn their way into the afterlife."

There was no doubt in Amelia's mind that Rennick meant every word, and she knew, if their roles were reversed, she'd mean it too.

30

Amelia stood beside Fawn in the laundry room, folding towels and telling her about everything that had happened the day before, while the men were in a meeting discussing the rebel attack.

"I saw Ora in the dining hall last night," Fawn remarked slyly. "She made a big fuss about the guards not allowing her to see Rennick last night."

Amelia scoffed at the audacity of that wretched woman. "We were supposed to banish her from the palace yesterday afternoon, but the rebels attacked."

Fawn whistled. "When will you tell her and, more importantly, can I be there to see it?"

"Me too," Echo said from the doorway where they stood sentry. "I'd love to see the look on her face."

Amelia slammed a folded towel into the basket with more force than necessary. "I can't wait to see her face, either. It's why Rennick hasn't told her yet; he said I could be the one to do it." The cloth in her hand wrinkled in her grasp. "He said she thinks she's his mate."

Fawn's jaw dropped. "She actually believes that?"

"Yep."

"I thought she only told the staff that to wield authority over us." Fawn glanced at Echo. "You should chop her head off. That'll shut her up."

"Fawn!" Amelia laughed. "You're as bad as Rennick."

"Her father is a council member," Echo replied. "It might be too hard to cover up her death."

"You two are awful." Amelia tried to stop her laughter. "Echo, are you married?"

The guard snorted. "To my job."

Fawn leaned in conspiratorially. "I've seen them flirting with one of the cooks in the kitchens."

Both women turned to Echo with devious smiles, and Amelia wiggled her eyebrows. "What's their name?"

"Her name is Beverly, and she's about this tall." Fawn held her hand even with Amelia's chest.

"That's enough," Echo grumbled. "How do you know so much, anyway?"

Fawn folded the last of the towels and dropped them into the basket. "Nothing is private in this place. If you sneeze, every staff member will know by the end of the day."

Amelia picked up one of the baskets and balanced it on her hip. "Do they still think I'm the king's whore?"

Fawn grinned. "No. Birdie told everyone she thinks you're the king's true mate."

"How would she know?" Echo mused, following the women into the hall.

"I don't know, but she's Amelia's biggest fan. Tells everyone how great of a queen you'll make."

Amelia's heart skipped a beat. "Do you think everyone will be receptive to a human queen?"

Fawn looked at her strangely. "You're not human."

"We're not telling anyone I'm fae." She adjusted the basket to keep it from slipping from her grip. "Claiming to be a hidden

heir of the Desert Kingdom would cause an uproar in both kingdoms." It didn't matter that she was a royal fae. She appeared
human, and they'd probably think she was lying.

"You blabbed your *very important* secret to Fawn without
pause," Echo pointed out. "Remind me to never tell you
anything."

Amelia bumped Echo's shoulder. "I trust her like I trust
you."

They climbed the stairs to the main floor of the palace,
almost running into another guard. "Thank the gods," he
muttered. "The king is looking for her," he told Echo, pointing at
Amelia.

"I have to deliver these." Fawn indicated to the basket in her
hand. "If you'll leave your basket here, I'll send someone to grab
them."

Amelia set the basket down and tried to follow the guard.
"I'll find you later."

Echo grabbed her shoulder, holding her back, and asked the
guard, "What is the reason?"

Another guard appeared around the corner, stopping when he
spotted them. "You found her?"

The first guard nodded. "Tell the others to call off the
search."

"Search?" Amelia looked between the two men.

"The king has every guard in the palace looking for you," he
replied. "We've been looking for almost an hour."

She pinched the bridge of her nose with a huff. "What is
wrong with him?"

Echo released Amelia's shoulder and chuckled. "Let's find
the king before he tears the palace apart."

Every guard they passed looked relieved, and the guard
leading them told the others to spread the word that she'd been
found.

Ridiculous.

He led them through the palace until Amelia recognized the path. "Is he in our rooms?"

The guard nodded, and Echo stopped him. "We've got it from here. Help the others call off the search."

"Yes, general." He bowed and left.

"General?" Amelia mouthed, but Echo ignored her.

Once back at Amelia and Rennick's rooms, she opened the door to find her mate in the sitting room, fiddling with something on the table.

"I'll see you later, Echo." She closed the door and spun around. "A palace wide search was a bit dramatic."

Rennick grinned and kissed her head. "Nothing is too dramatic when it comes to you, love."

"I'm not complaining because I love it, but why do you kiss my head so much? My hair can't taste very good." She kept her voice light and teasing, but she was genuinely curious. He kissed her head *a lot.*

Her mate cleared his throat. "To remind myself that you're really here and not another dream." He smoothed her hair back. "To make up for all the opportunities I missed over the last ten years."

For once, she hated his height because now she wanted to kiss him a million times a day, too. She crooked her finger for him to bend down and kissed his forehead. "I love it."

Cupping her chin, he kissed her lightly. "Good." He turned, picked up her bow and quiver from the table, and held them out.

She stared dumbly at the weapon. "What is this for?"

"To go hunting. You wished to go not two days ago. With the stress of yesterday and the upcoming coronation celebration, I wanted to do something fun for you." He flashed her a boyish smile that made her melt.

Amelia hated the idea of hunting but knew he liked it; that was the only reason she'd been willing to go a few days ago. In hindsight, she should have tried to fuck him instead, because now she wanted to do anything but.

The sentiment was sweet, and she'd do it if for no other reason than to make him happy, even if she'd rather eat glass. "Great." She smiled brightly, hoping it looked genuine.

The way his face lit up made it worthwhile.

She took the bow from his outstretched hand and set it aside. "What about Amos? Shouldn't we be with him? I'd like to get to know him better."

"He and my father are spending time together," Rennick replied, removing her coat from the hook by the door. "He was the only true father figure your brother had, and it's been about six months since they've seen each other."

"I'm glad he had someone." Having no father had to be better than having a father cruel enough that her brother felt a duty to kill him. "I'm going to miss Eddy."

Rennick looked around. "Where is Charlie?"

"He wanted outside this morning, and I haven't seen him since." He'd likely gone to hunt or relieve himself; he slipped outside periodically.

Rennick noticed the slippers on her feet and disappeared into their dressing room, returning with her green boots.

Amelia accepted them with a strained smile and sat down to put them on. "Where is Greta? I've been here three days and have yet to see her."

"I checked on her yesterday." He handed Amelia a scarf and gloves. "She's not far from here."

"Does she not like being around you?"

He scowled down at her. "Owls don't like being indoors. When I start training with my warriors again, she'll perch on the walls to watch."

"Since I'm a royal, what are the chances I'll get a *familiar* when we marry?" The thought excited her, but she didn't want to get her hopes up.

Rennick paused briefly. "Yes, I think you will."

A giddy thrill made her clap her hands. "I wonder what it will be! Hopefully, it gets along with Charlie."

Rennick chuckled. "Something tells me that won't be an issue. You'll find out tomorrow."

They'd agreed to wed the next day in a private ceremony with just their families and closest friends.

She shifted slightly, still adjusting to the bigger plug he'd placed inside her earlier. He'd do a bigger one tonight and then again tomorrow morning to prepare her for their wedding night. The thought both scared and excited her.

Once they finished bundling up, she and Rennick grabbed their gear and headed toward Amelia's worst nightmare.

31

Rennick tied their horses to a tree and glamoured them to be invisible in case a beast ventured to the tree line. They normally didn't, but he could never be too safe.

"We're walking into the woods?" Amelia asked, eyeing the forest skeptically. "Horses are faster if we need to escape."

He smirked. "The beasts can't see us."

Gulping, she moved closer to him. "Right."

As they walked, they talked about their upbringings as far back as they could remember. It pleased him to know the orphanage had always treated her well, but he could hear the loneliness in her voice when she spoke of her past.

The hurt she experienced from Amos's news made more sense because wanting nothing more than a family, wondering why they left you or if they'd come back, only to discover they knew where you were all along, must have been hard. She understood, of course, but that didn't make the feelings go away.

Everything she knew about herself turned on its head yesterday, and Rennick would give her all the time she needed to adjust.

"What toys did you play with as a child?" Amelia tapped her

chin playfully. "You seem like the type to come out of the womb making battle plans."

Chuckling, Rennick told her about the fuzzy stuffed lynx toy he'd carried everywhere. His mother would try to trade it for a new one, but he always knew and threw a fit until she gave it back. He didn't admit it, but he still had it packed away in a trunk under their bed.

Her eyes lit up. "You had a Charlie!"

"Did the orphanage provide you with toys?" Gods, he hoped so, otherwise he would send cart loads there tomorrow. "Dolls at least?" He would send a cart load, anyway.

She grimaced. "I have a confession."

"You still play with them?" he teased, but his smile dropped abruptly when she shuddered.

"I hate dolls. They're terrifying."

"You kept the doll I gave you." Unease stirred in his chest. "They must not scare you that much."

"I have another confession."

He stopped, the unease growing stronger. "You hated the doll."

She pulled at a string on her scarf, refusing to look him in the eye. "I wouldn't say *hate*." He stayed silent, waiting for her to tell the truth, and she threw her hands up. "Fine, it was awful. I screamed and threw it when I opened the box." The distraught look on her face was adorable, and he couldn't help but laugh. Her eyes turned to slits. "It's not that funny."

He covered his mouth to stave off his laughter, to no avail, and she picked up a handful of snow to throw at him. "You're the worst, you know that?"

Still laughing, he dodged the assault easily. "I wish I could have seen your face. That's why I roped Ora into helping me." He grimaced and added, "I wouldn't have had I known she thought she and I were mates." Amelia hesitated long enough for him to realize something else was amiss. "What is it?" Her teeth dug into her bottom lip, and he took a step forward. "Amelia."

"Before I say this, I need you to know that the thought behind your gifts made me love them, and I wouldn't get rid of them for anything."

A sinking feeling settled in his stomach. All these years he'd thought she'd loved everything he sent, but her words from the boarding house came back. *Ora and I have different tastes.*

"Everything Ora picked out was terrible. I think she purposefully sabotaged my gifts." She lifted the hem of her dress to show her green boots. "I don't even know where they'd sell these."

"I had them custom made." The pieces fell into place. "Ora said the color was popular, and that they had sold out in town."

Amelia rolled her lips together, and her eyes crinkled with amusement. "They're warm and sturdy, and they've lasted me years."

"The dresses?" he asked, already knowing the answer. He'd thought they were horrible, but what did he know?

"They fit perfectly, and I needed dresses that fit."

He reached around her and wound her braid around his fist to tilt her head back. "Tell me, were the dresses pretty?"

Her throat bobbed. "No. They're terrible, but I wear them, more so now than then. They didn't go to waste."

Amelia would banish Ora from the palace, and once Ora was thoroughly devastated and his mate had claimed her victory, he would kill Ora for what she'd done. She'd tortured his mate for years and made him the conduit.

A branch snapped, followed by a loud chuff, and they whirled around to find the culprit. A large lelker passed through the rainbow trees, its giant black head bobbing with each step. It was similar to an elk in the Human Kingdom, except horns ran the length of its neck like a horse's mane and its body was larger. All thoughts of Ora fled as the rush of the hunt took their place.

"What is that?" Amelia whispered in a panic.

"A lelker." Rennick slowly removed her bow so as not to make too much noise. "Are you ready, little mate?"

"Yes." Her voice shook, and it took her several tries to nock an arrow.

Rennick stalked the beast with his gaze, waiting for the perfect opening to move closer, but something in his chest smarted. A quick glance at his mate made him do a double take. "Are you crying, love? You're in no danger."

"I'm fine." The arrow trembled in her hold.

He'd seen her talent with a bow; her apprehension didn't make sense to him. Did she think he cared if she wasn't a perfect shot?

She lowered the weapon with tears streaming down her now pale face. "I can't do it."

He rubbed her back reassuringly. "It's okay if you miss. I won't think lesser of you. I miss from time to time." *No, I don't.*

"I don't want to kill it," she blubbered and swiped at her face. "I hate hunting, but you like it, and I wanted to do something you enjoyed, but I can't do it. I thought I could, but I can't."

Her words stole his own. She'd tried to do something that tore her to pieces for him? A protective rage filled him, and he grabbed her arrow and snapped it in half. The sound sent the lelker skittering away.

She'd chanced the scorn of others to wear the awful things he'd sent her, kept a doll that terrified her, and had agreed to kill a living creature, knowing it would destroy her, all to make him happy.

He'd never wanted anyone in his life more than he wanted her right now.

"It is taking everything in me not to fuck you here in the snow," he said roughly. "That you would do that for me... I love you."

Her gaze met his. "I love you too, Rennick. I'd do anything for you." She glanced at the broken arrow between them in the snow. "I'd try to, at least."

The explosion in his chest undid him. He slammed his lips to hers and picked her up. "Wrap your legs around me, love."

Her ankles locked behind his back, and he yanked at her skirts, swearing when he felt wool leggings underneath. "I need to touch you everywhere."

She removed her bulky scarf and pulled back. "Don't let me fall." Reaching down with both hands, Amelia gripped the crotch of her leggings. She tugged relentlessly at the fabric until it gave way and exposed her bare skin.

He groaned. "No underwear?"

"Move me down a little." Confused at first, he dropped her body lower, then he understood when her hands made quick work of undoing his pants to release his painfully hard dick.

He raised her to align himself with her entrance. "Hold tight."

"Wait," she gasped. Rennick held still. "What about the plug?"

He'd researched before retrieving her, learning everything there was to know about sex, and from what he'd been told, fucking her with the plug in should heighten things for both of them. "Wait and see," he purred before he seated himself fully inside of her.

She scratched at his shoulders. "It's—I—*Rennick*."

The plug made her pussy feel tighter around his dick, and stars danced in his vision. *Fuck.* "Ride my cock, little mate," he murmured against her ear. "Drench me."

Sex was still new to him, and the slow, torturous movements of her hips with the added tightness from the plug had him struggling to hold back his release.

A wide tree stood nearby, and he moved in front of it, leaning his shoulders against the trunk to give her a flatter plane. She straightened slightly and held on to his shoulders, quickening her movements for more friction. With one hand around her waist, he brought the other to his mouth, spit on his fingers, and lowered them to her clit.

Amelia jolted. "*Gods.*"

"Not even they can save you from me, love. Don't bother calling for them now."

She moved faster, digging her nails into his skin. If he bore her claw marks on his skin, he would never wear a shirt again; he'd never hated clothes as much as he did then.

Their breaths came in erratic pants, and her pussy clenched around him as her hazy eyes met his. Her hips rolled faster, her fingers held tighter, and all he could do was suffer the sweetest torture.

The need to touch her everywhere, *taste* her everywhere, and worship her the way she deserved was killing him, but he only had two hands.

He wanted to thrust his hips, to plunge deep, but he'd promised not to let her fall, and while the snow would make a soft landing, nothing killed arousal faster than cold, wet slush coating your skin.

Their moans and her slick body sliding against his were the only sounds in the quiet forest. Her tight cunt fit around him like a custom-made sheath, and the closer she came to her orgasm, the tighter she squeezed.

Groaning, he tried to stave off his own for her to finish first.

Her hips sped up as her cries came faster, and he cursed, moving his hand from her clit to her other hip to help quicken her movements until she shuddered around him and coated him with her cum.

He stood up straight, trying like hell to not slam her down too hard. Amelia wound her arms around his neck and pressed her lips to his. She murmured against them, "I love you, mate."

Rennick didn't come; he detonated with her name on his lips, filling her to the brim. He didn't know if she was on a tonic, nor did he care. Thinking of her being pregnant with his child made him want to destroy kingdoms to make it happen.

"I love you," he murmured back, their breaths mingling in the frigid air. "Forever."

Ora slipped out of the royal officiant's office with a bottle of holy oil tucked inside her pocket, one step closer to her goal.

She didn't know how, but she knew Amelia had brainwashed Rennick, and after she completed their mating bond, she would kill the bitch.

Ora hurried down the hall toward her father's office and poked her head inside with a wide smile. "Hi Daddy!"

Her father looked up and set down his quill. "Hi, sweet pea. What are you doing here?"

"I'm always here," she giggled, taking a seat in the chair across from him.

"I meant, what are you doing in my office?" He clasped his hands on his desk. "Rennick is gone today, and Finn is training."

That's why she was here.

She pouted. "I have other friends here, but I need to ask Rennick a question. We were to have a meeting yesterday, but the rebels attacked. Do you know where he went?"

He pressed his lips together. Once upon a time, her father thought Ora and Rennick were mates and that the king had lied about Rennick finding his mate to give the prince time to sow his wild oats before marriage. But ever since Amelia's arrival, Ora's father had been acting strangely. *Did he believe the rumors that Amelia was Rennick's mate?*

"He went hunting and will be back later this afternoon. I'm sure he will seek you out for that meeting. No need to go romping through the woods."

She stood before he finished speaking and rounded his desk to peck him on the cheek. "Thanks, Daddy."

"You're welcome. I'm sure Rennick will reschedule your meeting, if that's what you're worried about."

She was already at the door, waving in parting to her father as she slipped into the hall.

Ora knew exactly where her mate liked to hunt.

Ora picked her way through the woods, using the tracking skills the boys had taught her to find Rennick. To her dismay, she followed two sets of tracks, one much smaller than the other. *Amelia.*

Ora listened intently. She needed to dab the holy oil on her lips before confronting him.

If Rennick wouldn't recognize their bond, she would force him to complete it. He would see she was right all along.

She'd thought it over all night. First, she'd slather her tongue and lips with holy oil and bite her tongue hard enough to fill her mouth with blood. Taking him off guard would be hard, especially with Amelia there, but all she needed was to press her mouth to his to transfer the oil and then bite him hard enough to bleed. He'd have no choice but to swallow her blood. It was a foolproof plan.

Grinning from ear-to-ear, she hurried through the snow, following her mate's tracks to her impromptu wedding.

32

Amelia held her bow behind her back. "You're not breaking my bow."

Rennick folded his arms across his chest with a stubborn set to his mouth. "You don't like to hunt. I'm destroying everything Ora fooled me into buying you."

She raised her chin defiantly. "No, you won't. I told you I love the gifts because of their meaning. If you break my things, I won't speak to you for the rest of the day." It wasn't much of a threat, but it was enough.

He released a low growl of frustration. "You're being ridiculous. I will buy you a better version of everything to replace the old ones."

"I don't want a new necklace or boots or anything. I want the things I have."

Her mate balked. "Your necklace is awful, too?"

She covered her necklace and backpedaled. "If you break my necklace, I will never forgive you."

They were at an impasse. "I won't destroy your things," he conceded, "but I'm buying you new ones. Prepare to go shopping next week."

She flashed him a triumphant smile. "I plan on wearing one of my dresses and my boots tomorrow."

He looked horrified. "You will not get married in clothes you hate."

"You can't tell me what to do," she shot back, hiding a smile. Had she known he was this fun to rile up, she'd have done it sooner.

Her grave mistake was taking her eyes off him for three seconds, something she realized when he lifted her in the air and threw her over his shoulder like a sack of potatoes. Her bow fell to the ground, and the rest of her arrows slid out of their quiver.

"Put me down!" she laughed, screeching when he slapped her ass.

He popped her backside again. "You can't tell me what to do."

"But I dropped my bow." She kicked her feet lightly.

Chuckling, he lowered her to the ground, and she bent down to gather her things.

He grabbed her hips and tugged her against him. "I like you bent over like that."

"You're insatiable." She glanced at him over her shoulder. The animalistic look in his eye gave her an idea.

Rotating to face him, she pushed lightly on his chest and walked backward. "Let's make a deal."

He rubbed his jaw while looking her up and down suggestively. "I'm listening."

"If you can catch me, I'll let you fuck me bent over in the snow."

His eyes sparked, and he took a step forward, but she held out a hand. "Your legs are longer than mine, and you have fae speed. It's only fair that I get a head start."

His feral smile sent a thrill through her. "Run, little mate."

Returning his smile with a taunting one of her own, she flipped around and sprinted into the woods.

Rennick watched his mate disappear through the trees, knowing he'd be deep inside her within the next few minutes. Those thoughts came to a halt when Ora approached him from behind. "There you are," she purred.

He moved away from her, furious with himself for letting his guard down. He should have heard her coming from a mile away, but his lust-addled mind had focused solely on his mate.

"What are you doing here?" he demanded, sick of her conniving ways. He held up a hand to stop her reply. It didn't matter. "You need to leave the palace and never return. You are hereby forbidden to step foot on palace grounds."

Her loud gasp echoed through the trees. "You don't mean that."

"I have never meant anything more, Ora, and if you don't leave on your own accord, I will kill you. One way or another, you're leaving."

Her lip wobbled, and she advanced toward him. "Ren, it's *me*. We've known each other most of our lives."

"That's the only reason I have yet to stake your head on the front gates," he said, his voice like ice. "I can easily change my mind, and if Amelia sees you and it upsets her, I will."

"Are you here of your own free will?" she whispered, her eyes scanning the area.

Her wording threw him off guard. "I am, and you are not welcome. Leave. This is your last warning."

She whispered something, snapped her mouth shut, and winced. He expected her to argue, to beg him to let her stay, but she said nothing.

Her eyes widened, and she pointed behind him. He turned to assess, finding nothing. *A distraction,* he realized too late when she barreled into him. She crashed her lips to his and bit down hard enough to break his skin open. A metallic taste filled his mouth, and he shoved her away.

A searing pain heated his chest, and he fell to his knees. A foreign fury lit him from the inside out and mingled with his own. *Amelia.*

He started to stand, but Ora's words held him in place.

"See? I told you we were mates, *husband.*"

33

Amelia's mate should have found her by now. Knowing him, he was hiding and waiting to jump out and scare the shit out of her. As long as he fucked her again, she didn't care.

Jogging back the way she came, she careened around a tree and halted at the sight before her. Ora pointed somewhere in the distance. When Rennick turned to look, she charged him and slammed her body into his. Pure, unadulterated rage ripped through Amelia.

Without thinking, she sprinted forward, willing herself to be invisible. She didn't know if it'd work, but she had to try. If she remembered correctly, Rennick would see through her glamour, but Ora wouldn't. Her mate hit his knees, and her anger burned brighter. If Ora hurt him, she would die a slow death.

Amelia closed in on them and heard Ora claim Rennick as her husband. He roared with fury and climbed to his feet. Ora backed away from him, but before he could advance toward her, Amelia yelled, "*Stop!*"

Ora's death was hers.

Rennick whipped around, and he must have seen something on her face because he stepped aside. Amelia approached her mate and jerked the hunting knife from his boot as she stalked past him, willing the snow beneath her boots to appear undisturbed.

Ora spun in a circle, scanning the area. *"You're too late!"* she screamed at nothing but woods before turning to face Rennick. "We're married, and you're mine."

Amelia stepped behind her, dropped her glamour, and yanked Ora's head back by her hair. "No, the fuck he's not," she snarled, pressing her knife into Ora's neck hard enough to pierce the skin. "If you move, I will paint the snow with your blood."

Ora whimpered, her eyes pleading with Rennick. "Don't let her hurt your mate."

Amelia yanked on her hair harder. "Don't speak to him." Her eyes met Rennick's, and the sadistic fucker smiled so wide she thought his face might split in half. She dug her knife deeper into Ora's skin and leaned down. "When you get to hell, tell Orcus hello for me."

Ora struggled and screamed, but Amelia ripped the knife across her throat and held her in place to watch the life drain from her eyes.

As Ora grew limp in her grasp, reality came crashing back in. Amelia released the body and staggered back in shock. *I killed a person.*

Rennick gently led her away from the bloody scene, trying to soothe her.

"I-I killed her," she stammered, unable to look away from the blood-soaked snow.

Rennick held her chin and forced her to look at him. "It's okay, love. She touched what is yours. Had you not killed her, I would have."

"She called you her husband," she said, still in a daze. "You're mine."

Rennick pressed his forehead to hers and nodded. "I'm yours."

He pulled away and swiped his sleeve across his mouth. Amelia gasped at the blood coating his lips. "You're bleeding."

He spat a mouthful of blood on the ground. "She bit me."

Amelia's voice darkened. "She put her mouth on you?"

Rennick winked and licked his red lips. "I like seeing you this way."

"It's not funny," she snapped, but her annoyance turned to horror when she tried to push a stray hair out of her face. Blood coated her right hand, and she held it up. "Oh, my gods."

Her eyes rolled back in her head, and everything went black.

Rennick cradled a disgruntled Amelia in his arms as he walked back to the palace. He was worried about her; she'd cried *thinking* about killing a lelker—killing a human, no matter who it was, wasn't in her nature.

"I can walk," she protested for the hundredth time.

He leaned over and pecked the frown marring her pretty face. "You fainted. I might never let you walk again."

"You're ridiculous," she muttered. A companionable silence accompanied their steps for a while before she spoke again. "She wouldn't have stopped. Her obsession with you wouldn't have allowed her to."

Rennick held her tighter. "I know, love. I wasn't lying when I said had you not killed her, I would have. Either way, she was going to die in those woods today."

"I don't feel bad for killing her." She lifted her free hand helplessly. "Something inside me snapped."

"Killing her might not be considered justifiable to the world, but to me, what you did made me love you even more."

She mumbled something under her breath that sounded a lot like, *"You're terrible."*

His mouth spread into a wide smile. "But you like it."

With a heavy sigh, she rested her head against his chest. "I do." He peered down as she chewed on the inside of her cheek. "What will we tell everyone?"

"Nothing." He adjusted her in his arms. "A beast will find her before anyone else does."

"You don't know that."

"I poured wulfer bait on her before we left. One is probably dragging her away as we speak."

Amelia turned a little green. "What is a wulfer?"

"The beast we saw on our way into the Mountain Kingdom that made you jump into my lap." His eyes dipped to her lips. "You forced me to ride an hour with a painfully hard cock."

"*Rennick*," she laughed. "Is that all you think about?"

"No." He wiggled his eyebrows. "I'm a multitasker." That made her laugh harder, and he leaned down to kiss her forehead. "I'll never get tired of that sound." She took a deep breath, and her apprehension pressed into him. "What is it, love?"

"Why did she think you two were married?"

Rennick's face grew stormy. "She tried to force a marriage mating bond, but she's a fool. A marriage bond can't be formed if one party doesn't want it, whether or not they say they're present willing."

Her face lit with understanding, then twisted with disgust. "That's why you had blood on your mouth. If I could kill her again, I would."

The way she looked at him made Rennick believe he could fight an entire legion bare-handed and win, and when she flashed him a brilliant smile, he knew nothing could tear them apart. Anyone who tried would become another dead body in their wake.

34

Amelia and Rennick stood in their dressing room after washing off the day's events to get ready for dinner. She expected to feel some sense of wrongness for what she had done in the woods, but the remorse didn't come.

She hadn't killed Ora because the woman wanted her mate. He was six-foot-five of pure muscle, with a handsome face and a throne; everyone wanted him. She did it because even after being rejected time and again, Ora continued to chase Rennick in an attempt to steal him away. *That* Amelia wouldn't tolerate.

A steadying hand landed on her shoulder. "You're pale," Rennick observed, feeling her clammy head.

"There was a lot of blood," she muttered, reaching for her trout necklace. "You know it makes me queasy."

A large hand covered hers. "You don't have to wear that." He glowered at the necklace like it personally offended him. "I should have known someone who never fished wouldn't want a trout necklace."

"Unhand my necklace." She lightly smacked his hand, and he snatched it back.

"We can cancel tonight if you're not up to it. It's natural to be upset."

"I'm not upset." She circled the necklace around her neck and fastened it. "Ouch." The chain sat upon the still-raw bite mark on her neck. She'd forgotten to replace the bandage after bathing. "I need a new bandage or the chain will rub the scabs."

Rennick disappeared into the bathroom and returned with a metal box containing various medical supplies.

"Do you dress your own wounds?" she asked, poking around inside of the box.

"When they're small." He moved her hair to the side and examined her neck. "Hold up the chain."

"You'll be my wife tomorrow," he murmured when he was done. "I've been waiting for this day since we were fifteen."

She considered his words and pinched her eyebrows together. "Why fifteen?"

His hand fell from her neck and snaked around her waist. "After hearing your name, I felt a sense of duty to you as your mate, but then I saw you, and I knew no one else would do, mate or not."

"What do you mean, '*mate or not*?'"

He fingered the trout pendant hanging around her neck. "I'd never seen you before, and Finn described you the best he could. I spotted you and Clover leaving the orphanage that morning, but I didn't know who was who."

Her eyes widened slightly. "We're both tall and blonde."

He nodded. "I tried to focus on my mate's emotions, but nothing strong stuck out, and the longer I followed you, the more enraptured I became. You had the prettiest smile I'd ever seen, and the way you spoke to Clover about the book you were reading was intoxicating. Excitement shone through your eyes, and even though she barely replied, you kept going."

Amelia listened with fascination, wondering what she'd done to deserve this man as a mate.

"It didn't matter who I shared a bond with; it was you I wanted. The two of you climbed the schoolhouse steps, and another girl called your name to ask for something. I didn't hear what, because when I realized you were my mate, everything fell into place. For the first time since my mother's death, I was happy."

Heat pricked the backs of Amelia's eyes, and she stood on her toes to close the distance between them with a tender kiss. Their tongues tangled together, and she moaned when he bit her softly.

"I'll have dinner brought to us," he whispered against her lips, bringing her back to the real world.

"We can't skip dinner." She pulled back. "Everyone is expecting us."

He groaned and released her. "Lead the way, love."

Amelia clutched Rennick's hand in hers to ground herself. Not only would Callum and Amos be at dinner, so would the entire staff. At least, she assumed they would be since rumors she was the king's mate had likely made their way to the other side of Eden by now.

Tonight, they would officially announce her as Rennick's mate.

Rennick leaned down and hovered near her ear. "If at anytime you want to leave, we'll leave."

With a steadying breath, she squared her shoulders and stepped a bit closer to him. "I'm ready."

A guard opened the door, bowing to them both, and Amelia noticed him pause briefly when he saw her ears. She smiled kindly. They would not intimidate her.

When they entered the large room, Amelia scanned the

podium for her friends. She spotted Fawn sitting between Finn and Clover and relaxed.

Amelia's steps faltered. "Clover?"

She hadn't meant to draw everyone's attention, but she'd spoken loud enough to earn the curiosity of those near her, and when her eyes locked with her oldest friend's, she released Rennick's hand and ran.

It hit her then, the homesickness. She hadn't realized how much she needed a familiar face. Clover met her at the bottom of the podium steps and wrapped her in a hug.

"I knew you were my friend," she croaked against Clover's shoulder.

Clover pushed her back, looking devastated. "You thought we weren't friends?"

Amelia waved her off. "It's an inside joke I had with myself." She realized how stupid that sounded and added, "You rarely spoke, and sometimes I thought you were simply too polite to tell me to leave you alone, but deep down I knew that wasn't the case."

Clover laughed, a sound Amelia rarely heard. "I don't like to talk, but I like to listen. You always had a lot to say."

"Did you get my note? I dropped it in your mail slot at the house." Amelia's heart sped up at the guilty look on Clover's face. "What is it?"

"I moved home," she replied softly.

Moved *home*? Their home was the boardinghouse. Amelia fought to work out her friend's meaning because nothing made sense. If Clover hadn't received Amelia's note because she'd already moved, then that meant... Amelia's hand flew to her mouth. Surely, she was wrong. Clover wouldn't do that but, still, she voiced her fear. "You left without saying goodbye?"

Clover's hands twisted together as she took in Amelia's crestfallen expression. "I knew where you'd be and planned to visit after you settled in."

Amos approached them, his eyes glued to Clover. "We need to take this somewhere private."

Rennick agreed and shuffled them through a side door that led into an elegant sitting room with no other doors or windows.

"What is this place?" Amelia surveyed the room. "Why would a gaudy sitting room be connected to the dining hall?"

Rennick dropped a steel bar across the door to lock it. "It's a soundproof safe room for the royal family."

"I really need a map of the palace," Amelia muttered under her breath and turned to Amos. "Why are we in here?"

"I sent Clover to watch over you," he said, still staring at Clover, who studiously ignored him.

Amelia blinked. "What do you mean?"

Rennick closed the distance between them and placed his hand on her lower back.

"My father trained me to fight as well as any warrior from the time I could walk," Clover interjected, her voice softer than usual. "Your brother found me when I was thirteen and sent me to protect you."

"I don't understand." Amelia struggled to keep up. She didn't know how many more secrets she could handle. "You're a human, and he couldn't leave the Desert Kingdom until he was twenty-five."

Clover shifted uncomfortably and pushed her wild blonde hair behind her pointed ear. "Glamour. I'm from the Desert Kingdom."

Amelia gaped at her. "What about your family?" she asked, desperately hoping and praying her friend wasn't ripped from her loved ones. "Did they die?"

Clover glanced at Amos. "They're alive. They came to visit as often as they could."

Amelia's guilt over her brother carrying the burden of protecting her at such a young age was one thing, but forcing a young girl from her home? It was too much.

She whirled on Amos without thinking and slapped him as hard as she could. Clover flinched, but Amelia swore she saw the hint of a smile on her face. Rennick pushed Amelia behind him, and Amos stood open-mouthed, holding the side of his face.

"You forced a thirteen-year-old girl to leave her kingdom?" she shouted, lunging at him, but Rennick held her back. "How dare you? She was a *child.*"

"It's okay," Clover insisted, trying to calm Amelia down and failing miserably.

Amelia stopped struggling in her mate's hold and stared down at her friend. "Did you want to leave your family?"

Clover's mouth opened to say something before it clamped shut. When she avoided Amelia's gaze, Amelia bent over, ignoring Rennick's hands tightening on her hips. She quickly removed one of her slippers and launched it at her brother's head, but he deflected the blow with his forearms.

"Enough!" he yelled, clenching his fists.

"Yell at her again, Desert King, and you won't have a voice box to yell with," Rennick warned.

Amos threw his hands up. "You don't think I know what I've done?" The pain in his voice took Amelia by surprise and stopped her from grabbing her other shoe. "I didn't seek her out to send her away. She was training when I found her, and she was more skilled than I was at the time. So, I had a stupid idea to send her to you."

"Why?" Amelia demanded. "I'd been fine up until that point."

He stepped forward, as did Rennick. "Because when your mate came looking for you, I knew you'd have a bigger target on your back if anyone found out who you were to not only the Desert throne but to him." He ran a hand through his messy hair. "Clover was talented and young; no one would suspect her." He looked crushed beneath his guilt. "I was a kid, and I made a foolish decision."

She stared at him, waiting for him to continue, but he didn't. "And when you wised up? Why didn't you tell her she could go home?"

"He did," Clover spoke up. "When we were sixteen, he asked me to come back, but I told him no."

Amelia rubbed her forehead, not comprehending why the girl would stay when she had a family who loved her. "And you were okay with that? You didn't stay because you thought you owed something to the future king?"

Clover pressed her lips together and shook her head. "I had no desire to be in the Desert Kingdom, and I owe him nothing."

Amelia glanced at her brother. "I know you were only a child," she told him, "but that was a cruel thing to ask of her as her future king, and while I appreciate the sentiment, I'm forced to carry the guilt too."

"No one regrets my decision more so than me." The deep sadness in his voice made Amelia's heart break a little.

A bell next to the door rang in a merry pattern, and Rennick removed the steel beam to open it. Callum popped his head in. "Is everything all right?" He took stock of the room, pausing on Amos's red cheek.

"You three go ahead," Amelia told Clover, Rennick, and Callum. "Amos and I will be there shortly."

The others shuffled out, Rennick begrudgingly so.

Amos looked tired, the shadows under his eyes prominent, and Amelia wondered how long they'd been there. "I don't need another—"

She wrapped her arms around him, cutting him off mid-sentence, and he froze with his arms pinned beneath hers.

"I know you meant well." She released him and backed away. "All I wanted growing up was a family. I used to dream someone would show up to claim me. Knowing Clover was made to leave her own because of me is a hard bite to swallow."

Amos seemed haunted by demons Amelia couldn't begin to understand. "I regret it every day."

"We'll make sure she and her family are set for life," Amelia promised, with an awkward pat on his shoulder.

"I tried," he replied with a long sigh. "She refuses every time, but she and I will work it out later. We need to discuss our situation." He motioned between them. "You're the only family I have left, and I'd like to get to know you better."

Amelia hugged him again, and he stiffened under her affection. "You're not a hugger, are you?"

He tried to move, but she held tight. "I despise them," he said uncomfortably.

She laughed and let him go. "I'd like to get to know you, too." He smiled then, and she returned it tenfold. "Let's go eat before my mate hauls me over his shoulder in front of everyone."

35

Amelia straddled Rennick's lap on their bed as he caressed the bare skin of her back. They'd wanted time alone before their nuptials later that day.

Their mouths moved together, perfectly in sync, and he made an animalistic sound that shot straight to her core. She extracted herself from his hold and climbed off the bed. Rennick tried to follow, but she placed a hand on his shoulder to stop him from standing.

"What are you doing, little mate?"

Pre-cum leaked from the head of his cock, and she sank to her knees in front of him. His dick twitched when she wrapped her hand around the base, and he sucked air between his teeth. "If you start this, I won't be able to stop."

Leaning forward, she ran her tongue up the length of his shaft. "I don't want you to."

His head fell back with a tortured groan, and she licked again and took the tip into her mouth. There was a small knot near the head of his dick, and when she lightly scraped her teeth over it, he jumped and fisted her hair.

Smiling, she lowered her head as much as she could without

gagging, using her hand to make up the difference of his length. He whispered her name and wrapped her hair around his fist as he pulsed his hips.

"I wish you could see yourself," he rasped. She gagged when he hit the back of her throat. "Swallow, love." She gagged again, but tried to swallow him with every thrust. "Fuck, Amelia." He jerked back, freeing his cock from her lips, and held her in place while he came on her face, coating her with his salty release.

Stunned, she stared at him with cum dripping down her face. He silently stood, picked her up, and placed her on the bed. His hands moved gently over her face, rubbing in his cum like lotion.

She didn't know whether to be turned on or disgusted, but her thoughts were interrupted by his silky voice. "My turn." He kneeled beside the edge of the bed and rested his elbows between her legs. "Knees up."

When his mouth covered her sensitive skin, she sighed with relief and rolled her hips against his face. She hadn't realized how wound up she was until then, and his assault on her clit made her nerves go wild. His hot tongue ran through her folds and traced every inch of her as he lapped up her arousal like a starved man.

With his hair gripped tightly in her hands, she guided his head where she wanted him, preening when he hummed his approval.

"Rennick," she breathed when he pushed a large finger into her and pumped it a few times before adding another digit. He continued his torture until she thrashed around. He replaced his fingers with his face as she came. His stubble scratched against her pussy, sending more shocks through her.

The last of her climax subsided, and he gave her one last lick before pulling up to his knees to stare her in the eyes as he rubbed the proof of her orgasm into his skin.

"Don't try to wash me off your face," he drawled, crawling over her. "I won't allow it."

Rennick stood in the snow under the stars and the moon, staring at Amelia, who wore one of the unseemly dresses he'd given her all those years ago—an ugly brown thing with flowers in pink, purple, and red, and yellow vines. He was a fool. Green boots peeked out from under the hem, and her golden trout necklace hung around her neck. Two twists held her blonde hair away from her face, exposing her rounded ears, and her cheeks and nose were red from the cold.

Much to his dismay, she'd insisted on taking her coat off for the ceremony to "show off" her outfit. She would pay for that later.

When she caught his gaze, he made a show of licking his lips, and she shook her head. Before they left their rooms earlier, she'd locked herself in the bathroom and washed his cum from her face. He'd ignored her pleas for him to do the same, and while he'd already licked every drop of her from his lips, he enjoyed taunting her.

Clover, Fawn, Amos, Echo, and Birdie stood on Amelia's side, and his father, Finn, his maternal grandmother, and Reyna stood on Rennick's. Greta perched on a nearby tree, and Eddy sat at Amelia's feet wearing one of his coats. Charlie's absence did not go unnoticed, and Rennick feared he'd been wrong about the lynx being her *familiar*.

The royal officiant tipped his head to Rennick and Amelia. "Amelia Stratton, are you here by your own free will?"

Her nerves fluttered in Rennick's chest, yet she straightened her shoulders and nodded. "I am."

The officiant pulled out a small bottle and dabbed holy oil on his finger. Amelia bared her neck, and the man drew a line over the dip between her neck and shoulder. He ran through the same process with Rennick, and when they stood facing each other with oil-marked necks, Amelia's anxiety rose.

"I don't know if I can do this," she croaked quietly. "What if I faint?"

"You've only passed out once." He grinned. "If you do it again, I'll have your brother hold you up and Clover hold your mouth open, and we'll do it for you."

She narrowed her eyes. "You're not funny."

His lips twitched, causing her eyes to narrow more. "I wasn't joking, love."

The officiant cleared his throat. "Are you two ready?"

Amelia trembled at the sight of the tiny dagger in the officiant's hand.

"We're ready," Rennick announced. "Do you want to go first, love?"

She gulped. "I think you should go first." Squeezing her eyes tight, she leaned her head to the side to expose the oily side of her neck.

The officiant handed Rennick the dagger, and he held the tiny blade to the oil and sliced a line deep enough to draw blood, but shallow enough to not inflict any real damage.

Leaning forward, he licked the oil and blood from her skin and swallowed. He teasingly licked her again and kissed the spot behind her ear, laughing lightly when she shivered.

She opened her eyes and held out her shaky hand. "What if I kill you?"

To anyone else, it sounded like a joke, but Rennick felt her worry. "You won't."

They could have pricked their fingers instead, but he wanted to do it the old way. Some believed doing the holy blood exchange was strongest when done on the neck.

He presented his neck to her, placing his life in her hands, and when he felt the cold steel flick across his skin, he suppressed a laugh. *Did she even break the skin?*

She tapped him on the chest and motioned for him to bend down. "I can't reach you."

He lowered himself to one knee and held on to her hips.

"Get off the ground," she hissed, glancing at the others. "I just needed you to bend a little."

"I am where I have always been, love: at your feet, waiting for you to claim me as your own."

Amelia tried not to look at the drop of blood on Rennick's neck. Of all things the fae could do to seal a mating bond, it had to involve blood. She tentatively leaned forward and quickly licked the oil and blood away.

The metallic taste hit her tongue, but she refused to gag like a child. Instead, she stood tall, proud of herself for not falling over, but her victory was short-lived.

A burning pain hit her chest, and she fell to her knees with a strangled cry.

"Rennick," she rasped.

Rennick swore and reached for her. "What's happening to her?"

"I don't know, Your Majesty," the officiant replied frantically.

That couldn't be a good sign.

"She's fine, son," Callum said calmly. "Look at her chest."

The pain ebbed into a distant memory, and she breathed a sigh of relief and held Rennick's arm for stability. "It's gone. I'm okay."

She looked up and everyone stared at her with various looks ranging from shock to awe.

"Look at her chest."

"What's wrong with my chest?" She glanced down at her ugly dress to find dark lines on her skin. "I don't understand."

Rennick reached for her collar and, before she could protest, ripped it slightly, earning himself a glare.

"I told you I wanted to keep this dress," she admonished.

He smiled a mile wide. "Look."

More black lines swirled across the left side of her chest into a design. "What is it?"

"It's your *familiar* mark," Amos said, unbuttoning his shirt. He opened it slightly to reveal a tattoo of a fennec fox.

She looked at Eddy and back to Amos's chest. "I get a *familiar*?"

The information sank in, and she reached for the top of her dress to rip it more, but Rennick stopped her. "If you show any more of your chest, I will have to kill every man here."

She stood and brushed the snow from her dress. "You're ridiculous. I need a mirror."

"My room is closest," Fawn offered. She looked at the others. "But it won't fit everyone."

A light blur caught Amelia's eye in the distance. Squinting, she smiled at the tan lynx bounding toward her. "Charlie!"

He wove around the others and stopped at her feet. *"Sorry I'm late."*

She spun around. It wasn't a voice, and she massaged her temples. "Did anyone else catch that, or am I going crazy?"

Rennick laid a hand on her lower back. "Charlie is your *familiar*, love. Whatever you felt was him."

"They can talk?" she whispered, too stunned to say much else.

"In a way," Callum confirmed, leaning down to stroke Charlie's fur. "You can sense his thoughts through the bond."

She squatted in front of Charlie. "Why couldn't I hear him before now?"

Callum straightened. "My guess is the bond wasn't strong enough. It takes fifteen years for a royal's magic to mature enough to bond with a *familiar*. I'm surprised Charlie came to you early." He eyed Amelia. "It's interesting, indeed."

"Tell him to stop staring at you like that, or I'm going to claw his eyes out," Charlie pushed down the bond.

Amelia sputtered out a laugh. *"You sound like Rennick."*

"What did he say?" Rennick asked her.

She waved a hand dismissively. "Nothing important." Charlie's feline mouth turned down, and Amelia stifled another laugh. Of course, her *familiar* would be a lynx version of her husband.

Callum turned to the others. "Why don't we offer our congratulations and let the happy couple have the night to themselves?" Following his own lead, he embraced his son and whispered something in his ear. Rennick hugged him tighter, nodding. Callum released him and opened his arms to Amelia. "Welcome to the family, little one."

She stepped into his embrace. "Thank you."

He released her with a fatherly smile. "I look forward to getting to know you better." He nodded to his son, gave Amelia's shoulder a squeeze, and walked away.

Finn took his place and stood in front of Amelia with his hands behind his back and a sheepish smile on his face. "I'm sorry I've been avoiding you." He glanced at Rennick. "Had your husband seen me anywhere near you, he would have ripped my head off."

Rennick grunted, and Amelia elbowed him in the stomach. "I'm going to hug him, and if you try to stop me, you won't touch me tonight."

Rennick growled. Actually *growled,* but he wasn't the only one. She glared at Charlie. "Stop it. Both of you." Finn engulfed her in his arms and held her tight. "I know what you did for us, and I'm sorry you had to shave your head." She stage-whispered the last part, earning a snort from Rennick.

Finn released a full belly laugh and extracted himself from her hold. "He's a good man, and he deserved to be happy. I was happy to do it."

"No, you weren't," Rennick laughed. "I had to bribe you."

Finn shrugged. "And your bribes made me happy."

Rennick shoved his shoulder, almost knocking him over, but brought him back in for a hug. "I am forever indebted to you. Anything you need, it's yours."

"I guess Ora finally got the message," Finn remarked with knowing eyes. Rennick dipped his chin, and his friend nodded. "It was the right call. She would have hurt Amelia, eventually. Congratulations, you two."

Amelia studied Finn as he walked away. He just found out they'd killed his childhood friend and he'd shrugged it off like it was nothing. Either he never liked Ora, or he hid his emotions well.

Clover wandered over, bashful as ever, and offered Amelia a hug. "Congratulations." She released her and added, "Don't be upset with your brother."

Amelia spotted Amos brooding a couple of yards away. "I understand his motivations were good, but he shouldn't have forced you to give up your home."

Clover ran a hand nervously through the ends of her hair. "Your brother didn't force me. He'd never do that." She looked away and Amelia thought she saw a sheen of tears in her eyes. "I'm not saying what happened was right, but he didn't force me by any means. I could have said no."

Amelia sensed there was more to the story, but she didn't want to pry. "How long will you stay? I've never heard you speak this much, and I don't want to miss my chance to ask you a million questions about yourself."

Clover smiled sadly. "I'll answer them someday, but I'm leaving tonight."

"Like hell you are," Amos all but yelled as he stalked their way. "You're not crossing the border at night."

Her nostrils flared slightly, and she closed her eyes. Taking a deep breath, she opened them and said, "You are not my keeper, Amos."

"I am your *king*," he seethed. "You're not leaving."

Rennick and Amelia watched the two square off. Never in a million years did Amelia think Clover would argue with anyone, least of all a fae king.

"You owe me the right to do as I please." Though Clover's voice remained quiet, it was anything but meek. "Haven't you done enough?"

"Don't ask this of me," Amos pleaded softly. "You know I can't let you go alone."

Clover scoffed. "It never bothered you before."

The venom in her words made Amelia's eyes widen.

Amos cracked his neck and swept his arm wide. "Then do as you please, *Your Highness*."

Your Highness?

Clover turned back to Amelia and Rennick. "I'll write soon." They hugged quickly, and she stormed off.

Rennick kept quiet, studying Amos with a knowing look. "Go."

Amos' mouth tightened, and he nodded his thanks. "I'm sorry, Amelia, but I can't stay. I promise to return when I can."

It hit her then, and her eyes almost popped out of her head. "She's your mate."

"I have to go before she gets too far," he said, ignoring her revelation. "I love you."

She stared at her brother's retreating back. "Clover and I have the same birthday?"

Rennick threw his head back in laughter. "That's what you got from that?" He leaned in and kissed the top of her head. "Let's thank the rest of our guests and retire for the night."

Rennick took off his coat and hung it on a hook by their sitting room door. He scanned Amelia from head to toe. "You're cold."

"I'm fine," she replied through chattering teeth. "I want to see my mark."

"I remember the excitement when I got mine." He trailed after her into the dressing room and unbuttoned the back of her torn dress. "When I saw the owl on my chest, I'd never been more disappointed." He pushed the fabric off her shoulders. "But then I met Greta, and she was exactly what I needed to see you. The gods always know best. Remember that."

Amelia stepped out of her dress and kicked it aside. "Charlie is perfect."

The lynx seemed temperamental at best, but Rennick didn't argue. "Are you ready to see?"

Amelia spun around and moved her hair to the side. Her eyes ate up the lynx imprinted on her skin, and she twisted to look at Rennick with an excited gleam in her eye. "Do you like it?"

His hands ran down her sides, caressing her curves. "I love it." One hand curved over her ass and squeezed. "Do you know what else I love?" He pushed under the edge of her underwear and ran a finger over the plug in her backside. "The fact that after tonight, every part of you will be mine."

She sucked in a sharp breath and met his gaze in the mirror. "What are you waiting for?"

Nothing. He ripped the underwear from her body and kneeled behind her. "Bend over, love." She braced her hands on the mirror and bent forward. His hand slid over her back and pushed lightly. "More."

For a moment she didn't move, but then she walked her hands down the mirror, giving him the perfect access. He leaned forward and licked her already wet slit, and she jumped slightly.

Soft skin gave under his hands when he grabbed her hips and pressed her body against his face as he feasted on her until her legs shook. She begged him for more and he obliged, probing her entrance with his tongue as he used his thumb to work her clit until her knees buckled. Her body jerked with her orgasm, and he held her firm against his face until he'd extracted every last drop from her.

"Gods, Rennick," she moaned with a shaky breath.

He gave her one last lick and stood. "I'll be right back."

After retrieving the bottle of intimate oil and a towel, he took his place behind her on the floor. She sat on her heels, staring at her *familiar* mark in the mirror. "It really is pretty."

"Everything about you is pretty." He unscrewed the jar's lid. "On your hands and knees, love."

Her eyes flashed with eagerness as she got into position.

"Are you ready?" She nodded and closed her eyes. Moving the plug side to side, Rennick gently slid it out and placed it on the towel. He lightly oiled his cock, lifted to his knees, and fisted his shaft. "Amelia." She opened her eyes and looked at him in the mirror. "Are you sure this is okay?"

Her sweet smile knocked the wind out of him. "More than sure."

The head of his cock nudged her back entrance. "Watch us in the mirror, little mate."

Ever so slowly, he pushed into her. There was resistance, but he reminded her to bear down, and once his head pushed through her tight ring of muscles, her body let him in fully. Her mouth fell open, and his head fell back.

"I'm going to let you adjust," he said roughly. "Breathe." Once he saw her breathing slowly and her eyes returned to his, he pulled back and pushed in again, hissing at the tightness.

"Rennick," she whispered and dropped her head.

His eyes moved to where their bodies joined. "Fuck, baby, you're taking my cock like a godsdamned dream." His pace quickened, and Amelia braced a hand on the mirror.

She cried out and pushed against him when he strummed her clit, the movement pushing him deeper. Their sounds of pleasure filled the room alongside the slapping of their skin and, when she finally came, he wasn't far behind. His stamina grew each time they were intimate, but holding out for her was still difficult.

His cock pumped out his release, marking her completely. He hissed as he pulled out, and once he'd cleaned them both, they climbed into bed, kissing each other goodnight.

As Rennick stared at his wife's sleeping form, he thought back to every letter, every trip to the Human Kingdom, and every sleepless night he'd laid awake and wondered about her.

It felt surreal to finally have her here with him, and now that he'd had her, no one in this life or the next could take her from him.

36

Days later, Rennick and Amelia greeted their guests as they filed into the dining hall for the coronation celebration. The large room had been transformed into a ballroom with tables sprinkled around the dance floor. It was impressive, to say the least.

A few council members from the Desert Kingdom gave her curious stares, and she knew they took note of the similarities between her and their kingdom's royal family. She wondered if any of them had been friends with her mother. *Do any of them know who I am?* Her decision to wear a high-neck dress that hid her *familiar* mark proved to be a wise decision, because if they didn't already know who she was, a mate possessing a *familiar* mark would have given her away.

The Tropical King and Queen arrived next, introducing themselves and offering their congratulations before disappearing inside.

A tall, statuesque woman with ebony skin and black hair pulled into a tight knot approached them. *It couldn't be... could it?* Though she'd never met the woman, Amelia would recognize her face anywhere. The Human Queen wore a small tiara and a white dress adorned with crystals. Rennick bowed. "Thank you for coming. Let me introduce you to my wife."

The woman stared intently at Amelia with an affectionate smile on her face. "I have waited twenty-five years to meet you, dear." She held out her hand. "I'm Charlotte, and this is my husband, Hollis." Her elegant hand gestured to a handsome man with pale freckled skin and fiery red hair that Amelia recognized as well. She'd learned about the royals of the Human Kingdom in school, but she never thought she'd get to meet them.

Knowing what Queen Charlotte did for her made the meeting even more surreal.

The Human King stepped forward and took Amelia's hand in his own, kissing her fingers. "It's a pleasure, Amelia."

Amelia couldn't stop staring at the woman in front of her. Her throat tightened with emotion. "Thank you." She didn't have to explain. It was clear by the knowing look on Charlotte's face that she understood.

Charlotte's eyes shined, and Amelia sensed the woman held back emotions of her own. Charlotte reached out and grasped Amelia's hand, squeezing it lightly. "I would love to sit and chat when you have time."

Amelia nodded dumbly. "I'd like that, too. Lunch tomorrow?"

"That sounds perfect, dear." After trading quick pleasantries with Rennick, the human royals left to find their seats.

Rennick leaned down. "Are you all right, love?"

Before she could answer, a man standing about six-foot-two or six-foot-three with a muscular, lean build sauntered toward them with a lazy smile. His hair was a mix between brown and blond, his jawline strong, and his light grey eyes danced with mischief.

He wore trousers with a button-down shirt and militant style jacket similar to Rennick's, but where Rennick's was white, this man's was a bright blue that made his eyes pop. He exuded raw sex appeal and arrogance, and Amelia surmised he was the Garden King.

"Rennick," he drawled, sticking out his hand, "it's nice to finally meet you in person. I apologize for not coming sooner."

"Think nothing of it," Rennick replied, shaking the man's hand before motioning to Amelia. "This is my wife, Amelia."

Something flickered across the Garden King's face, momentarily breaking the cavalier mask he donned well. He flashed her a charming smile and brought her hand to his mouth. "It's a pleasure to meet you." He kissed her hand in a way that would have flustered her had she not met Rennick. "I'm Dean."

Rennick yanked Amelia to his side. "Careful how you look at my wife."

Dean chuckled, the sound smooth and velvety. "Easy, Mountain King. I only meant to greet her properly." He winked and walked away before Rennick could rip his innards out.

It didn't escape her notice that Dean didn't wait for her to return his greeting, probably out of self-preservation. Dean was lucky Charlie wasn't here. He would have bitten his leg before Amelia could stop him.

Once all the guests were greeted, she and Rennick joined the others on the podium. Callum announced Rennick's reign and marriage, and after a heartfelt toast, dinner was served.

The podium housed the other royal families and their council members, the Mountain Kingdom's council members, and Rennick and Amelia's closest friends.

Birdie and Fawn insisted on sitting with the other staff, but Amelia wouldn't have it. Echo had no compunction about joining the royal table and immediately began shoving food into their mouth.

Tully, Ora's father, was notably absent due to the letter his daughter had left the night before. It stated she couldn't bear to see Rennick with another and that she wouldn't be returning to the Mountain Kingdom anytime soon.

Finn's idea.

Their table erupted with laughter when Echo said something utterly inappropriate, drawing the attention of those around them. Amelia noticed Dean's head snap up, his fist rubbing over his chest as he scanned the other tables on the podium before stopping on theirs.

Odd.

A server who looked to be in his early twenties tapped Fawn on the shoulder. She turned with a wide smile that turned into a scream when the boy was ripped backwards and thrown to the ground by a possessed-looking Dean.

Fawn scrambled out of her chair to get away from the Garden King, but he snagged her around the waist and tugged her against him. His chest heaved as he stared into her scared eyes. No one in the room moved. They recognized a royal claiming what was theirs.

"I thought you were dead," Dean rasped, lifting her into his arms.

Fawn kicked her legs and thrashed around. "Put me down!"

He lowered her to the ground and stared at her with wonder. "You're stunning, Fawn."

She backpedaled until she bumped into her chair. "How do you know my name?"

The room watched the two with unwavering attention, hanging onto every word of the drama unfolding before them. Damned palace gossips.

"I've known your name since I was thirteen years old. My father had men searching the four fae kingdoms for you." He stopped with a pained expression. "But when we were fourteen, I felt agonizing pain, followed by a deep sorrow." Fawn trembled under Dean's intense gaze. "And then I felt nothing at all."

Callum, ever the father of reason, stood and approached the two. "Let me take you two somewhere private, where you can discuss things without prying eyes."

Fawn composed herself and schooled her features into the picture of calm, but Amelia saw the quick flash of panic in her eyes. "You're his mate," Amelia said softly. "He won't hurt you."

"I'm only half fae." She turned to Dean. "There's been a mistake."

"There is no mistake, darling." He caressed her cheek, looking at her with enough adoration to make the entire room swoon. "You are mine, and I'm not leaving here without you."

"Come." Callum wrapped his arm around Fawn's shoulders. Dean didn't look happy with another man touching her, but he was wise enough to let it go.

The poor server still lay on the floor in a state of shock, and Echo rolled their eyes and hauled the boy to his feet. "You're lucky he didn't kill you."

The boy fainted.

EPILOGUE
SEVEN YEARS LATER

"Corrigan, if you don't put him down, you'll be mucking the stables for a week!" Amelia shouted across the palace play yard they had built a few years ago.

Well, *Rennick* had it built. It stood inside of the palace walls and was reminiscent of a mini training arena but with lush grass and green ivy climbing its high stone walls. A glass dome covered the top to keep the snow out and the heat in, but tiny openings placed strategically in the stone allowed for enough airflow to keep it from getting stuffy.

Structures made for climbing, swinging, jumping, and other various activities littered the inside. It was what children's dreams were made of.

Guards stood at the gates day and night to ensure no one snuck in, and before the children entered, someone had to do a perimeter check, but Amelia hadn't expected anything less from her husband.

Corrigan, their six-year-old daughter, dropped Wren, Finn's four-year-old son, unceremoniously, and when he hit the ground, he stood on chubby legs and glared at her. He was a miniature version of his father, with dark hair, golden brown skin, and strong features. The only thing he'd inherited from his mother were his aquamarine eyes. He often stayed at the palace while his parents trained with the other warriors.

Corrigan looked like Amelia but with brilliant red hair like Rennick's mother. Her personality, however, was a direct copy of Rennick's. Gods help them all.

Rennick burst out of a nearby playhouse with a growl, holding his arms up like a beast. Both kids ran with a mixture of screams and giggles, tugging at Amelia's heartstrings. He swooped Corrigan into one arm and Wren into the other, spinning them around as they wiggled and kicked their feet, their laughter bouncing off the walls.

Greta perched atop one of the play structures, watching Rennick and the children. From the time Corrigan was born, the owl could be found perched near wherever she was when outside, keeping watch like her personal guard.

It surprised Amelia that owls lived as long as Greta had, but Callum explained that *familiars* lived as long as their bonded instead of the normal lifespan of their species. She was glad to hear it, because if Charlie died before her, she would be inconsolable.

Over the years, Charlie had become one of her closest companions who purposefully irritated Rennick. Despite their grumblings about each other, she knew they secretly loved one another. She occasionally caught Rennick leaving Charlie new blankets in his bed when he thought no one was looking.

Charlie zoomed around Rennick and the children, making the kids giggle harder. Something scratched at the bottom of Amelia's dress, whining for her attention.

She looked down and her face lit up. "Eddy!" Picking up the big-eared fox, she nuzzled the side of his neck. "You better find Birdie and have her put on your coat before Rennick sees."

She laughed at the memory of Amos admitting that the times Eddy fought against wearing his warm clothes were because he'd begged the fox not to wear them while they were connected. He said it was demeaning.

Rennick had turned ten shades of red and told Amos that Eddy could have died of hypothermia because of his boyish pride, and that the fox would wear his sweaters when in their kingdom. Amos had reluctantly agreed, but conveniently always forgot Eddy's coats at home.

As if Rennick didn't have an entire trunk full.

Eddy knowingly licked the side of Amelia's face and jumped down to find Birdie.

"Uncle Amos and Aunt Clover are here," Amelia called out as she crossed the large yard.

Charlie's ears perked up seconds before he darted toward the exit, presumably to find Eddy. Those two were thick as thieves. She asked Charlie if the *familiars* could speak to each other, and he'd looked at her like she was stupid and walked off. She still didn't know the answer.

Both kids wiggled until Rennick set them down, and the way Corrigan screamed Amos's name made Rennick glower after them.

"Don't worry, love," Amelia cooed, petting his arm. "She loves you more."

"Where have you been?" he asked, pulling her close to kiss the top of her head. "I missed you."

"I was gone for two hours," she laughed. "I received word back from Fawn. They'll be here in a fortnight."

"Can you two separate long enough to tell your favorite brother hello?" a familiar voice grumbled.

Amelia rolled her eyes and turned to her brother. "Don't be dramatic."

A three-year-old girl with Amos' eyes and Clover's wild blonde hair hid behind Amos' legs. As heir to the Desert Kingdom, Rose shouldn't be able to leave her kingdom, but everything changed three years ago when Corrigan slipped from

Amelia's grasp and ran through barrier, destroying it.

As the first heir born of two blood-born royal fae, Corrigan's magic had always been strong for her age, even by royal fae standards. Rennick and Amelia just hadn't realized *how* strong until the day she undid what the gods had put into place thousands of years ago.

Rennick crouched down and opened his arms with a warm smile. Rose smiled back shyly and ran into his embrace, nuzzling into his chest.

"Hi Uncle Rennick." She had her mother's quiet voice and demeanor but wasn't quite as shy.

Amos's eyes turned to slits, and Amelia pushed him lightly. "You two are terrible. Your daughters love you more than the other. Happy?"

"No," they said at the same time.

Rennick stood with Rose in his arms and joined Clover, Corrigan, and Wren by the entrance.

"Have you spoken with Roman?" she asked her brother. Roman was the Tropical King, and one of Amos' best friends.

The Tropical King and Queen were an anomaly in Eden. Roman's original mate, Vivian, broke their royal mating bond by secretly marrying another man. That had never happened before, and no one knew what it meant for the Tropical Kingdom's royal bloodline. When Roman turned twenty-five, the gods granted him a new mate—Violet, Vivian's twin sister.

"Clover received a letter from Violet last week. Said she's been really sick since finding out she was pregnant." He rubbed his jaw and chuckled. "I bet Roman has summoned every healer in Eden to help her and threatened to kill any who failed."

She rolled her eyes. "Why the gods sent you four overprotective mother hens to rule the fae kingdoms at the same time is beyond me. They should have spread you guys out." Amelia shuddered. "Do you remember how sick I was with Corrigan?"

Amos took a pointed step away from her. "You puked on my shirt when I hugged you."

"You smelled like cooked ham," she said defensively. "There is no worse smell than hot meat."

"For the last time, it wasn't me who smelled like ham," he argued, using the same defense he'd been using for six-and-a-half years "It was the ham on the table."

She lifted a dismissive shoulder. "I didn't puke until I hugged you."

"You're impossible."

She bumped against him. "But you love me."

"Unfortunately." He slung an arm around her shoulders, walking them toward the others. "We need to take Rose inside to rest, but we'll see you tonight at dinner."

Amos held out his arms and took Rose from Rennick, blowing on her rounded cheek. Amelia hugged Clover and informed her of Fawn's planned arrival before bidding her goodbye.

"*Echo*," Amelia yelled, waving when a familiar head of dark hair popped around the edge of the entrance. "Can you take Amos and Clover to Birdie, please? She'll show them to their rooms."

The guard gave her a mock salute, and Amelia mouthed, *"Fuck you,"* making them both laugh.

After they'd gone, Rennick shushed the children and cupped a hand behind his ear. "I think I hear a monster."

The kids screamed and ran off, but Rennick grabbed Corrigan from behind and set her on his shoulders. She squealed and covered his eyes. "I caught the monster!"

He held his hands out, pretending to feel around.

"Mommy, run!" Corrigan shrieked, but it was too late. Rennick's hand grasped her shoulder.

He gasped in mock horror and set their daughter on the

ground. "What do we do if the queen gets caught by the monster? How do we save her?"

"Magic kisses and hugs!" Corrigan bellowed. Amelia squatted down and steadied herself against the onslaught of kisses peppering her cheeks from Corrigan as Wren wrapped his arms around her from behind. "Thank you for saving me," she said enthusiastically, pressing a hand to her chest.

Rennick leaned down and swept her into his arms. "I think you need one more to be sure. We wouldn't want a big scary monster to carry you off to a faraway land."

He smiled against her lips because they both knew one already had.

CURRENT AND UPCOMING WORKS

For release date info, sign up for my newsletter (only sent for releases and free books). Go to

beacons.ai/jamieapplegatehunter *for the sign up link*

VINCULA REALM

The Umbra King (Rory & Caius part 1)

Aeternum (Rory & Caius part 2)

Silenced Fate (Sam & Stassi) TBD

FAE KINGS OF EDEN (STANDALONES)

Viciously Yours (Rennick & Amelia)

Untitled (Roman & Violet) 2024

Untitled TBD

Untitled TBD

UNTITLED SERIES (STANDALONES)

4 book series (Release dates TBD 2024/2025)

ABOUT THE AUTHOR

"I'm always thinking one step ahead, like a carpenter that makes stairs."

-Andy Bernard

LET'S CONNECT

For links to my website, newsletter, socials, and more, visit

beacons.ai/jamieapplegatehunter

TikTok
@jah.hdj.books

Instagram
@jah.hdj.books

ACKNOWLEDGMENTS

To my husband, Ray, for being my biggest hype man and making sure I have time to work sans children. I love you.

My bookish group chat friends: Smut Sluts (Vyc & Kaylie), Books & Trash Bags (Kate & Maddie), High School Drama Book Club (Brynne & Heather), Ratpatootie Can Eat A Bag of Dicks (Kit, Janessa, & Heather), and Morally Grey Side Hoez (Amber, Genie, Lu, and Kalista). I love you all.

There are so many other friends in the bookish community who deserve to be in here, too, but I have a goldfish brain, and if I left someone out, I'd never forgive myself. You guys know who you are!

Zoe Holland for being an amazing artist who will go back and forth with me to perfect my vision. She has brought many of my characters to life, and I will forever sing her praises.

Cooper Darling-Tallent for helping me write the letters from 13, 14, 15, and 16-year-old Rennick to make them sound more age-appropriate. You're much cooler than I am.

Sage & Helena for helping polish this book in a way I never could.

And everyone at Brower Literary, who are the nicest people to work with. I'm thankful to have you all on my side.

Thank you all!

CONTENT WARNINGS

Not suitable for those under 18 years-old.

Graphic violence and death, gore, death of an immediate family member, morally black decisions that are irredeemable by the main characters, orphaned heroine, sexually explicit scenes, and mature language.

Printed in the USA
CPSIA information can be obtained
at www.ICGtesting.com
CBHW032302181024
16045CB00033B/808